POPULAR NOVELS
BY
Mrs. Mary J. Holmes.

1.—TEMPEST AND SUNSHINE.
2.—ENGLISH ORPHANS.
3.—HOMESTEAD ON THE HILLSIDE.
4.—'LENA RIVERS.
5.—MEADOW BROOK.
6.—DORA DEANE.
7.—COUSIN MAUDE.
8.—MARIAN GREY.
9.—DARKNESS AND DAYLIGHT.
10.—HUGH WORTHINGTON.
11.—CAMERON PRIDE.
12.—ROSE MATHER.
13.—ETHELYN'S MISTAKE.
14.—MILLBANK.
15.—EDNA BROWNING.
16.—WEST LAWN.
17.—EDITH LYLE.
18.—MILDRED *(New)*.

"Mrs. Holmes is a peculiarly pleasant and fascinating writer. Her books are always entertaining, and she has the rare faculty of enlisting the sympathy and affections of her readers, and of holding their attention to her pages with deep and absorbing interest."

All published uniform with this volume. Price $1.50 each. Sold everywhere, and sent *free* by mail, on receipt of price,
BY
G. W. CARLETON & CO., Publishers,
New York.

MILDRED.

A Novel.

BY
Mrs. MARY J. HOLMES,

AUTHOR OF

EDITH LYLE—EDNA BROWNING—TEMPEST AND SUNSHINE—'LENA RIVERS—WEST LAWN—MARIAN GREY—HUGH WORTHINGTON—ETHELYN'S MISTAKE, ETC., ETC.

"—— Love soweth here with toil and care,
But the harvest-time of Love is there."
SOUTHEY.

NEW YORK:
G. W. *Carleton & Co.*, Publishers.
LONDON: S. LOW & CO.
MDCCCLXXVII.

CONTENTS.

CHAPTER	PAGE
I.—The Storm, and what it Brought.	9
II.—Village Gossip.	27
III.—Nine Years Later.	35
IV.—Oliver and Mildred visit Beechwood.	50
V.—Lawrence Thornton and his Advice.	60
VI.—What came of it.	72
VII.—Lilian and Mildred.	93
VIII.—Lawrence and his Father.	111
IX.—Lawrence at Beechwood.	119
X.—The River.	131
XI.—Lawrence Deceived and Undeceived.	142
XII.—The Proposal.	157
XIII.—The Answer.	173
XIV.—What Followed.	201
XV.—The Sun Shining through the Cloud.	214
XVI.—The Ebbing of the Tide.	228
XVII.—The Deserted Hut.	238
XVIII.—The Guests at the Hotel.	256
XIX.—Lawrence and Oliver.	276
XX.—Oliver and Mildred.	285
XXI.—The Meeting.	299
XXII.—Natural Results.	314
XXIII.—Conclusion.	321

MILDRED.

CHAPTER I.

THE STORM, AND WHAT IT BROUGHT.

'HE sultry September day was drawing to a close, and as the sun went down, a dark thunder-cloud came slowly up from the west, muttering in deep undertones, and emitting occasional gleams of lightning by way of heralding the coming storm, from which both man and beast intuitively sought shelter. Ere long the streets of Mayfield were deserted, save by the handsome carriage and span of spirited grays, which went dashing through the town toward the large house upon the hill, the residence of Judge Howell, who paid no heed to the storm, so absorbed was he in the letter which he held in his hand, and which had roused him to a state of fearful excitement. Through the gate, and up the long avenue, lined with

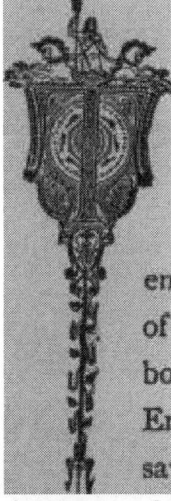

giant trees of maple and beech, the horses flew, and just as the rain came down in torrents they stood panting before the door of Beechwood.

" Bring me a light! Why isn't there one already here ? " roared the Judge, as he stalked into his library, and banged the door with a crash scarcely equalled by the noise of the tempest without.

" Got up a little thunder-storm on his own account! Wonder what's happened him now !" muttered Rachel, the colored housekeeper, as she placed a lamp upon the table, and then silently left the room.

Scarcely was she gone when, seating himself in his arm chair, the Judge began to read again the letter which had so much disturbed him. It was post-marked at a little out-of-the-way place among the backwoods of Maine, and it purported to have come from a young mother, who asked him to adopt a little girl, nearly two months old.

" Her family is fully equal to your own," the mother wrote ; " and should you take my baby, you need never blush for her parentage. I have heard of you, Judge Howell. I know that you are rich, that you are com-p.aratively alone, and there are reasons why I would rather my child should go to Beechwood than any other spot in the wide world. You need her, too,—need something to comfort your old age, for with all your money, you are far from being happy."

" The deuce I am ! " muttered the Judge. " How did the

trollop know that, or how did she know of me, any way ? i/take a child to comfort my old age ! Ridiculous ! I'm not old,—I'm only fifty,—just in the prime of life; but I hate young ones, and I won't have one in my house ! I'm tormented enough with Rachel's dozen, and if that madame brings hers here, I'll "

The remainder of the sentence was cut short by a peal of thunder, so long and loud that even the exasperated Judge was still until the roar had died away ; then, resum ing the subject of his remarks, he continued :

"Thanks to something, this letter has been two weeks on the road, and as she is tired of looking for an answer by this time, I sha'n't trouble myself to write,—but what of Richard ?—I have not yet seen why he is up there in New Hampshire, chasing after that Hetty, when he ought to have been home weeks ago ;" and taking from his pocket another and an unopened letter, he read why his only son and heir of all his vast possessions was in New Hampshire " chasing after Hetty," as he termed it.

Hetty Kirby was a poor relation, whom the Judge's wife had taken into the family, and treated with the utmost kindness and consideration ; on her death-bed she had committed the young girl to her husband's,care, bidding him be kind to Hetty for her sake. In Judge Howell's crusty heart there was one soft, warm spot,—the memory of his wife and beautiful young daughter, the latter of whom died within a few months after her marriage. They

had loved the orphan Hetty, and for their sakes, he had kept her until accident revealed to him the fact that to his son, then little more than a boy, there was no music so sweet as Hetty's voice,—no light so bright as that which shone in Hetty's eye.

Then the lion was roused, and he turned her from his door, while Richard was threatened with disinheritance if he dared to think again of the humble Hetty. There was no alternative but to submit, for Judge Ho well's word was law, and, with a sad farewell to what had been her home so long, Hetty went back to the low-roofed house among the granite hills, where her mother and half-imbe cile grandmother were living.

Richard, too, returned to college, and from that time not a word had passed between the father and the son concerning the offending Hetty until now, when Richard wrote that she was dead, together with her grandmother, —that news of her illness had been forwarded to him, and immediately after leaving college, in July, he had hastened to New Hampshire, and staid by her until she died.

"You cancusefe me for it if you choose," he said, " but it will not make the matter better. I loved Hetty Kirby while living, I love her memory now that she is dead; and in that little grave beneath the hill I have buried my heart forever."

The letter closed by saying that Richard would possibly

be home that night, and he asked that the carriage might be in wailing at the depot.

The news of Hetty's death kept the Judge silent for a moment, while his heart gave one great throb as he thought of the fair-haired, blue-eyed girl, who had so often ministered to his comfort.

"Poor thing, she's in heaven, I'm sure," he said; " and if I was ever harsh to her, it's too late to help it now. I always liked her well enough, but I did not like her making love to Richard. He'll get over it, too, even if he does talk about his heart being buried in her grave. Stuff and nonsense ! Just as if a boy of twenty knows where his heart is. Needn't tell me. He'll come to his senses after he's been home a spell, and that reminds me that I must send the carriage for him. Here, Ruth," he continued, as he saw a servant passing in the hall, " tell Joe not to put out the,horses, or if he has, to harness up again. Richard is coming home, and he must meet him at the station."

Ruth departed with the message and the Judge again took up the letter in which a child had been offered for his adoption. Very closely he scrutinized the handwriting, but it was not a familiar one to him. He had never seen it before, and, tearing the paper in pieces, he scattered them upon the floor.

The storm by this time had partially subsided, and he heard the carriage wheels grinding into the gravel as Joe

drove from the house. Half an hour went by, and then the carriage returned again; but Richard was not in it, and the father sat down alone to the supper kept in waiting for his son. It was a peculiarity of the Judge to retire precisely at nine o'clock ; neither friend nor foe could keep him up beyond that hour, he said ; and on this even ing, as on all others, the lights disappeared from his room just as the nine o'clock bell was heard in the distance, But the Judge was nervous to-night. The thunder which at intervals continued to roar, made him restless, and ten o'clock found him even more wakeful than he had been an hour before.

"What the plague ails me?" he exclaimed, tossing un easily from side to side, " and what the deuce can that be ? Rachel's baby as I "live ! What is she doing with it here ? If there's anything I detest, it is a baby's squall. Just hear that, will you ? " and raising himself upon his elbow he listened intently to what was indisputably an infant wail, rising even above the storm, for it had commenced raining again, and the thunder at times was fearfully loud.

" Screech away," said the Judge, as a cry, sharper and more prolonged, fell upon his ear; " screech away till you split your throat; but I'll know why a Christian man, who hates children, must be driven distracted in his own house," and stepping into the hall, he called out, at the top of His voice, " Ho, Rachel!" but no Rachel made her appearance; and a little further investigaticn sufficed to

show that she had retired to the h'ttle cottage in the back yard, which, in accordance with a Southern custom, the Judge, who was a Virginian, had built for herself and her husband. Rachel was also a native of Virginia, but for many years she had lived at Beechwood, where she was now the presiding genius,—and the one servant whom the Judge trusted above all others. But she had one great fault, at which her master chafed terribly; she had nearly as many children as the fabled woman who lived in a shoe. Indeed there seemed to be no end to the little darkies who daily sunned themselves upon the velvety sward in front of their cabin door, and were nightly stowed away in the three wide trundle-beds, which Rachel brought forth from unheard-of hiding-places, and made up near her own. If there was one thing in the world more than another which the Judge professed to hate, it was children, and when Rachel innocently asked him to name her twelfth, he answered wrathfully :

"A dozen,—the old Harry !—call it FINIS, —and let it be so,—do you hear ? "

" Yes, marster," was the submissive answer, and so Finis, or JFmn, for short, was the name given to the child, which the Judge fancied was so disturbing him, as, lean ing over the banister, he called aloud to Rachel, "to stop that noise, and carry Finn back where he belonged."

" She has carried him back, I do believe," he said to himself, as he heard how still it was below, and retiring

to his room, he tried again to sleep, succeeding so far as to fall away into a doze, from which he was aroused by a thunder-crash, which shook the massive building to its foundation, and wrung from the watch-dog, Tiger, who kept guard without, a deafening yell.

But to neither of these sounds did the Judge pay the least attention, for, mingled with them, and continuing after both had died away, was that same infant wail, tuned now to a higher, shriller note, as if the little creature were suffering from fear or bodily pain.

" Might as well try to sleep in bedlam ! " exclaimed the exasperated Judge, stepping from his bed a second time, and commencing to dress himself, while his nervousness and irritability increased in proportion as the cries grew louder and more alarming.

Striking a light and frowning wrathfully at the sour, tired-looking visage reflected by the mirror, he descended the stairs and entered the kitchen, where everything was in perfect order, even to the kindlings laid upon the hearth for the morning fire. The cries, too, were fainter there and could scarcely be heard at all, but as he retraced his steps and came again into the lower hall, he heard them distinctly, and also Tiger's howl. Guided by tlie sound, he kept on his way until he reached the front door, when a thought flashed upon him which rendered him for an instant powerless to act. What if that Maine woman, tired of waiting for an answer to her letter, had

taken some other way of accomplishing her purpose ? What if he should find a baby on his steps ! But I sha'n't," he said, decidedly; I won't, and if I do, I'll kick it into the street, or something," and emboldened by this resolution he unlocked the door, and shading the lamp with his hand, peered cautiously out into the darkness.

With a cry of delight Tiger sprang forward, nearly upsetting his master, who staggered back a pace or two, and then, recovering himself, advanced again toward the open door.

" There's nothing here," he said, thrusting his head out into the rain, which was dropping fast through the thick vine leaves which overhung the lattice of the portico.

As if to disprove this assertion, the heavens for an instant blazed with light, and showed him where a small white object lay in a willow basket beneath the seat built on either side of the door. He knew it was not Finn, for the tiny fingers which grasped the basket edge were white and pure as wax, while the little dimples about the joints involuntarily carried him back to a time when just such a baby hand as this had patted his bearded cheek or pulled his long black hair. Perhaps it was the remembrance of that hand, now cold in death, which prompted him to a nearer survey of the contents of the basket, and setting down his lamp, he stooped to draw it forth, while Tiger stood by trembling with joy that his vigils were ended, and that human aid '*ad come at last to the helpless crea-

ture he had guarded with the faithfulness peculiar to his race.

It was a fair, round face which met the judge's view as he removed the flannel blanket, and the bright, pretty eyes which looked up into his were full of tears. But the Judge hardened his heart, and though he did not kick the baby into the rain, he felt strongly tempted so to do, and glancing toward the cornfield not far away, where he fancied the mother might be watching the result, he screamed :

" Come here, you rnadame, and take the brat away, for I sha'n't touch it, you may depend upon that."

Having thus relieved his mind, he was about to re-enter the house, when, as if divining his intention, Tiger planted his huge form in the doorway, and effectually kept him back.

" Be quiet, Tiger, be quiet," said the Judge, stroking his shaggy mane; but Tiger refused to move, until at last, as if seized by a sudden instinct, he darted toward the basket, which he took in his mouth, and carried into the hall.

"It sha'n't be said a brute is more humane than myself," thought the Judge, and leaving the dog and the baby together, he stalked across the yard, and, pounding on Rachel's door, bade her come to the house at once.

But a few moments elapsed ere Rachel stood in the hall, her eyes protruding like harvest apples when she

saw the basket and the bat>y it contained. The twelve young Van Brunts sleeping in their three trundle-beds, had enlarged her motherly heart, just as the Judge's lonely condition had shrivelled his, and kneeling down she took' the wee thing in her arms, called it a " little honey," and then, woman-like, examined its dress, which was of the finest material, and trimmed with costly lace.

" It's none of your low-flung truck," she said. " The edgin' on its slip cost a heap, and its petticoats is all worked with floss."

" Petticoats be hanged 1" roared the Judge. " Who cares for worked petticoats ? The question is, what are we to do with it ? "

" Do with it ? " repeated Rachel, hugging it closer to her bosom. "Keep it, in course. Tears like it seems mighty nigh to me," and she gave it another squeeze, this time uttering a faint outcry, for a sharp point of some thing had penetrated through the thin folds of her ging ham dress. " Thar's somethin' fastened to 't," she said, and removing the blanket, she saw a bit of paper pinned to the infant's waist. "This may 'splain the matter," she continued, passing it to the Judge, who read, in the same handwriting of the letter: " God prosper you, Judge Howell, in proportion as you are kind to my baby, whom I have called Mildred?

" Mildred!" repeated the judge, " Mildred be "

He did not finish the sentence, for he seemed to hear

far back in the past a voice much like his own, saying aloud :

" I, Jacob, take thee, Mildred, to be my wedded wife."

The Mildred taken then in that shadowy old church had been for years a loving, faithful wife, and another Mil dred, too, with starry eyes and nut-brown hair had flitted through his halls, calling him her father. The Maine woman must surely have known of this when she gave her offspring the only name in the world which could possibly have touched the Judge's heart. With a per plexed expression upon his face, he stood rubbing his hands together, while .Rachel launched forth into a stream of baby-talk, like that with which she was wont to edify her twelve young blackbirds.

" For Heaven's sake, stop that! You fairly turn my stomach," said the Judge, as she added the finishing touch by calling the child " a pessus 'ittle darlin' dumplin' 1" " You women are precious big fools with babies ! "

" Wasn't Miss Milly just as silly as any on us ? " asked Rachel, who knew his weak point; " and if she was here to-night, instead of over Jordan, don't you believe she'd take the little critter as her own ? "

"Thafs nothing to do with it," returned the Judge. " The question is, how shall we dispose of it—to-night, I mean, for in the morning I shall see about its being taken to the poor-house."

" The poor-house 1" repeated Rachel "Ain't it writ

on that paper, 'The Lord sarve you and yourn as you sarve her and hern' ? Thar's a warnin' in that which I shall mind ef you don't. The baby ain't a-goin' to the poor-house. I'll take it myself first. A hen don't scratch no harder for thirteen than she does for twelve, and though Joe ain't no kind o' count, I can manage some how. Shall I consider it mine ? "

" Yes, till morning," answered the Judge, who really had no definite idea as to what he intended doing with the helpless creature thus forced upon him against his will.

He abhorred children,—he would not for anything have one abiding in his house, and especially this one of so doubtful parentage ; still he was not quite inclined to cast it off, and he wished there was some one with whom to advise. Then, as he remembered the expected coming of his son, he thought, " Richard will tell me what to do !" and feeling somewhat relieved he returned to his chamber, while Rachel hurried off to her cabin, where, in a few words, she explained the matter to Joe,- who, being naturally of a lazy temperament, was altogether too sleepy to manifest emotion of any kind, and was soon snoring as loudly as ever.

In his rude pine cradle little Finn was sleeping, and once Rachel thought to lay the stranger baby with him ; but proud as she was of her color and of her youngest born, too, she felt that there was a dividing line over

which she must not pass, so Finn was finally removed to the pillow of his sire, the cradle re-arranged, and the baby carefully lain to rest.

Meantime, on his bedstead of rosewood, Judge Howell tried again to sleep, but all in vain were his attempts to woo the wayward goddess, and he lay awake until the moon, struggling through the broken clouds, shone upon the floor. Then, in the distance, he heard the whistle of the night express, and knew it was past mid night.

" 1 wish that Maine woman had been drowned in Passa-maquoddy Bay !" said he, rolling his pillow into a ball and beating it with his fist. " Yes, I do, for I'll be hanged if I .want to be bothered this way ! Hark ! I do believe she's prowling round the house yet," he continued, as he thought he caught the sound of a footstep upon the gravelled walk.

He was not mistaken in the sound, and he was about getting up for the third and, as he swore to himself, the last time, when a loud ring of the bell, and a well-known voice, calling: " Father! father ! let me in," told him that not the Maine woman, but his son Richard, had come. Hastening down the stairs, he unlocked the door, and Richard Howell stepped into the hall, his boots bespattered with mud, his clothes wet with the heavy rain, and his face looking haggard and pale by the dim light of the lamp his father carried in his hand.

" Why, Dick ! " exclaimed the Judge, " what ails you ? You are as white as a ghost."

"I am tired and sick," was Richard's reply. "I've scarcely slept for several weeks."

" Been watching with Hetty, I dare say," thought the Judge ; but he merely said: " Why didn't you come at seven, as you wrote you would ? "

"I couldn't conveniently," Richard replied: "and, as I was anxious to get here as soon as possible, I took the night express, and have walked from the depot. But what is that ? " he continued, as he entered the sitting-room, and saw the willow-basket standing near the door.

" Dick," and the Judge's voice dropped to a nervous whisper,—" Dick, if you'll believe me, some infernal Maine woman has had a baby, and left it on our steps. She wrote first to know if I'd take it, but the letter was two weeks coming. I didn't get it until to-night, and, as I suppose she was tired of waiting, she brought it along right in the midst of that thunder-shower. She might have known I'd kick it into the street, just as I said I would,—the trollop ! "

" Oh, father!" exclaimed the more humane young man, "you surely didn't treat the innocent child so cruelly !"

"No, I didn't, though my will was good enough," answered the father. "Just think of the scandalous reports that are certain to follow. It will be just like that gossiping Widow Simms to get up some confounded

yarn, and involve us both, the wretch! But I sha'n't keep it,—I shall send it to the poor-house."

And, by way of adding emphasis to his words, he gave the basket a shove, which turned it bottom side up, and scattered over the floor sundry articles of baby-wear, which had before escaped his observation.

Among these was a tiny pair of red morocco shoes ; for the " Maine woman," as he called her, had been thought ful both for the present and future wants of her child.

" Look, father," said Richard, taking them up and holding them to the light. "They are just like those sister Mildred used to wear. You know mother saved them, because they were the first; and you have them ttill in your private drawer."

Richard had touched a tender chord, and it vibrated at once, bringing to his father memories of a little soft 3 fat foot, which had once been encased in a slipper much like the one Richard held in his hand. The patter of that foot had ceased forever, and the soiled, worn shoe was now a sacred thing, even though the owner had. grown up to beautiful womanhood ere her home wae made desolate.

"Yes, Dick," he said, as he thought of all this. " It-is like our dear Milly's, and what is a little mysterious, the baby is called Mildred, too. It was written on a bit of paper, and pinned upon the dress."

" Then you will keep her, won't you ? and BeechwooJ will not be so lonely," returned Richard, continuing after a pause, "Where is she, this little lady? I am anxious to pay her my respects."

"Down with Rachel, just where she ought to be," said the Judge ; and Richard rejoined, " Down with all those negroes ? Oh, father, how could you ? Suppose it were your child, would you want it there ? "

"The deuce take it— 'tain't mine — there ain't a drop of Howell blood in its veins, the Lord knows, and as for my lying awake, feeding sweetened milk to that Maine woman's brat, I won't do it, and that's the end of it. I won't, I say, — but I knew't would be just like you to want me to keep it. You have the most unaccountable taste, and always had. There isn't another young man of your expectations, who would ever have cared for that - "

"Father," and Richard's haiiV was laid^upon the Judge's arm. " Father, Hetty is dead, and we will let her rest, but if she had lived, I would have called no other woman my wife."

"And the moment you had called her so, I would have disinherited you, root and branch," was the Judge's savage answer. " I would have seen her and you and your chil dren starve before I would have raised my hand. The heir of Beechwood marry Hetty Kirby ! Why, her father was a blacksmith and her mother a factory girl, — do you hear?"

Richard made no reply, and striking another light, he went to his chamber, where varied and bitter thoughts kept him wakeful until the September sun shone upon the wall, and told him it was morning. In the yard below he heard the sound of Rachel's voice, and was reminded by it of the child left there the previous night. He would see it for himself, he said, and making a hasty toilet, he walked leisurely down the well-worn path which led to the cottage door. The twelve were all awake, and as he drew near, a novel sight presented itself to his view. In the rude pine cradle, the baby lay, while over it the elder Van Brunts were bending, engaged in a hot discussion as to which should have "the little white nigger for their own." At the approach of Richard their noisy clamor ceased, and they fell back respectfully as he drew near the cradle. Richard Howell was exceedingly fond of children, and more than one of Rachel's dusky brood had he held upon his lap, hence it was, perhaps, that he parted so gently the silken rings of soft brown hair, clustering around the baby's brow, smoothed the velvety cheek, and even kissed the parted lips. The touch awoke the child, who seemed intuitively to know that the face bending so near to its own was a friendly one, and when Richard took it in his arms, it offered no resistance, but rather lovingly nestled its little head upon his shoulder, as he wrapped its blanket carefully ahput it, and started for the house.

CHAPTER II.

VILLAGE GOSSIP.

ITTLE MILDRED lay in the willow basket, where Richard Howell had placed her when he brought her from the cabin. Be tween himself and father there had been a spirited controversy as to what should be done with her, the one insisting that she should be sent to the poor-house, and the other that she should stay at Beechwood. The dis cussion lasted long, and they were still lingering at the breakfast table, when Rachel came in, her appearance indicating that she was the bearer of some important message.

" If you please," she began, addressing herself to the Judge, " I've jest been down to Cold Spring after a buck et o' water, for I feel mighty like a strong cup of hyson this mornin', bein' I was so broke of my rest, and the pump won't make such a cup as Cold Spring "

" Never mind the pump, but come to the point at once," interposed the Judge, glancing toward the basket

with a presentiment that what she had to tell concerned the little Mildred.

" Yes, that's what I'm coming to, ef I ever get thar. You see, I ain't an atom gossipy, but bein' that the Thomp son door was wide open, and looked invitin' like, I thought I'd go in a minit, and after fillin' my bucket with water,—though come to think on't, I ain't sure I had filled it,—had I ? Let me see,—I b'lieve I had, though I ain't sure "

Rachel was extremely conscientious, and no amount of coaxing could have tempted her to go on until she had settled it satisfactorily as to whether the bucket was filled or not. This the Judge knew, and he waited patiently un til she decided that "the bucket was filled, or else it wasn't, one or t'other," any way, she left it on the grass, she said, and went into Thompson's, where she found Aunt Hepsy " choppin' cabbage and snappin' at the boy with the twisted feet, who was catching flies on the winder."

"I didn't go in to tell 'em anything particular, but when Miss Hawkins, in the bedroom, give a kind of lone some sithe, which I knew was for dead Bessy, I thought I'd speak of our new baby that come last night in the basket; so I told 'em how't you wanted to send it to the poor-house, but I wouldn't let you, and was goin' to nuss it and fotch it up as my own, and then Miss Hawkins looked up kinder sorry-like, and says, ' Rather than suffer that, I'll take it in place of my little Bessy.'

" You or'to of seen Aunt Hepsy then,—but I didn't stay to hear her blow. I clipped it home as fast as ever I could, and left my bucket settin' by the spring."

"So you'll have no difficulty in ascertaining whether you filled it or not," slyly suggested

Richard. Then, turning to his father, he continued, " It strikes me favorably, this letting Hannah Hawkins take the child, inasmuch as you are so prejudiced against it. She will be kind to it, I'm sure, and I shall go down to see her at once."

There was something so cool and determined in Richard's manner, that the Judge gave up the contest without another word, and silently watched his son as he hurried along the beaten path which led to the Cold Spring.

Down the hill, and where its gable roof was just discernible from the windows of the Beechwood mansion, stood the low, brown house, which, for many years, had been tenanted by Hezekiah Thompson, and which, after his decease, was still occupied by Hepsabah, his wife. Only one child had been given to Hepsabah,—a gentle, blue-eyed daughter, who, after six years of happy wifehood, returned to her mother,—a widow, with two little fatherless children,—one a lame, unfortunate boy, and the other a beautiful little girl. Toward the boy with the twisted feet, Aunt Hepsy, as she was called, looked askance,-while all the kinder feelings of her nature seemed called into being by the sweet, winning ways of the baby Bessy ; but when one bright September day they laid the little one

away beneath the autumnal grass, and came back to their home without her, she steeled her heart against the entire world, and the wretched Hannah wept on her lonely pillow, uncheered by a single word of comfort, save those her little Oliver breathed into her ear.

Just one week Bessy had lain beneath the maples when Rachel bore to the cottage news of the strange child left at the master's door, and instantly Hannah's heart yearned toward the helpless infant, which she offered to take for her own. At first her mother opposed the plan, but when she saw how determined Hannah was, she gave it up, and in a most unarniable frame of mind was clearing her « breakfast dishes away, when Richard Howell appeared, asking to see Mrs. Hawkins. Although a few years older ' than himself, Hannah Thompson had been one of Richard's earliest playmates and wannest friends. He knew her disposition well, and knew she could be trusted; and when she promised to love the little waif, whose very helplessness had interested him in its behalf, he felt sure that she would keep her word.

Half an hour later and Mildred lay sleeping in Bessy's cradle, as calmly as if she were not the subject of the most wonderful surmises and ridiculous conjectures. On the wings of the wind the story flew that a baby had been left on Judge Howell's steps,—that the Judge had sworn it should be sent to the poor-house; while the son, who came home at twelve o'clock at night, covered with mud

and wet to the skin, had evinced far more interest in the stranger than was at all commendable for a boy scarcely out of his teens.

" But there was no tellin' what young bucks would do, or old ones either, for that matter! " so at least said Widow Simms, the Judge's bugbear, as she donned her shaker and palm-leaf shawl, and hurried across the fields in the direction of Beechwood, feeling greatly relieved to find that the object of her search was farther down the hill, for she stood somewhat in awe of the Judge and his proud son. But once in Hannah Hawkins' bedroom, with her shaker on the floor and the baby on her lap, her tongue was loosened, and scarcely a person in the town who could by any possible means have been at all connected with the affair, escaped a malicious cut. The infant was then minutely examined, and pronounced the very image of the Judge, or of Captain Harrington, or of Deacon Snyder, she could not tell which.

" But I'm bound to find out," she said; " I sha'n't rest easy nights till I do."

Then suddenly remembering that a kindred spirit, Polly Dutton, who lived some distance away, had probably not yet heard the news, she fastened her palm-leaf shawl with her broken-headed darning-needle, and bade Mrs. Haw-kins good-morning just as a group of other visitors was announced.

All that day, and for many succeeding ones, the cottage was crowded with curious people, who had come to see the sight, and all of whom offered an opinion as to the parentage of the child. For more than four weeks a bevy of old women, with Widow Simms and Polly Button at their head, sat upon the character of nearly every person they knew, and when at last the sitting was ended and the verdict rendered, it was found that none had passed the ordeal so wholly unscathed as Richard Howell. It was a little strange, they admitted, that he should go to Kiah Thompson's cottage three times a day; but then he had always been extremely fond of children, and it was but natural that he should take an interest in this one, particularly as his father had set his face so firmly against it, swearing heartily if its name were mentioned in his presence, and even threatening to prosecute the Widow Simms if she ever again presumed to say that the brat resembled him or his.

With a look of proud disdain upon his handsome, boy ish face, Richard, who on account of his delicate health had not returned to college, heard from time to time what the gossipping villagers had to say of himself, and when at last it was told to him that he was exonerated from all blame, and that some had even predicted what the result would be, were his interest in the baby to con tinue until she were grown to womanhood, he burst into a merry laugh, the first which had escaped him since he came back to Beechwood.

"Stranger things than that had happened," Widow Simms declared, and she held many a whispered confer ence with Hannah Hawkins as to the future, when Mil dred would be the mistress of Beechwood, unless, indeed, Richard died before she were grown, an event which seem ed not improbable, for as the autumn days wore on and the winter advanced, his failing strength became more and more perceptible, and the same old ladies, who once before had taken his case into consideration, now looked at him through medical eyes and pronounced him just gone with consumption.

Nothing but a sea voyage would save him, the physi cian said, and that to a warm, balmy climate. So when the spring came, he engaged a berth on board a vessel bound for the South Sea Islands, and after a pilgrimage to the obscure New Hampshire town where Hetty Kirby was buried, he came back to Beechwood one April night to bid his father adieu.

It was a stormy farewell, for loud, angry words were heard issuing from the library, and Rachel, who played the part of eaves-dropper, testified to hearing Richard say : " Listen to me, father, I have not told you all." To which the Judge responded, " I'll stop my ears before I'll hear another word. You've told me enough already; and, from this hour, you are no son of mine. Leave me at once, and my curse go with you."

With a face as white as marble, Richard answered, " I'll go father, and it may be we shall never meet again; but, in the lonesome years to come, when you are old and sick, and there is none to love you, you'll remember what you've said to me to-night."

The Judge made no reply, and without another word Richard turned away. Hastening down the Cold Spring path, he entered the gable-roofed cottage, but what passed between himself and Hannah Hawkins no one knew, though all fancied it concerned the beautiful baby Mil dred, who had grown strangely into the love of the young man, and who now, as he took her from her crib, put her arms around his neck, and rubbed her face against his own.

" Be kind to her, Hannah," he said. " There are none but ourselves to care for her now;" and laying her back in her cradle, he kissed her lips and hastened away, while Hannah looked wistfully after him, wondering much what the end would be.

CHAPTER III.

NINE YEARS LATER.

NINE times the April flowers had blossomed and decayed ; nine times the summer fruits had ripened and the golden harvest been gathered in ; nine years of change had come and gone, and up the wooded avenue which led to Judge HowelPs residence, and also to the gable-roofed cottage, lower down the hill, two children, a boy and a girl, were slowly wend ing their way. The day was balmy and bright, and the grass was as fresh and green as when the summer rains were falling upon it, while the birds were singing of their nests in the far off south land, whith er ere long they would go. But not of the birds, nor the grass, nor the day, was the little girl thinking, and she did not even stop to steal a flower or a stem of box from the handsome grounds of the cross old man, who many a time has screamed to her from a distance, bidding her quit her childish depredations ; neither did she pay the least attention to the old decrepit Tiger, as he trotted slowly down to meet her, licking her bare feet and look ing wistfully into her face as if he would ask the cause of her unwonted sadness.

"Come this way, Clubs," she said to her companion, as they reached a point where two paths diverged from the main road, one leading to the gable-roof, and the other to the brink of a rushing stream, which was sometimes dignified with the name of river. " Come down to our play-house, where we can be alone, while I tell you some thing dreadful."

Clubs, as he was called, from his twisted feet, obeyed, and, in a few moments, they sat upon a mossy bank be neath the sycamore, where an humble playhouse had been built,—a playhouse seldom enjoyed, for the life of that little girl was not a free and easy one.

" Now, Milly, let's have it; " and the boy Clubs looked inquiringly at her.

Bursting into tears she hid her face in his lap and sobbed :

" Tell me true,—true as you live and breathe,—ain't I your sister Milly, and if I ain't, who am I? Ain't I any body ? Did I rain down as Maria Stevens said I did ? "

A troubled, perplexed expression flitted over the pale face of the boy, and awkwardly smoothing the brown head resting on his patched pantaloons, he answered:

"Who told you that story, Milly; I hoped it would be long before you heard it 1 "

"Then 'tis true,—'tis true; and that's why grandma scolds me so, and gives me such stinchin' pieces of cake, and not half as much bread and milk as I can eat. Oh, dear, oh, dear,—ain't there anybody anywhere that owns me? Ain't I anybody's little girl?" and the poor child sobbed passionately.

It had come to her that day, for the first time, that she was not Mildred Hawkins, as she had supposed herself to be, and coupled with the tale was a taunt concerning her uncertain parentage. But Mildred was too young to understand the hint; she only comprehended that she was nobody,—that the baby Bessy she had seen so often in her dreams was not her sister,—that the gentle, loving woman, who had died of consumption two years before, was nothing but her nurse,—and worse than all the rest, the meek, patient, self-denying Oliver, or Clubs, was not her brother. It was a cruel thing to tell her this, and Maria Stevens would never have done it, save in a burst of passion. But the deed was done, and like a leaden weight Mildred's heart had lain in her bosom that dreary afternoon, which, it seemed to her, would never end. Anxiously she watched the sunshine creeping along the floor, and when it reached the four o'clock mark, and her class, which was the last, was called upon to spell, she drew a long sigh of relief, and taking her place, mechanically toed the mark, a ceremony then never omitted in a New England school.

But alas for Mildred; her evil genius was in the ascendant, for the first word which came to her was missed, as was the next, and the next, until she was ordered back to her seat, there to remain until her lesson was learned. Wearily she laid her throbbing head upon the desk, while the tears dropped fast upon the lettered page.

"Grandma will scold so hard and make me sit up so late to-night," she thought, and then she wondered if Clubs would go home without her, and thus prevent her from asking him what she so much wished to know.

But Clubs never willingly deserted the little maiden, and when at last her lesson was learned and she at liberty to go, she found him by the road-side piling up sand with his twisted feet, and humming a mournful tune, which he always sung when Mildred was in disgrace.

"It was kind in you to wait," she said, taking his offered hand. "You are real good to me;" then, as she remembered that she was nothing to him, her lip began to quiver, and the great tears rolled down her cheeks a second time.

"Don't, Milly," said the boy soothingly. "I'll help you if she scolds too hard."

Mildred made no reply, but suffered him to think it was his grandmother's wrath she dreaded, until seated on the mossy bank, when she told him what she had heard, and appealed to him to know if it were true.

"Yes, Milly," he said at length, "'tis true! You ain't my sister! You ain't any relation to me! Nine years ago, this month, you were left in a basket on Judge Howell's steps, and they say the Judge was going to kick you into the street, but Tiger, who was young then, took the basket in his mouth and brought it into the hall!"

Involuntarily Mildred wound her arms around the neck of the old dog, who lashed the ground with his tail, and licked her hand as if he knew what it were all about.

Clubs had never heard that she was taken to Rachel's cabin, so he told her next of the handsome, dark-eyed Richard, and without knowing why, Mildred's pulses quickened as she heard of the young man who befriended her and carried her himself to the gable-roof.

"I was five years old then," Oliver said; "and I just remember his bringing you in, with your great long dress hanging most to the floor. He must have liked you, for he used to come every day to see you till he went away!"

"Went where, Clubs? Went where?" and Mildred started up, the wild thought flashing upon her that she would follow him even to the ends of the earth, for if he had befriended her once he would again, and her desolate heart warmed toward the unknown Richard, with a strange feeling of love. "Say, Clubs, where is he now?" she continued, as Oliver hesitated to answer. "He is not dead,—you shan't tell me that!"

" Not dead that I ever heard," returned Oliver; " though nobody knows where he is. He went to the South Sea Islands, and then to India. Mother wrote to him once, but he never answered her ! "

" I guess he's dead then," said Mildred, and her tears flowed fast to the memory of Richard Howell, far off on the plains of Bengal.

Ere long, however, her thoughts took another channel, and turning to Oliver, she said :

" Didn't mother know who I was ? "

Oliver shook his head and answered : " If she did she never told, though the night she burst that blood-vessel and died so suddenly, she tried to say something about you, for she kept gasping * Milly is,—Milly is,—' and when she couldn't tell, she pointed towarehBeechwood."

" Clubs ! " and Mildred's eyes grew black as midnight, as she looked into the boy's face, " Clubs, Judge Howell is my father ! for don't you mind once that the widow Simms said I looked like the picture of his beautiful daughter, which hangs in the great parlor. I mean to go up there some day, and ask him if he ain't."

"Oh, I wouldn't! I wouldn't!" exclaimed Oliver, utterly confounded at the idea of Mildred's facing the crusty, ill-natured Judge, and asking if he were not her father. " He'd pound you with his gold-headed cane. He hates you! "and Oliver's voice sunk to a whisper. " He hates you because they do say you look like him, and act like him, too, when you are mad."

This last remark carried Mildred's thoughts backward a little, and for several moments she sat perfectly still; then leaving Tiger, whom all the time she had been fond ling, she came to Oliver's side, passed her hands caress ingly over his face, smoothed his thin, light hair, timidly kissed his forehead, and whispered beseechingly :

" I am % awful ugly, sometimes, I know. I scratched you once, Clubs, and stepped on your crooked feet, but I love you, oh, you don't know how much ; and if I ain't your sister, you'll love me just the same, won't you, precious Oliver. I shall die if you don't."

There were tears on the meek, patient face of Oliver, but before he could reply to this appeal, they were star tled by the loud, shrill cry of

" Mildred,—Mildred Hawkins !—what are you lazin' away here for ? I've been to the school-house and every where. March home this minute, I say," and adjusting her iron-bowed specs more firmly on her sharp, pointed nose, Hepsy Thompson came toward the two delin quents, frowning wrathfully, and casting furtive glances around her, as if in quest of Solomon's prescription for children who loitered on the road from school. At the sight of the ogress, Mildred grew white with fear, while Oliver, winding his arm protectingly around her, whis pered in her ear:

" You are sorry I am not your brother, but you must be glad that she ain't youi granny !" and he jerked his elbow toward Aunt Hepsy, who by this time had come quite near.

Yes, Mildred was glad of that, and Oliver's remark was timely, awakening within her a feeling of defiance toward the woman who had so often tyrannized over her. In stead of crying or hiding behind Oliver, as she generally did when the old lady's temper was at its boiling-point, she answered boldly :

" I was kept after school for missing, and then I coaxed Clubs out here to tell me who I am, for I know now I ain't Mildred Hawkins, arid you ain't my granny either."

It would be impossible to describe the expression of Hepsy's face, or the attitude of her person, at that mo ment, as she stood with her mouth open, her green calash hanging down her back, her nose elevated, and her hands upraised in astonishment at what she had heard. For a time after Hannah's death, Mrs. Thompson had tolerated Mildred simply because her daughter had loved her, and she could not wholly cast her off; but after a few weeks she found that the healthy, active child could be made useful in various ways, and had an opportunity presented itself, she would not have given her up. So she kept her, and Mildred now was little more than a drudge, where once she had been a petted and half-spoiled child. She washed the dishes, swept the floors, scoured the knives, scrubbed the door-sill, and latterly she had been initiated into the mysteries of shoe-closing, an employment then very common to the women and children of the Bay State. By scolding and driving, early and late, Aunt Hepsy managed to make her earn fifteen cents a day, and as this to her was quite an item, she had an object for wishing to keep Mildred with her. Thus it was not from any feeling of humanity that she with others remained silent as to Mildred's parentage, but simply because she had an undefined fancy that, if the child once knew there was no tie of blood between them, she would some day, when her services were most needed, resent the abuses heaped upon her, and go out into the world alone. So when she heard from Mildred herself that she did know,— when the words, "You are not my granny," were hurled at her defiantly, as it were, she felt as if something she had valued was wrested from her, and she stood a moment uncertain how to act.

But Hepsy Thompson was equal to almost any emergency, and after a little she recovered from her astonishment, and replied :

" So you know it, do you ? Well, I'm glad if somebody's saved me the trouble of telling you how you've lived on us all these years. S'posin I was to turn you out-doors, where would you go or who would you go to?"

Mildred's voice trembled, and the tears gathered in her large, dark eyes, as she answered :
11 Go to mother, if I could find her."

" Your mother !" and a smile of scorn curled Hepsy's withered lips. " A pretty mother you've got. If she'd cast you off when a baby, it's mighty likely she'd take you now."

Every word which Hepsy said stung Mildred's sensitive nature, for she felt that it was true. Her mother had cast her off, and in all the wide world there was no one to care for her, no place she could call her home, save the cheerless gable-roof, and even there she had no right. Once a thought of Richard flitted across her mind, but it soon passed away, for he was probably dead, and if not, he had forgotten her ere this. All her assurance left her, and burying her face in Oliver's lap, she moaned aloud :

" Oh, Clubs, Clubs, I most wish I was dead. Nobody wants me nowhere. What shall I do ? "

"Do?" repeated the harsh voice of Hepsy. "Go home and set yourself to work. Them shoes has got to be stitched before you go to bed, so, budge, I say."

There was no alternative but submission, and with a swelling heart Mildred followed the hard woman up the hill and along the narrow path and into the cheerless kitchen, where lay the shoes which she must finish ere she could hope for food or rest.

" Let me take them upstairs," she said ; " I can work faster alone," and as Hepsy made no objection, she hurried to her little room beneath the roof.

Her head was aching dreadfully, and her tears came so fast that she could scarcely see the holes in which to put her needles. The smell of the wax, too, made her sick, while the bright sunlight which came in through the western window made her still more uncomfortable. Tired, hungry, and faint, she made.but little progress with her task, and was about giving up in despair, when the door opened cautiously and Oliver came softly in. He was a frail, delicate boy, and since his mother's death Hepsy had been very careful of him.

"He couldn't work," she said; "and there was no need of it either, so long as Mildred was so strong and healthy."

But Oliver thought differently. Many a time had he in secret helped the little, persecuted girl, and it was for this purpose that he had sought her chamber now.

"Grandmother has gone to Widow Simms's to stay till nine o'clock," he said, " and I've come up to take your place. Look what I have brought you ; " and he held to view a small blackberry pie, which his grandmother had made for him, and which he had saved for the hungry Mildred.

There was no resisting Oliver, and Mildred yielded him her place. Laying her throbbing head upon her scanty pillow, she watched him as he applied himself diligently to her task. He was not a handsome boy; he was too pale,—too thin,—too old-looking for that, but to Mildred, who knew how good he was, he seemed perfectly beautiful, sitting there in the fading sunlight and working so hard for her.

" Clubs," she said, " you are the dearest boy in all the world, and if I ever find out who I am and happen to be rich, you shall share with me. I'll give you more than half. I wish I could do something for you now, to show how much I love you."

The needles were suspended for a moment, while the boy looked through the window far off on the distant hills where the sunlight still was shining.

"I guess I shall be dead then," he said, "but there's one thing you could do now, if you would. I don't mind it in other folks, but somehow it always hurts me when you call me Clubs. I can't help my bad-shaped feet, and I don't cry about it as I used to do, nor pray that God would turn them back again, for I know He won't. I must walk backwards all my life, but, when I get to Heaven, there won't be any bad boys there to plague me and call me Reel-foot or Clubs ! Mother never did; and almost the first thing I remember of her she was kissing my poor crippled feet and dropping tears upon them ! "

Mildred forgot to eat her berry pie ; forgot her aching head,—forgot everything in her desire to comfort the boy, who, for the first time in his life, had, in her presence, murmured at his misfortune.

"I'll never call you Clubs again," she said, folding her arms around his neck. " I love your crooked feet; I love every speck of you, Oliver, and, if I could, I'd give you my feet, though they ain't much handsomer than yours, they are so big!" and she stuck up a short, fat foot, which, to Oliver, seemed the prettiest he had ever seen.

"No, Milly," he said, "I'd rather be the deformed one. I want you to grow up handsome, as I most know you will!" and, resuming his task, he looked proudly at the bright little face, which bade fair to be wondrously beautiful.

Mildred did not like to work if she could help it, and, climbing upon the bed, she lay there while Oliver stitched on industriously. But her thoughts were very busy, for she was thinking of the mysterious Richard, wondering if he were really dead, and if he ever had thought of her when afar on the Southern seas. Then, as she remembered having heard that his portrait hung in the drawing-room at Beechwood, she felt a strong desire to see it; and why couldn't she ? Wasn't she going up there, some day, to ask the Judge if he were not her father ? Yes, she was ! and so she said again to Oliver, telling him how she meant to be real smart for ever so long, till his grandmother was good-natured and would let her go. She wotid wear her best calico gown and dimity pantalets, while Oliver should carry his grandfather's cane, by way of imitating 'the Judge, who might thus be more impressed with a sense of his greatness.

Although he lived so near, Oliver had never had more than a passing glance of the inside of the great house on the hill, and now that the first surprise was over, he began to feel a pleasing interest in the idea of entering its spacious halls with Mildred. They would go some day, he said, and he tried to frame a good excuse to give the Judge, who might not be inclined to let them in. Mildred, on the contrary, took no forethought as to what she must say; her wits always came when needed, and, while Oliver was thinking, she fell away to sleep, resting so quietly that she did not hear him go below for the bit of tallow candle necessary to com plete his task; neither did she see him, when his work was done, bend over her as she slept. Very gently he arranged her pillow, pushed back the hair which had fallen over her eyes, and then, treading softly on his poor warped feet, he left her room and sought his own, where his grandmother found him sleeping, when at nine o'clock she came home from Widow Simms's.

Mildred's chamber was visited next, the old lady start ing back in much surprise, when, instead of the little figure bending over her bench, she saw the shoes all finished and put away, while Mildred, too, was sleep ing,—her lips and hands stained with the berry pie, a part of which lay upon the chair.

"It's Oliver's doings," old Hepsy muttered, while thoughts of his crippled feet rose up in time to prevent an explosion of her wrath.

She could maltreat little Mildred, who had no mar or blemish about her, but she could not abuse a deformed boy, and she went silently down the stairs, leaving Oliver to his dreams of Heaven, where there were no crippled boys, and Mildred to her dreams of Richard, and the time when she would go to Beechwood, and claim Judge Ho well for her sire.

CHAPTER IV.
OLIVER AND MILDRED VISIT BEECHWOOD.

ILDRED had adhered to her resolution of being smart, as she termed it, and had suc ceeded so far in pleasing Mrs. Thompson that the old lady reluctantly consented to giving her a half holiday, and letting her go with Oliver to Beechwood one Saturday after noon. At first Oliver objected to accompany ing her, for he could not overcome his dread of the cross Judge, who, having conceived a dislike for Mildred, extended that dislike even to the inoffensive Oliver, always frowning wrathfully at him, and seldom speaking to him a civil word. The girl Mildred the Judge had only seen at a distance, for he never went near the gable-roof, and as he read his prayers at St. Luke's, while Hepsy screamed hers at the Metho dist chapel, there was no chance of his meeting her at church. Neither did he wish to see her, for so many stories had been fabricated concerning himself and the little girl, that he professed to hate the sound of her name.

MILDRED VISITS BEECHWOOD. *>l

He knew her figure, though, and never did she pass down the avenue, and out into the highway, on the road tc school, but he saw her from his window, watching her un til out of sight, and wondering to himself who she was, and why that Maine woman had let her alone so long ! It was just the same when she came back at night. Judge Howell knew almost to a minute when the blue paste board bonnet and spotted calico dress would enter the gate, and hence it was that just so sure as she stopped to pick a flower or stem of box (a thing she seldom failed to do), just so sure was he to scream at the top of his voice •

" Quit that, you trollop, and be off, I say." 4

Once she had answered back :

" Yow,yow,yow ! who's afraid of you, old cross-patch ! " while through the dusky twilight he had discerned the flourish of a tiny fist!

Nothing pleased the Judge more than grit, as he called it, and shaking his portly sides, he returned to the house, leaving the audacious child to gather as many flowers as she pleased. In spite of his professed aversion, there was, for the Judge, a strange fascination about the little Mildred, who, on one Saturday afternoon, was getting herself in readiness to visit him in his fortress. Great pains she took with her soft, brown hair, brushing it until her arm ached with the exercise, and then smoothing it with her hands until it shone like glass. Aunt Hepsy Thompson was very neat in her household arrangements,

and the calic D dress which Mildred wore was free from the least taint of dirt, as were the dimity pantalets, the child's especial pride. A string of blue wax beads was suspended from her neck, and when her little straw bon net was tied on, her toilet was complete.

Oliver, too, entering into Mildred's spirit, had spent far more time than usual before the cracked looking-glass which hung upon the wall; but he was ready at last, and issued forth, equipped in his best, even to the cane which Mildred had purloined from its hiding-place, and which she kept concealed until Hepsy's back was turned, when she adroitly slipped it into his hand and hurried him away.

It was a hazy October day, and here and there a gay-colored leaf was dropping silently from the trees, which grew around Beechwood. In the garden through which the children passed, for the sake of coming first to Ra chel's cabin, many bright autumnal flowers were in blos som ; but for once Mildred's fingers left them untouched. She was too intent upon the house, which, with its numer ous chimneys, balconies, and windows, seemed to frown gloomily down upon her.

" What shall you say to the Judge ? " Oliver asked, and Mildred answered :

" I don t know what I shall say, but if he sasses me, it's pretty likely I shall sass him back."

Just then Rachel appeared in the door, and, spying the two children as they came through the garden-gate, she shaded l.er eyes with her tawny hand, to be sure she saw aright.

" Yes, 'tis Mildred Hawkins," she said; and she cast a furtive glance backward through the wide hall, toward the sitting-room, where the Judge sat, dozing in his willow chair.

" Was it this door, under these steps, that I was left ? " asked Mildred in a whisper, but before Oliver could reply Rachel had advanced to meet them.

Mildred was not afraid of her, for the good-natured negress had been kind to her in various ways, and going boldly forward, she said :

" I've come to see Judge Howell. Is he at home ? "

Rachel looked aghast, and Mildred, thinking she would not state her principal reason for wishing to see him, con tinued, " I want to see the basket I was brought here in and everything."

"Do you know then ? Who told you?" and Rachel looked inquiringly at Oliver, who answered : " Yes, she knows. They told her at school."

The fact that she knew gave her, in Rachel's estimation, some right to come, and motioning her to be very cau tious, she said : " The basket is up in the garret. Come still, so as not to wake up the Judge," and taking off her own shoes by way of example, she led the way through the hall, followed by Oliver and Mildred, the latter of whom could not forbear pausing to look in at the room where the Judge sat unconsciously nodding at her.

" Come away," whispered Oliver, but Mildred would Lot move, and she stood gazing at the Judge as if he had been a caged lion.

Just then Finis, who being really the last and youngest, was a spoiled child, yelled lustily for his mother. It was hazardous not to go at his bidding, and telling the children to stand still till she returned, Rachel hurried away.

"Now then," said Mildred, spying the drawing-room door ajar, " we'll have a good time by ourselves," and taking Oliver's hand, she walked boldly into the parlor, where the family portraits were hanging.

At first her eye was perfectly dazzled with the elegance of which she had never dreamed, but as she became some what accustomed to it, she began to look about and make her observations.

" Isn't this glorious, though! Wouldn't I like to live here !" and she set her little foot hard down upon the velvet carpet.

" Good afternoon, ma'am," said Oliver in his meekest tone, and Mildred turned just in time to see him bow to what he fancied to be a beautiful young lady smiling down upon them from a gilded frame.

"The portraits ! the portraits ! " she cried, clapping her hands together, and, in an instant, she stood face to face with Mildred Howell, of the " starry eyes and nut-brown hair."

But why should that picture affect little Mildred so strangely, causing her to hold her breath and gaze up at it with childish awe. It was very, very beautiful, and hundreds had admired its girlish loveliness; but to Mil dred it brought another feeling than that of admiration,— a feeling as if that face had looked at her many a time from the old, cracked glass at home.

" Oliver," she said, " what is it about the lady ? Who is she like, or where have I seen her before ? "

Oliver was quite as perplexed as herself; for the features of Mildred Howell seemed familiar even to him. He had somewhere seen their semblance, but he did not think of looking for it in the little girl, whose face grew each moment more and more like the one upon the canvas. And not like that alone, but also like the portrait beyond,—the portrait of Richard Howell. Mildred had not noticed this yet, though the mild, dark eyes seemed watching her every moment, just as another pair of living eyes were watching her from the door.

Mildred's scream of joy had penetrated to the ears of the sleeping Judge, rousing him from his after-dinner nap, and causing him to listen again for the voice which sounded like an echo from the past. The cry was not repeated, but through the open door he heard distinctly the childish voice, and shaking off his drowsiness he started to see who the intruders could be.

Judge Howell did not believe in the supernatural. Indeed, he scarcely believed in anything, but when he first

caught sight of Mildred's deep, brown eyes, and sparkling face, a strange feeling of awe crept over him, for it seemed as if his only daughter had stepped suddenly from the canvas, and going backward, for a few years, had come up before him the same little child, whose merry laugh and winsome ways had once made the sunlight of his home. The next instant, however, his eye fell upon Oliver •, and then he knew who it was. His first impulse was to scream lustily at the intruder, bidding her begone, but there was something in the expression of her face which kept him silent, and he stood watching her curiously, as, with eyes upturned, lips apart, and hands clasped nervously together, she stood gazing at his daughter, and asking her companion who the lady was like.

Oliver could not tell, but to the Judge's lips the answer sprang, " She's like you." Then, as he remembered that others had thought the same, his wrath began to rise ; for nothing had ever so offended him as hearing people say that Mildred Hawkins resembled him or his.

" You minx ! " he suddenly exclaimed, advancing into the room, " what are you doing here and who are you, hey?"

Oliver colored painfully, and looked about for some safe hiding-place, while Mildred, poising her head a little on one side, unflinchingly replied :

" 1 am Mildred. Who be you ? "

" Did I ever hear such impudence ?" muttered the

Judge, and striding up to the child, he continued, in his loudest tones, " Who in thunder do you think I am ? "

Very calmly Mildred looked him in the face and deliberately replied :

"I think you are my father ; anyway, I've come up to ask if you ain't."

" Great Heavens ! " and the Judge involuntarily raised his hand to smite the audacious Mildred, but before the blow descended his eyes met those of Richard, and though it was a picture he looked at, there was something in that picture which stayed the act, and his hand came down very gently upon the soft brown hair of the child who was so like both son and daughter.

" Say," persisted Mildred, emboldened by this very perceptible change in his demeanor, "be you my father, and if you ain't, who is? Is heV And she pointed toward Richard, whose mild, dark eyes seemed to Oliver to smile approvingly upon her.

Never bf-fore in his life had the Judge been so uncertain as to whether it were proper to scold or to laugh. The idea of that little girl's coming up to Beech wood, and claiming hi .n for her father was perfectly preposterous, and yet in spite of himself there was about her something he could not resist,—she seemed near to him,—so near that for one brief instant the thought flitted across his brain that he would keep her there with him, and not let her go back to the gable-roof where rumor said she was far from

being happy. Then as he remembered all that had been said, and how his adopting her would give rise to greater scandal, he steeled his heart against her and replied, in answer to her questions, " You haven't any father, and never had. Your mother was a good-for-nothing jade from Maine, who left you here because she knew I had money, and she thought maybe I'd keep you and make you my heir. But she was grandly mistaken. I sent you off then and I'll send you off again, so begone you baggage, and don't you let me catch you stealing any more flowers, or calling me names, either, such as ' old cross-patch.' I 'ain't deaf; I heard you."

" You called me names first, and you are a heap older than I am," Mildred answered, moving reluctantly toward the door, and coming to a firm stand as she reached the threshold.

" What are you waiting for ? " asked the Judge, and Mildred replied, " I ain't in any hurry, and I shan't go un til I see that basket I was brought here in."

"The" plague you won't," returned the Judge, now growing really angry. "We'll see who's master; and taking her by the shoulder, he led her through the hall, down the steps, and out into the open air, followed by Oliver, who having expected some such denouement, was not greatly disappointed.

" Let's go back," he said, as he saw indications of what he called, " one of Milly's tantrums." But Milly would

not stir until she had given vent to her wrath, looking and acting exactly like the Judge, who, from an upper window, was watching her with mingled feelings of amusement and admiration.

"She's spunky, and no mistake," he thought, " but I'll be hanged if I don't like the spitfire. Where the plague did she get those eyes, and that mouth so much like Mil dred and Richard ? She bears herself proudly, too, I will confess," he continued, as he saw her at last cross the yard and join Rachel, who, having found him in the par lor when she came back from quieting Finn, had stolen away unobserved.

Twice the Judge turned from the window, and as often went back again, watching Mildred, as she passed slowly through the garden, and half wishing she would gather some of his choicest flowers, so that he could call after her and see again the angry flash of her dark eyes. But Mildred did not meddle with the flowers, and when her little straw bonnet disappeared from view, the Judge be gan to pace the floor, wondering at the feeling of loneli ness which oppressed him, and the voice which whispered that he had turned from his door a second time the child who had a right to a place by his hearthstone and a place in his heart, even though he were not her father.

CHAPTER V.

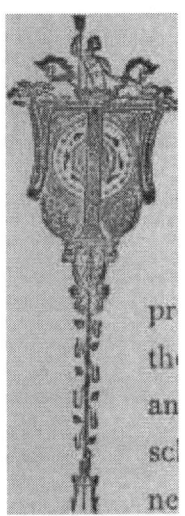

LAWRENCE THORNTON AND HIS ADVICE.

HE fact that Mildred had dared go up to Beechwood and claim Judge Howell as her father, did not tend in the least to im prove her situation, for regarding it as proof that she would, if she could, abandon the gable-roof, Aunt Hepsy became more un-amiable than ever, keeping the child from school, and imposing upon her tasks which never could have been performed but for Oli ver's assistance. Deep and dark were the waters through which Mildred was passing now, and in the coining future she saw no ray of hope, but behind that heavy cloud the sun was shining bright and only a little way beyond, the pastures lay all green and fair.

But no such thoughts as these intruded themselves up on her mind on the Sabbath afternoon when, weary and dejected, she stole from the house, unobserved even by Oliver, and wended her way to the river bank. It was a warm November day, and seating herself upon the with ered grass beneath the sycamore, she watched the faded leaves as they dropped into the stream and floated silent ly away. In the quiet Sabbath hush there was something very soothing to her irritated nerves, and she ere long fell asleep, resting her head upon the twisted roots, which made almost as soft a pillow as the scanty one of hen's feathers on which she was accustomed to repose.

She had not lain there long when a footstep broke the stillness, and a boy, apparently about fourteen or fifteen years of age, drew near, pausing suddenly as his eye fell upon the sleeping child.

"Belongs to some one of the Judge's poor tenants, I dare say," he said to himself, glancing at her humble dress, and he was about passing her by, when something in her face attracted his attention, and he stopped for a nearer view.

"Who is she like?" he said, and he ran over in his mind a list of his city friends, but among them all there was no face like this one. " Where have I seen her ? "** he continued, and determining not to leave the spot un til the mystery was solved, he sat down upon a stone near by. " She sleeps long; she must- be tired," he said at last, as the sun drew nearer to the western horizon, and there were still no signs of waking. "I know she's mighty uncomfortable with her neck on that sharp point/' he continued, and drawing near he substituted himself for the gnarled roots which had hitherto been Mildred's pillow.

Something the little girl said in her sleep of Oliver, whom she evidently fancied was with her, and then her brown head nestled down in the lap of the handsome boy, who smoothed her hair gently, while he wondered more and more whom she was like. Suddenly it came to him, and he started so quickly that Mildred awoke, and with a cry of alarm at the sight of an entire stranger, sprang to her feet as if she would run away. But the boy held her back, saying pleasantly :

" Not so fast, my little lady. I haven't held you till my arms ache for nothing. Come here and tell me who you are."

His voice and manner both were winning, disarming Mildred of all fear, and sitting down, as he bade her do, she answered :

"I am Mildred,—and that's all."

" Mildred,—and that's all! " he repeated. " You sure ly have some other name ! Who is your father ? "

" I never had any, Judge Ho well says, and my mother put me in a basket, and left me up at Beechwood, ever so long ago. It thundered and lightened awfully, and I wish the thunder had killed me before I was as tired and sorry as I am now. There's nobody to love me anywhere but Richard and Oliver, and Richard, I guess, is dead, while Oliver has crippled feet, and if he grows to be a man he can't earn enough for me and him, and I'll have to stay with grandmother till I die. Oh, I wish it could

be now; and I've held my breath a lot of times to see if I couldn't stop breathing, but I always choke and come to life !"

All the boy's curiosity was roused. He had heard before of the infant left at Judge Howell's, and he knew now that she sat there before him,—a much-abused, neglected child, with that strange look upon her face which puzzled him just as it had many an older person.

" Poor little girl," he said. " Where do you live, and who takes care of you ? Tell me all about it;" and adroitly leading her on, he learned the whole story of her life,—how sinCe the woman died she once thought was her mother she had scarcely known a happy day. Old Hepsy was so cross, putting upon her harder tasks than she could well perform,—beating her often, and tyranniz ing over her in a thousand different ways.

" I used to think it was bad enough when I thought she was related," said Mildred, "but now I know she hain't no right, it seems a hundred times worse,—and I don't know what to do."

"I'd run away," suggested the boy; and Mildred re plied :

" Run where ? I was never three miles from here in my life."

" Run to Boston," returned the boy. " That's where I live. Cousin Geraldine wants a waiting-maid, and though she'd be mighty overbearing, father would be

good, I guess, and so would Lilian,—she's just about your size."

" Who is Lilian ? " Mildred asked, and he replied :

" I call her cousin, though she isn't at all related. Father's sister Mary married Mr. Veille, and died when Geraldine was born. Ever so many years after uncle married again and had Lilian, but neither he nor his second wife lived long, and as father was appointed guar dian for Geraldine and Lilian, they have lived with us ever since. Geraldine is proud, but Lilian is a pretty little thing. You'll like her if you come."

" Should you be there ?" Mildred asked, much more interested in the handsome boy than in Lilian Veille.

" I shall be there till I go to college," returned the boy ; " but Geraldine wouldn't let you have much to say to me, she's so stuck up, and feels so big. The boys at school told me once that she meant I should marry Lilian, but I sha'n't if I don't want to."

Mildred did not answer immediately, but sat thinking intently, with her dark eyes fixed upon the stream running at her feet. Something in her attitude reminded the boy a second time of the resemblance which had at first so impressed him, and turning her face more fully toward him, he said :

11 Do you know that you look exactly as my mother did?"

Mildred started eagerly. The old burning desire to

know who she was, or whence she came, was awakened, and grasping the boy's hand, she said :

"Maybe you're my brother, then. Oh, I wish you was! Come down to the brook, where the sun shineg ; we can see our faces there and know if we look alike."

She had grasped his arm and was trying to draw him forward, when he dashed all her newly-formed hopes by saying:

"It is my step-mother you resemble; she that was the famous beauty, Mildred Howell."

"That pretty lady in the frame?" said Mildred, rather sadly. " Widow Simms says I look like her. And was she your mother ? "

" She was father's second wife," returned the boy, " and I am Lawrence Thornton, of Boston."

Seeing that the name, " Lawrence Thornton," did not impress the little girl as he fancied it would, the boy pro ceeded to give her an outline history of himself and fam ily, which last, he said, was one of the oldest, and richest, and most aristocratic in the city.

" Have you any sisters ? " Mildred asked, slOi Law rence replied:

" I had a sister once, a good vjeal older than I am. I don't remember her much, for when I was five years old, —that's ten years ago,—she ran off with her music teacher, Mr. Harding, and never came back again; and

about a year later, we heard that she was dead, and that there was a girl-baby that died with her "

" Yes ; but what of the beautiful lady, your mother ? * chimed in Mildred, far more interested in Mildred Howell than in the baby reported to have died with Lawreruce's sister Helen.

Lawrence Thornton did not know that the far-famed " starry eyes " of sweet Mildred Howell had wept bitter tears ere she consented to do her father's bidding and wed a man many years her senior, and whose only daughter was exactly her own age ; neither did he know how from the day she wore her bridal robes, looking a very queen, she had commenced to fade,—for Autumn and May did not go well together, even though the former were gilded all over with gold. He only had a faint re membrance that she was to him a playmate rather than a mother, and that she seemed to love to have him kiss her and caress her fair round cheek far better than his father. So he told this last to Mildred, and told her, too, how his father and Judge Howell both had cried when they stood together by her coffin.

"And Richard," said Mildred,—" was Richard there ?"

Lawrence did not know, for he was scarcely four years old when his step-mother died.

"But I have seen Richard Howell," he said; " I saw him just before he went away. He came to Boston to see Cousin Geraldine, I guess, for I've heard since that

Judge Howell wanted him to marry her when she got big enough. She was only thirteen then, but that's a way the Howells and Thorntons have of marrying folks a great deal older than themselves. You don't catch me at any such thing, though. How old are you, Mildred?"

Lawrence Thornton hadn't the slightest motive in ask ing this question, neither did he wait to have it answered; for, observing that the sun was really getting veiy low in the heavens, he arose, and, telling Mildred that dinner would be waiting for him at Beechwood, where he was now spending a few days, he bade her good-by, and walked rapidly away.

As far as she could see him Mildred followed him with her eyes, and when, at last, a turn in the winding path hid him from her view, she resumed her seat upon the twisted roots and cried, for the world to her was doubly desolate now that he was gone.

" He was so bright, so handsome," she said, " and he looked so sorry like when he said ' poor little Milly !' Oh, I wish he would stay with me always !"

Then she remembered what he had said to her of going to Boston, and she resolved that when next old Hepsy's treatment became harsher than she could bear, she would surely follow his advice and run away to Boston, perhaps, and be waiting-maid to Miss Geraldine Veille. She had no idea what the duties of a waiting-maid were, but no situation could be worse than her present one, and then

Lawrence would be there a portion of the time at least. Yes, she would certainly run away, she said ; nor was it very long ere she had an opportunity of carrying her resolution into effect, for as the weather grew colder, Hepsy, who was troubled with rheumatism and corns, became intolerably cross and one day punished Mildred fo"r a slight offense far more severely than she had ever done before.

"I can't stay,—I won't stay,—I'll go this very night! " thought Mildred, as blow after blow fell upon her uncovered neck and arms.

Then as her eye fell upon the white-faced Oliver, who apparently suffered more than herself, she felt a moment's indecision. Oliver would miss her,—Oliver would cry when he found that she was gone, but Lawrence Thornton would get him a place as chore boy somewhere near her, and then they would be so happy in the great city, where Hepsy's tongue could not reach them. She did not think that money would be needed to carry her to Boston, for she had been kept so close at home that she knew little of the world, and she fancied that she had only to steal away to the depot unobserved, and the rest would follow, as a matter of course. The conductor would take her when she told him of Hepsy, as she meant to do, and once in the city anybody would tell her where Lawrence Thornton lived. This being satisfactorily settled, her next step was to pin up in a

cotton handkerchief her best calico dress and pantalets, for if the Lady Geraldine were proud as Lawrence Thornton had said, she would want her waiting-maid to look as smart as possible.

Accordingly the faded frock and dimity pantalets, which had not been worn since that memorable visit to Beech-wood, were made into a bundle, Mildred thinking the while how she would put them on in the woods, where there was no danger of being detected by old Hepsy, who was screaming for her to come down and fill the kettle.

"It's the last time I shall do it," thought Mildred, as she descended the stairs and began to make her usual preparation for the supper, and the little girl's step was lighter at the prospect of her release from bondage.

But every time she looked at Oliver, who was suffering from a sick headache, the tears came to her eyes, and she was more than once tempted to give up her wild project of running away.

" Dear Oliver," she whispered, when at last the supper was over, the dishes washed, the floor swept, and it was almost time for her to go. " Dear Oliver," and going over to where he sat, she pressed her hand upon his throbbing temples,—" you are the dearest, kindest brother that ever was born, and you must remember how much I love you, if anything should happen."

Oliver did not heed the last part of her remark, he

only knew he liked to have her warm hand on his forehead, it made him feel better, and placing his own thin fingers over it he kept it there a long time, while Mildred glanced nervously at the clock, whose constantly moving minute hand warned her it was time to go. Immediately after supper Hepsy had taken her knitting and gone to spend the evening with Widow Simms, and in her absence Mildred dared do things she would otherwise have left undone. Kneeling down by Oliver and laying her head upon his knee, she said :

" If I should die or go away forever, you'll forgive me. won't you, for striking you in the barn that time, and laughing at your feet. I was mad, or I shouldn't have done it, I've cried about it so many times," and she laid her hand caressingly upon the poor, deformed feet turned backward beneath her chair.

" Oh, I never think of that," answered Oliver; " and if you were to die, I should want to die, too, 'twould be so lonesome without little Milly."

Poor Milly! She thought her heart would burst, and nothing but a most indomitable will could have sustained her ; kissing him several times she arose, and making some excuse, hurried away up to her room. It took but a moment to put on her bonnet and shawl, and stealing noiselessly down the stairs, she passed out into the winter darkness, pausing for a moment beneath the uncurtained window, to gaze at Oliver, sitting there alone, the dim fire-light shining on his patient face and falling on his hair. He did not see the brown eyes filled with tears, nor the forehead pressed against the pane, neither did he hear the whispered words, " Good-by, darling Oliver, good-by," but he thought the room was darker, while the shadows in the corner seemed blacker than before, and he listened eagerly for the footsteps coming down, but listened in vain, for in the distance, with no company save the gray December clouds and her own bewildered thoughts, a little figure was hurrying away to the far-off city,— and away to Lawrence Thornton.

CHAPTER VI.
WHAT CAME OF IT.

EPSY'S clock, which was thought by its mistress to regulate the sun, was really a great deal too slow, and Mildred had scarcely gone half the way to the Mayfield station, when she was startled by the shrill scream of the engine, and knew that she was left behind.

" Oh, what shall I do ? " she cried. " I can't go back, for maybe Hepsy's home before now, and she would kill me sure. My arm aches now where she struck me so hard, the old good-for-nothing. I'd rather stay here alone in the woods," and sinking against a log Mildred began to cry.

Not for a moment, however, did she regret what she had done. The dreary gable-roof seemed tenfold drearier to her than the lonesome woods, while the winter wind, sighing through leafless trees, was music compared with Hepsy's voice. The day had not been very cold, but the night was chilly, and not a single star shone through the leaden clouds. A storm was coming on, and Mildred felt the snow-flakes dropping on her face.

"I don't want to be buried in the snow and die," she ught, "for I ain't very good; I'm an awful sinner, nny says, and sure to go to perdition, but I ain't so tain about that. God wouldn't be very hard on a little girl who has been treated as mean as I have. He'd make some allowance for my dreadful bringing up. I wonder if He is here now ; Oily says He is everywhere, and if He is and can see me in my tantrums He can see me in the dark. I mean to pray to Him just as good as I can, and ask. Him to take care of me; " and kneeling by the old log; with the darkness all about her, and the snow-flakes falling thickly upon her upturned face, she began a prayer :h was a strange mixture of what she had heard at St. :e's, where she had once been with Oliver, what she had often heard at the prayer meetings which she had frently attended with Aunt Hepsy, and of her real self as thought and felt.

She began : " Have mercy upon us, miserable sinners, for if I know my own heart, I think I have made a new consecration of all that I have and all that I am since we last met, and henceforth I mean to,—mean to, "

Here the mere form of words left her, and the child y spoke out and told her trouble to God. "Qh, Jesus," she said,, "if you be really here, and if can hear what I say, as Oily says you can, I wish i come up close to me, right here by the log, so I needn't feel afraid while I tell you how granny has whip-4 ped me so many times for 'most nothing, and never let me have a real doll or do anything I wanted to, and I've been so unhappy there, and wicked, too, and mad at her, and called her ugly names behind her back, and would to her face, only I dassent, and I've made mouths at her and wished I could lick her, and have even in my tantrums been mean to Oily, and twitted him about his twisted feet, and pulled his hair and spit at him as fast as I could spit, and loved him all the time, and now I've runned away and the cars have left me when I was going in them to Boston to see Lawrence Thornton and be Miss Geral-dine's waiting-maid, and it's dark and cold and snowy here in the woods, and I am afraid of something, I don't know what, and I can't go back to granny, who would almost skin me alive, and she ain't my granny either; some Maine woman sent me to Judge Hovvell, in a thunder storm and basket, and I'm nobody's little girl; so, please, Jesus, take care of me and tell me where to go and what to do, and I'm so sorry for all my badness, especially to Oily, for Christ's sake, Amen."

This was a very long prayer for Milly, who had never before said more than " Now I lay me," or the Lord's prayer ; but God saw and heard the little desolate child, and answered her touching appeal.

" There, I feel better and not so lonesome, already," she said, as she rose from her knees and groped around to find some better place of shelter than the old log afforded.

Suddenly, as she came to an opening in the trees, she saw, in the distance, the light shining out from the library windows of Beechwood ; and the idea crossed her brain that she would go there, and if Judge Howell turned her off, as he did before, she'd go to Tiger's kennel and sleep with him. Mildred's impulses were usually acted upon, and she was soon traversing the road to Beechwood, feel ing with each step that she was drawing nearer to her home.

" Widow Simms says I have a right here," she thought, as she passed silently through the gate. " And I almost believe so, too. Any way, I mean to tell him I've come to stay;" and, without a moment's hesitation, the courageous child opened the door, and stepped into the hall.

Judge Howell sat in his pleasant library, trying to in terest himself in a book, but a vague feeling of loneliness oppressed him, and as often as he read one page, he turned backward to see what had gone before.

" It's of no use," he said, at last; " I'm not in a reading mood; " and closing his eyes, he leaned back in his arm chair, and thought of much which had come to him dur ing the years gone by,—thought first of his gentle wife,— then of his beautiful daughter,—and then of Richard, whom he had cursed in that very room. Where was he now ? Were the waters of the Southern seas chanting wild music over his ocean bed ? Did the burning sun of

?6 WHAT CAME OF IT.

Bengal look down upon his grave ?—or would he come back again some day, and from his father's lips hear that the old man was sorry for the harsh words that he had spoken? Then, by some sudden transition of thought, he remembered the night of the storm, and the infant left at his door. He had never been sorry for casting it off, he said, and yet, had he kept her,—were she with him this wintry night, he might not be so dreary sitting alone.

" There they go ! " said a childish voice, and as his gold-bowed specs fell to the floor, the Judge started up, and lo, there upon a stool, her bonnet and bundle on a chair, and her hands folded demurely upon her lap, sat the veritable object of his thoughts, even little Mildred.

Through the half-closed door she had glided so noise lessly as not to disturb his reverie, and sitting down upon the stool at his feet, had warmed her hands by the blaz ing fire, removed her hood, smoothed back her hair, and then watched breathlessly the slow descent of the specs from the nose of the Judge, who, she fancied, was sleep ing. Lower, and lower, and lower they came, and when at last they dropped, she involuntarily uttered the excla mation which roused the Judge to a knowledge of her presence.

" What the deuce,—how did you get in, and what are you here for ? " asked the Judge, feeling, in spite of him self, a secret satisfaction in having her there, and know ing that he was no longer alone.

Fixing her clear, brown eyes upon him, Mildred an swered :

" I walked in, and I've come to stay."

"The plague you have," returned the Judge, vastly amused at the quiet decision with which she spoke. " Come to stay, hey ? But suppose I won't let you, what then ? "

"You will," said Mildred ; "and if you turn me out, I shall come right in again. I've lived with Oliver's grand mother as long as I am going to. I don't belong there, and to-night I started to run away, but the cars left me, and it was cold and dark in the woods, and I was kind of 'fraid, and asked God to take care of me and tell me where to go, and I corned right here."

There was a big lump in the Judge's throat as he listened to the child, but he swallowed it down, and point ing to the bundle containing Mildred's Sunday clothes, said, " Brought your things, too, I see. You'll be want ing a closet and a trunk to put them in, I reckon."

The quick-witted child detected at once the irony in his tone, and with a quivering lip she answered :

" They are the best I've got. She never bought me anything since mother died. She's just as cross as she can be, too, and whips me so hard for nothing,—look," and rolling up her sleeve she showed him more than one red mark upon her arm.

Sour and crusty as the Judge appeared, there were soft spots scattered here and there over his heart, and though the largest was scarcely larger than a pin's head, Mildred had chanced to touch it, for cruelty to any one was some thing he abhorred.

"Poor little thing," he said, taking the fat, chubby arm in one hand, and passing the other caressingly over the marks,—" poor little thing, we'll have that old she-dragon 'tended to," and something very like a tear, both in form and feeling, dropped upon the dimpled elbow. " What makes you stare at me so ? " he continued, as he saw how the wondering brown eyes were fixed upon him.

" I was thinking," answered Mildred, " how you ain't such a cross old feller as folks say you be, and you'll let me stay here, won't you? I'd rather live with you than Lawrence Thornton "

" Lawrence Thornton ! " repeated the Judge. " What do you know of him ? Oh, yes, I remember now that he spoke of finding you asleep; but were you running away to him ? "

In a few words Mildred told him what her intentions had been, and then said to him again :

" But I shall stay here now and be your little girl."

" I ain't so sure of that," answered the Judge, adding, as he saw her countenance fall: " What good could you do me ? "

Mildred's first thought was, " I can wash the dishes and scrub the floor; " then as she remembered that servants did these things at Beechwood, she stood a moment un certain how to answer. At last, as a new idea crossed her mind, she said : " When you're old and lonesome, there'll be nobody to love you if I go away, and you'll be sorry " if you turn me off."

Why was it the Judge started so quickly and placed his hand before his eyes, as if to assure himself that it was little Mildred standing there and not his only boy,—not Richard, who long ago had said to him:

" In the years to come, when you are old and lone some, you'll be sorry for what you've said to-night."

Those were Richard's words, while Mildred's were :

"You'll be sorry if you turn me off."

It would seem that the son, over whose fate a dark mystery hung, was there in spirit, pleading for the help less child, while with him was another Mildred, and looking through the eyes of brown so much like her own, she said, " Take her father, you will need her some time ! "

And so, not merely because Mildred Hawkins asked him to do it, but because of the unseen influence which urged him on, the Judge drew the little girl closer to his side, and parting back her rich, brown hair, said to her pleasantly, " You may stay to-night, and to-morrow night, and if I don't find you troublesome, perhaps you may stay for good."

Mildred had not looked for so easy a conquest, and

this unexpected kindness wrung from her eyes great tears, which rolled silently down her cheeks.

" What are you crying for ? " asked the Judge. " You are not obliged to stay. You can go back to Hepsy any minute,—now, if you want. Shall I call Rachel to hold the lantern ? "

"He made a motion toward the bell-rope, while Mildred, in an agony of terror, seized his arm, telling him " she was only crying for joy; that she'd die before she'd go back ! " and adding fiercely, as she saw he had really rung the bell: " If you send me away I'll set your house on fire ! "

The Judge smiled quietly at this threat, and when Rachel appeared in answer to his ring, he said, " Open the register in the chamber above, and see that the bed is all right, then bring us some apples and nuts,—and,— wait till I get done, can't you,—bring us that box of prunes. Do you love prunes, child ? "

" Yes, sir, though I don't know what they be," sobbed Mildred, through the hands she had clasped over her face when she thought she must go back.

She knew she was not going now, and her eyes shone like diamonds as they flashed upon the Judge a look of gratitude. It wasn't lonesome now in that handsome library where Mildred sat, eating prune after prune, and apple after apple, while the Judge sat watching her with an immense amount of satisfaction, and, thinking to him-

self how, on the morrow, if he did not change his mind, he would inquire the price of feminine dry goods, a thing he had not done in years. In his abstraction he even forgot that the clock was striking nine, and, half an hour later, found him still watching Mildred, and marvelling at her enormous appetite for nuts and prunes. But he remem bered, at last, that it was his bed time, and, again ringing for Rachel, he bade her take the little girl upstairs.

It was a pleasant, airy chamber where Mildred was put to sleep, and it took her a long time to examine the fur niture and the various articles for the toilet, the names of which she did not even know. Then she thought of Oliver, wondering what he would say if he knew where she was; and, going to the window, against which a driving storm was beating, she thought how much nicer it was to be in that handsome apartment than back in her little bed beneath the gable roof, or even running away to Boston after Lawrence Thornton.

The next morning when she awoke, the snow lay high-piled upon the earth, and the wind was blowing in fearful gusts. But in the warm summer atmosphere pervading the whole house, Mildred thought nothing of the storm without. 'She only knew that she was very happy, and when the Judge came down to breakfast, he found her singing of her happiness to the gray house-cat, which she had coaxed into her lap.

*' Shall she eat with you or wait ? " asked Rachel, a
little uncertain whether to arrange the table for two or one.

"With me, of course, you simpleton," returned the Judge; " and bring on some sirup for the cakes,—or honey ; which do you like best, child ? "

Mildred didn't know, but guessed that she liked both, and both were accordingly placed upon the table,—the Judge forgetting to eat in his delight to see how fast the nicely browned buckwheats disappeared.

" She'll breed a famine if she stays here long," Rachel muttered, while Finn looked ruefully at the fast decreas ing batter.

But Mildred's appetite was satisfied at last, and she was about leaving the table, when Hepsy's sharp, shrill voice was heard in the hall, proclaiming to Rachel the aston ishing news that Mildred Hawkins had run away and been frozen to death in a snow bank,—that Clubs, like a fool, had lost his senses and gone raving distracted, call ing loudly for Milly and refusing to be comforted unless she came back.

Through the open door Mildred heard this last, and darting into the hall she asked the startled Hepsy to tell her if what she had said were true. Petrified with astonishment, Hepsy was silent for an instant, and then in no mild terms began to upbraid the child, because she was not frozen to death as she had declared her to be.

"Never mind," said Mildred, "but tell me of Oliver. Is h* sick, and does he ask for me ? "

The appearance of the Judge brought Hepsy to herself, and she began to tell the story. It seemed that she had staid with Widow Simms until after ten, and when she reached home she found Clubs distracted on account of Mildred's absence, He had looked all through the house, and was about going up to Beechwood, when his grandmother returned and stopped him, say ing that Mildred had probably gone to stay with Lottie Brown, as she had the previous day asked permission so to do and been refused. So Oliver had rested till morning, when he insisted on his grandmother's wad ing through the drifts to see if Milly really were at Mr. Brown's.

" When I found she wasn't," said Hepsy, " I began to feel a little riled myself, for I knowed that she had the ugliest temper that ever was born, and, says I, she's run away and been froze to death, and then such a rumpus as Oliver made. I thought he'd go "

Her sentence was cut short by a cry of joy from Mil dred, who, from the window, caught sight of the crippled boy moving slowly through the drifts, which greatly im peded his progress. Hastening to the door she drew him in out of the storm, brushed the snow from his thin hair, and folding her arms about him, sobbed out," Oliver, I ain't dead, but I've run away. I can't live with her any more,

though if you feel so bad about it, maybe I'll go back. Shall I ? "

Before Oliver could reply, Hepsy chimed in, "Go back, to be sure you will, my fine madame. I'll teach you what is what;" and seizing Mildred's hood, which lay upon the hat-stand, she began to tie it upon the screaming child, who struggled violently to get away, and succeeding at last ran for protection behind the Judge.

" Keep her, Judge Howell, please keep her," whispered Oliver, while Mildred's eyes flashed out their gratitude to him for thus interfering in her behalf.

"Woman ! " and the Judge's voice was like a clap of thunder, while his heavy boot came down with a ven geance as he grasped the bony arm of Hepsy, who was making a dive past him after Mildred. " Woman, get out of my house ! Quick too, and if I catch you here again after anybody's child, I'll pull every hair out of your head. Do you hear, you she-dragon ? Begone, I say ; start. Move faster than that! " and he accelerated her move ments with a shove, which sent her quite to the door, where she stood for an instant, threatening to take the la\v of him, and shaking her fist at Mildred, who, holding fast to the coat-skirts of the Judge, knew she had nothing to fear.

After a moment Hepsy began to cry, and assuming a deeply injured tone, she bade Oliver " Come."

Not till then had Mildred fully realized that if she stayed at Beechwood she must be separated from her beloved playmate, and clutching him as he arose to follow his grandmother, she whispered, " If you want me, Oliver, I'll go."

He </*V/want her, oh, so much, for he knew how lonely the gable-roof would be without her, but it was far better that she should not return, and -so, with a tremendous effort the unselfish boy stilled the throbbings of his heart, and whispered back : " I'd rather you'd stay here, Milly, and maybe h€ll let me come some time to see you."

" Every day, every day," answered the Judge, who could not help admiring the young boy for preferring Mildred's happiness to his own. "There, I'm glad that's over," he said, when, as the door closed upon Hepsy and Oliver, he led Mildred back to the breakfast room, asking her if she didn't want some more buckwheats.

But Milly's heart was too full to eat, even had she been hungry. Turn which way she would, she saw only the form of a cripple boy moving slowly through the drifts, back to the dark old kitchen, which she knew would that dismal day be all the darker for her absence. It was all in vain that the Judge sought to amuse her by showing her all his choice treasures and telling her she was now his little girl and should call him father if she liked. The sad, despondent look did not leave her face for the entire day, and just as it was growing dark, she laid her brown head upon the Judge's knee, as he sat in

his arm-chair, and said mournfully, " I guess I shall go back."

"I guess you won't," returned the Judge, running his fingers through her soft hair, and thinking how much it was like his own Mildred's.

" But I ought to," answered the child. " Oliver can't do without me. You don't know how much he likes me, nor how much I like him. He's missing me so now, I know he is, and I'm afraid he's crying, too. Mayn't I go?"

Mildred's voice was choked with tears, and Judge Howell felt them dropping upon his hand, as he passed it caressingly over her face. Six months before he had professed to hate the little girl sitting there at his feet, and crying to go back to Oliver, but she had grown strangely into his love within the last twenty-four hours, and to himself he said :

" I will not give her up."

So after sitting a time in silence, he replied :

" I can do you more good than this Oliver with his crooked feet."

"Yes, yes," interrupted Mildred, "but it's because his feet are crooked that I can't leave him all alone, and then he loved me first, when you hated me and swore such awful words if I just looked at a flower."

There was no denying this,—but the Judge was not convinced, and he continued by telling her how many

new dresses he would buy her,—how in the spring he'd get her a pony and a silver-mounted side-saddle "

" And let me go to the circus ? " she said, that having hitherto been the highest object of her ambition.

"Yes, let you go to the circus," he replied; "and to Boston and everywhere." •

The bait was a tempting one, and Mildred wavered for a moment,—then just as the Judge thought she was satis fied, she said:

" But that won't do Oliver any good."

" Hang Oliver! " exclaimed the Judge ; " I'll tell you what I'll do. I'll have a lady governess to come into the house and teach you both. So you will see him every day. I'll get him some new clothes "

" And send him to college when he's big enough ? " put in Mildred. " He told me once he wished he could go."

" Great Peter, what next will you want ? But I'll think about the college; and if he learns right smart, and you behave yourself, I reckon maybe I'll send him."

The Judge had no idea that Oliver would learn " right smart," for he did not know him, and he merely made the promise by way of quieting Mildred, who, with this prospect in view, became quite contented in her new quarters, though she did so wish Oliver could know it that night, and looking up in the Judge's face, she said :

" It's such a little bit of a ways down there,—couldn't
you go and tell him, or let me. It seems forever till to morrow."

Had the Judge been told the previous day that Mildred Hawkins could have persuaded him to brave that fierce northeaster, he would have scoffed at the idea as a most preposterous one, but now, looking into those shining eyes of brown, lifted so pleadingly to his, he felt all his sternness giving way, and before he knew what he was doing, or why he was doing it, he found himself plowing through the snow-drifts which lay between Beechwood and the gable-roof, where he found Oliver sitting before the fire with a sad, dejected look upon his face as if all the happiness of his life had suddenly been taken from him. But he brightened at once when he saw the Judge and heard his errand. It would be so nice to be with Milly every day and know that she was beyond the reach of his grandmother's cruelty, and bursting into tears he stammered out his thanks to the Judge, who without a sign of recognition for old Hepsy, who was dipping candles with a most sour expression on her puckered lips, started back through the deep snow-drifts, feeling more than repaid, when he saw the little, eager face pressed against the pane, and then heard a sweet, young voice calling him " the best man in the world."

And Mildred did think him the embodiment of every virtue, while her presence in his house worked a marvelous change in him. He had something now to live for,
and his step was always more elastic as he drew near his home, where a merry-hearted, frolicsome child was sure to welcome his coming.

"The little mistress of Beechwood," the people began to call her, and so indeed she was, ruling there with a high hand, and making both master and servant bend to her will, particularly if in that will Oliver were concerned. He was her first thought, and she tormented the Judge until he kept his promise of having a governess, to whom Oliver recited each day as well as herself.

Once during the spring Lawrence Thornton came again to Beechwood, renewing his acquaintance with Mildred, who, comparing him with other boys of her acquaintance, regarded him as something more than mortal, and after he was gone, she was never weary of his praises. Once in speaking of him to her teacher, Miss Harcourt, she said, " He's the handsomest boy I ever saw, and he knows so much, too. I'd give the world if Oliver was like him," and Mildred's sigh as she thought of poor lame Oliver was echoed by the white-faced boy without the door, who had come up just in time to hear her remarks. He, too, had greatly admired Lawrence Thornton, and it had, perhaps, been some satisfaction to believe that Mildred had not observed the difference between them, but he knew, now, that she had, and with a bitter pang, as he thought of his deformity, he took his accustomed seat in the school-room.

" I can never be like Lawrence Thornton," he said to himself. " I shall always be lame, and small, and sickly, and by and by, maybe, Milly will cease to love me."

Dark, indeed, would be his life, when the sun of Mildred's love for him was set, and his tears fell fast, erasing the figures he was making on his slate.

" What is it, Oily ? " and Mildred nestled close by his side, taking his thin hand in her own chubby ones- and looking into his face.

Without the least reserve he told her what it was, and Mildred's tears mingled with his as he said that his twisted feet were a continual canker worm,—a blight on all his hopes of the future when he should have attained the years of a man. The cloud was very heavy from which Mildred could not extract some comfort, and after a mo ment she looked up cheerily, and said :

" I tell you, Oliver, you can't be as handsome as Law rence, nor as tall, nor have such nice straight feet, but you can be as good a scholar, and when folks speak of that Mr. Hawkins, who knows so much, I shall be so proud, for I shall know it is Oliver they mean."

All unconsciously Mildred was sowing in Oliver's mind the first seeds of ambition, though not of a worldly kind. He did not care for the world. He cared only for the opinion of the little brown-eyed maiden at his side It is true he would have endured any amount of torture if, in the end, he might look like Lawrence Thornton; but

as this could not be, he determined to resemble him in something,—to read the same books,—to learn the same things,—to be able to talk about the same places, and if, in the end, she said he was equal to Lawrence Thornton, he would be satisfied. So he toiled both early and late, far outetripping Mildred and winning golden laurels, in the opinion of Miss Harcourt and the Judge, the latter of whom became, in spite of himself, deeply interested in the pale student, who before three years were gone, was fully equal to his teacher.

Then it was that Mildred came again to his aid, saying to the Judge one day, " Oliver has learned all Miss Har court can teach him, and hadn't you better be looking out for some good school, where he can be fitted for college ? "

" Cool!" returned the Judge, tossing his cigar into the grass and smiling down upon her. " Cool, I declare. So you think I'd better fit him for college, hey? "

" Of course, I do," answered Mildred; " you said you would that stormy day long ago, when I cried to go back and you wouldn't let me."

" So I did, so I did," returned the Judge, adding that " he'd think about it."

The result of this thinking Mildred readily foresaw, and she was not at all surprised when, a few days afterwards, the Judge said to her, " I have made arrangements for Clubs to go to Andover this fall, and if he behaves himself I shall send him to college, I guess; and,—come back

here, you spitfire," he cried, as he saw her bounding away with the good news to Oliver. But Mildred could not stay for more then. She must see Oliver, who could scarcely find words with which to express his gratitude to the man who, for Mildred's sake, was doing so much for him. ^

Rapidly the autumn days stole on, until at last one Sep tember morning Mildred's heart was sore with grief, and her eyes were red with weeping, for Oliver was gone and she was all alone.

" If yqn mourn so for Clubs, what do you think I shall do when you, too, go off to school ? " said the Judge.

" Oh, I sha'n't know enough to go this ever so long," was Mildred's answer, while the Judge, thinking how lonely the house would be without her, hoped it would be so ; but in spite of his hopes, there came a day, just four teen years after Mildred was left on the steps at Beech-wood, when the Judge said to Oliver, who had come home, and was asking for his playmate :

" She's gone to Charlestown Seminary, along with that Lilian Veille, Lawrence Thornton makes such a fuss about, and the Lord only knows how I'm going to live without her for the next miserable three years."

CHAPTER VII.

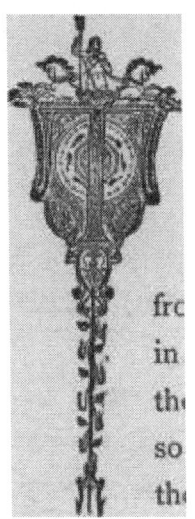

LILIAN AND MILDRED.

THE miserable three years are gone, or nearly so, and all around the Beechwood mansion the July sun shines brightly, while the summer shadows chase each other in frolicsome glee over the velvety sward, and in the maple trees the birds sing merrily, as if they know that the hand which has fed them so often with crumbs will feed them again on the morrow. In the garden, the flowers which the child Milly loved so well are blossoming in rich pro-fusion, but their gay beds present many a broken stalk to day, for the Judge has gathered bouquet after bouquet with which to adorn the parlors, the library, the chambers, and even the airy halls, for Mildred is very fond of flowers, and when the sun hangs just above the woods and the engine-whistle is heard among the May field hills lying to the westward, Mildred is coming home, and stored away in some one of her four trunks is a bit of paper saying that its owner has been graduated with due form, and is a finished-up young lady.

During the last year the Judge had not seen her, for business had called him to Virginia, and, for a part of the time, Beechwood had been closed and Mildred had spent her long vacation with Lilian, who was now to accompany her home. With this arrangement the Judge hardly knew whether to be pleased or not. He did not fancy Lilian. He would a little rather have Mildred all to himself a while ; but when she wrote to him, saying : " May Lilian come home with me ? It would please me much to have her,"—he answered "Yes," at once ; for now, as of old, he yielded his wishes to those of Mildred, and he waited impatiently for the appointed day, which, when it came, he fancied would never end.

Five o'clock, said the fanciful time-piece upon the marble mantle, and, when the silver bell rang out the next half-hour, the carnage came slowly to the gate, and with a thrill of joy the Judge saw the girlish head protruding from the window, and the fat, white hand wafting kisses towards him. He had no desire now to kick her into the street,—no wish to send her from Beechwood,—no inclination to swear at Widow Simms for saying she was like himself. He was far too happy to have her home again, and, kissing her cheeks as she bounded to his side, he called her " little Spitfire," just as he used to do, and then led her into the parlor, where hung the picture of another

Mildred, who now might well be likened to herself, S&VQ that the dress was older-fashioned and the hair a darker brown.

" Oh, isn't it pleasant here?" she cried, dancing about the room. " Such heaps of flowers, and, as I live, a new piano! It's mine, too!" and she fairly screamed with joy as she saw her own name, " MILDRED HOWELL," engraved upon it.

" It was sent home yesterday," returned the Judge, enjoying her delight and asking for some music.

" Not just yet," returned Mildred, " for, see, Lilian and I are an inch deep with dust ;" and gathering up their shawls and hats, the two girls sought their chamber, from which they emerged as fresh and blooming as the roses which one had twined among her flowing curls, and the other had placed in the heavy braids of her rich brown hair.

"Why is not Oliver here?" Mildred asked, as they were about to leave the supper-table, " or does he think, because he is raised to the dignity of a Junior, that young ladies are of no importance ? "

" I invited him to tea," said the Judge, " but he is suffering from one of his racking headaches. I think he studies too hard, for his face is white as paper, and the veins on his forehead are large as my finger; so I told him you should go down there when I was sick of you."

"Which I shall make believe is now," said Mildred,

laughingly, and taking from the hall-stand her big stn hat, she excused herself to Lilian, and hurrying down t Cold Spring path, soon stood before the gable-roof doc where old Hepsy sat knitting and talking to herself,- a habit which had come upon her with increasing years.

At the sight of Mildred she arose, and dropping a low curtsey, began in her fretful, querulous way : " I wonder now if you can stoop to come down here; but I s'po it's Oliver that's brought you. It beats all how folks th gets a little riz will forget them that had all the trouble of bringin* 'em up. Ofiver is up charmber with the headache, and I don't b'lieve he wants to be disturbed."

"Yes, he does," said Mildred, and lifting the old-fasioned wooden latch, she was soon climbing the crazy stairs which creaked to her bounding tread.

Of his own accord, and because he knew it won please Mildred, the Judge had caused what was once her chamber at the gable roof to be finished off and fitt< into a cozy library for Oliver, who when at home spent many a happy hour there, bending sometimes over his books, and thinking again of the years gone by, and (' the little girl who had often cried herself to sleep with those very walls. It was well with her now, he knew, and he blessed God that it was so, even though his po feet might never tread the flowery path in which it w given her to walk. He had not seen her for nearly two "years, but she had written to him regularly, and from her

letters he knew she was the same warm-hearted, impulsive Milly who had once made all the sunshine of his life. She had grown up very beautiful, too, for among his class mates were several whose homes were in Charlestown, and who, as a matter of course, felt a deep interest in the Seminary girls, particularly in Miss Howell, who was often quoted in his presence, his companions never dreaming that she was aught to the " club-footed Lexicon," as they called the studious Oliver.

Lawrence Thornton, too, when he came to the college commencement, had said to him playfully :

" Clubs, your sister Milly, as you call her, is very Beautiful, with eyes like stars and hair the color of the chestnuts I used to gather in the Mayfield woods. If I A-ere you, I should be proud to call her sister."

And Oliver was proud; but when the handsome,
•nanly figure of Lawrence Thornton had vanished through
-.he door, he fancied he breathed more freely, though
why he should do so he could not tell, for he liked to
ear Mildred praised.

"I shall see her for myself during this vacation," be 'bought; and after his return to Beechwood he was i early as impatient as the Judge for her arrival. "She "ill be home to-day," he thought on the morning when e knew she was expected, and the sunlight dancing on >.ie wall seemed all the brighter to him.

He had hoped to meet her at Beechwood, but his 5 enemy, the headache, came on in time to prevent his do ing so, and with a sigh of disappointment he went to his little room, and leaning back in his easy-chair, counted the lagging moments until he heard the well-known step upon the stairs, and knew that she had come. In a mo ment she stood beside him, and was looking into his white, worn face, just as he was gazing at her in all her glowing, healthy beauty. He had kissed her heretofore when they met,—kissed her when they parted; but he dared not do it now, for she seemed greatly changed. He had lost his little, romping, spirited Milly, and he knew there was a dividing line between himself and the grown young lady standing before hinft But no such thoughts intruded themselves upon Mildred; Oliver, to her, was the same good-natured boy who had waded barefoot with her in the brook, picked "huckleberries" on the hills and chesfnuts in the wood. She never once thought of him as a man, and just as she was wont to do of old, just so she did now,—she wound her arms around his neck, and kissing his forehead, where the blue veins were swelling, she told him how glad she was to be there with him again,—told him how sorry she was to find him so feeble and thin, and lastly, how proud she was when she heard from Lawrence Thornton that he was first in his class, and bade fair to make the great man she long ago predicted he would make. Then she paused for his reply, half expecting that he would complimer t her in return, for Mildred was well used to flattery, and rather claimed it as her due.

Oliver read as much in her speaking eyes, and when, laying her hat upon the floor, she sat down upon a stool at his feet, he laid his hand fondly on her hair, and said :

"You are very, very beautiful, Milly ! "•

"Oh, Oliver ! " and the soft, brown eyes looked up at him wistfully,—"you never yet told me a lie; and now, as true as you live, do you think I am handsome,—as hand some, say, as Lilian Veille ? "

"You must remember I have never seen Miss Veille," said Oliver, "and I cannot judge between you. Mr. Thornton showed me her photograph, when he was in Amherst; but it was a poor one, and gave no definite idea of her looks."

"Did Lawrence have her picture ?" Mildred asked quickly, and, in the tone of her voice Oliver detected what Mildred thought was hidden away down in the deep est corner of her heart.

But for this he did not spare her, and he said : " I fancied they might be engaged."

"Engaged, Oliver ! " and the little hand resting on his knee trembled visibly. " No, they are not engaged yet; but they will be some time, I suppose, and they'll make a splendid couple. You must come up to-morrow and call on Lilian, She is the sweetest, dearest girl you ever sawl"

Oliver thought of one exception, but he merely an swered : " Tell me of her, Milly, so I can be somewhat prepared. What is she like ? "

"She is a little mite of a thing," returned Mildred, " with the clearest violet-blue eyes, the tiniest mouth and nose, the longest, silkiest, golden curls, a complexion pure as wax, and the prettiest baby ways,—why, she's afraid of everything; and in our walks I always constitute myself her body-guard, to keep the cows and dogs from looking at her."

"Does she know anything ? " asked Oliver, who, taking Mildred for his criterion, could scarcely conceive of a sensible girl being afraid of dogs and cows.

"Know anything ! " and Mildred looked perfectly aston ished. "Yes, she knows as much as any woman ever ought to know, because the men,—that is, real, nice men such as a girl would wish to marry, —always prefer a wife with a sweet temper and ordinary intellect, to a spirited and more intellectual one; don't you think they do?"

Oliver did not consider himself a " real nice man,— such as a girl would wish to marry," and so he could not answer for that portion of mankind. He only knew that for him there was but one temper, one mind, one style of beauty, and these were all embodied in Mildred Howell, who, without waiting for his answer, continued :

" It is strange how Lilian and I came to love each other
so much, when we are so unlike. Why, Oliver, they called me the spunkiest girl in the Seminary, and Lilian the most amiable; that's when I first went there ; but we did each other good, for she will occasionally show some spirit, while I try to govern my temper, and have not been angry in ever so long. You see, Lilian and I roomed to gether. I used to help her get her lessons \ for somehow she couldn't learn, and, if she sat next to me at recitation, I would tell her what to answer, until the teacher found it out, and made me stop. When Lilian first came to Charlestown, Lawrence was with her; she was fifteen then, and all the girls said they were engaged, they acted so. I don't know how, but you can imagine, can't you ? "

Oliver thought he could, and Mildred continued : " I was present when he bade her good-by, and heard him say, * You'll write to me, Fairy ?' that's what he calls her. But Lilian would not promise, and he looked very sorry. After we had become somewhat acquainted, she said to me one day, * Milly, everybody says you write splendid compositions, and now, won't you make believe you are me, and scribble off a few lines in answer to this ? ' and she showed me a letter just received from Lawrence Thornton.

" I asked why she did not answer it herself, and she said, * Oh, I can't; it would sicken him of me at once, for I don't know enough to write decently ; I don't always spell straight, or get my grammar correct. I never know when to use to or too, or just where the capitals belong; *
so after a little I was persuaded, and wrote a letter, which she copied and sent to Lawrence, who expressed himself sc much delighted with what he called ' her playful, pleas ant style,' that I had to write again and again, until now I do it as a matter of course, though it does hurt me sometimes to hear him" praise her, and say he never knew she had such a talent for writing,"

" But she will surely undeceive him ? " Oliver said, be ginning to grow interested in Lilian Veille.

" Oh, she can't now," rejoined Mildred, for she loves him too well, and she says he would not respect her if he knew it."

" And how will it all end ? " asked Oliver, to which Mildred replied:

"End in their being married, of course. He always tells her how much he likes her—how handsome she is, and all that,"

There was the least possible sigh accompanying these words, and Oliver, who heard it, smoothed again the shin ing braids, as he said, " Milly, Lawrence Thornton told me you were very beautiful, too, with starry eyes and hair the color of rich brown chestnuts."

"Did he, sure? what else did he say ? " and assuming a kneeling position directly in front of Oliver, Mildred buttoned and unbuttoned his linen coat, while he told her everything he could remember of Lawrence Thornton's remarks concerning herself.

" He likes me because Lilian does, I suppose," she said, when he had finished. "Did I tell you that his father and Geraldine,—that's Lilian's half-sister,—have always intended that he should marry Lilian ? She told me so herself, and if she hadn't, I should have known it from

Geraldine, for you know I have been home with Lilian ever so many times, besides spending the long vacation there. I couldn't bear her,—this Geraldine ; she talked so insultingly to me, asking if I hadn't the least idea who I was, anu saying once, right before Lawrence Thornton, that she presumed my mother was some poor, ignorant country girl, who had been unfortunate, and so disposed of me that way ! I could have pulled every black hair out of her head ! " and Mildred, who, in her excitement loosened a button in Oliver's coat, looked much like the Mildred of old,—the child who had threatened to set fire to the Judge's house if he sent her back to Hepsy.

"Mildred," said Oliver, smiling in spite of himself, and thinking how beautiful she looked even in her anger, " shall I tell you who /think you ar<! ? "

"Yes, yes," and the wrathful expression of the soft, dark eyes disappeared at once. "Who am I, Oliver?"

"I don't know for certain," he replied, "but I think you are Richard Howell's daughter. Any way, you are the very counterpart of his sister's picture."

"Mrs. Thornton, you mean," returned Mildred.

There's a portrait of her at Lawrence's home. Almost everybody spoke of the resemblance while I was there ; and once some one made a suggestion similar to yours, but Mr. Thornton said he knew every inch of ground Richard had gone over from the time he was twelve years old until he went away, and the thing wasn't possi ble,—that the resemblance I bore to the Hcwells was merely accidental. I don't like Mr. Thornton. He's just as proud as Geraldine, and acted as if he were afraid Lawrence would speak to me. It was ' Lawience, Lilian wants you ;' ' Lawrence, hadn't you better take Lilian to ride, while I show Miss Howell my geological speci mens.' Just as though I cared for those old stones. He needn't trouble himself, though, for I don't like Lawrence half as well as I do you. But I must go back to Lilian, •^s&efll wonder that I leave her so long."

" Lilian is here," said a childish voice, and both Oliver and Mildred started quickly, as a little figure advanced from its position near the doorway, where, for the last two minutes, it had been standing.

Oliver's first thought was, " she has heard all Mildred said; she had no business to come up so quietly," and with his previously formed impressions of the little lady, he was not prepared to greet her very cordially. But one glance at the baby face which turned towards him as Mildred said: "This is Oliver, Miss Veille," convinced him that, if she had heard anything, it had not offended

her. Indeed, Lilian Veille belonged to the class of whom it has been truly said, " they do not know enough to be offended."

She was a good-natured, arniable girl, and though usually frank and open-hearted, she would sometimes stoop to deceit, particularly if her own interests were con cerned. At home she had been petted and caressed until she was a thoroughly spoiled, selfish child, exacting from others attentions and favors which she was never willing to render back. All this Oliver saw before she had been ten minutes in his presence, but he could not dislike her any more than he could have disliked a beau tiful, capricious baby ; and he began to understand in part why Mildred should feel so strong an attachment for her. She was naturally very familiar and affectionate, and as Mildred had resumed her seat upon the stool, she, sat down upon the floor, and laying both her soft hands on Oliver's knee, began to talk with him as if she had known him all her life, stipulating, on the start, that he shouldn't say a word to her of books, as she detested the whole thing.

" Mildred will tell you how little I know," she said. "She used to do my sums, translate my French, write my compositions, and some of my letters, too. Do you know Lawrence, Mr. Hawkins?"

Oliver replied that he had seen him, and Lilian continued:

"Isn't he splendid? All the Boston girls are ready to pull caps over him, but he don't care for any of them. I used to think maybe he'd fall in love with Milly; but,— Geraldine says she knows too much for a man like him really to care for; and I guess she does, for anybody can see I'm a simpleton,—and he certainly likes me the best,—don't he, Milly? Why, how red your cheeks are,—and no wonder, it's so hot in this pent-up room. Let's go down," and without waiting for an answer, Lilian tripped down the stairs, followed by Mildred and Oliver,—the latter having forgotten his headache in the pleasure of seeing his former playmate.

"Now where?" asked Lilian, as they emerged into the open air.

"Home, I guess," said Mildred, and bidding Oliver good-night, they went back to Beechwood, where they found the Judge impatiently waiting for them. He wanted some music, he said, and he kept Mildred, who was a fine performer, singing and playing for him until it was long after his bed-time, and Lilian began to yawn very decidedly.

"She was bored almost to death," she said, as she at last followed Mildred up the stairs. "She didn't like Beechwood at all, thus far,—she did wish Lawrence Thornton would come out there," and with a disagreeable expression upon her pretty face, she nestled down among her pillows, while Mildred, who was slower in hex movements, still lingered before the mirror, brushing her rich brown hair.

Suddenly Lilian started up, exclaiming: "I've got it, Milly, I've got it."

"Got what?" asked Mildred, in some surprise, and Lilian rejoined, "Lawrence comes home from Chicago to-night, you know, and when he finds I'm gone, he'll be horridly lonesome, and his father's dingy old office will look dingier than ever. Suppose I write and invite him to come out here, saying you wish it, too?"

"Well, suppose you do," returned Mildred with the utmost gravity. "There's plenty of materials in my desk. Will you write sitting up in bed?" and in the eyes which looked every way but at Lilian there was a spice of mischief.»

(f You hateful thing," returned Lilian. "You know well enough that when I say f f am going to write to Law rence,' I mean you are going to write. He's so completely hoodwinked that I cannot now astonish him with one of my milk-and-water epistles. Why, I positively spell worse and worse, so Geraldine says. Think of my putting an h in precious!"

"But Lawrence will have to know it some time," persisted Mildred, "and the longer it is put off the harder it will be for you."

"He needn't know either," said Lilian. "I mean to have you give me ever so many drafts to carry home, and if none of them suit the occasion Geraldine must write, though she bungles awfully. And when I'm his wife, I sha'n't care if he does know. He can't help himself then. He'll have to put up with his putty head."

"But will he respect you, Lily, if he finds you deceived him to the last?" Mildred asked; and with a look very much like a frown in her soft blue eyes, Lilian replied: "Now, Milly, I believe you are in love with him yourself, and do this to be spiteful, but you needn't. His father and Geraldine have always told him he should marry me,—and once when some one teased him of you, I heard him say that he shouldn't want to marry a woman unless he knew something of her family, for fear they might prove to be paupers, or even worse. Oh, Milly, Milly, I didn't mean to make you cry!" and jumping upon the floor, the impulsive Lilian wound her arms around

Mildred, whose tears were dropping fast.

Mildred could not have told why she cried. She only knew that Lilian's words grated harshly, but hers was a sunshiny nature, and conquering all emotion, she returned Lilian's caress and said: "I will write the letter, Lily,—write it to-night if you like."

"I knew you would. You're a splendid girl," and giving her another hug Lilian jumped back into bed, and made herself quite comfortable while Mildred knotted up her silken hair and brought out her desk preparatory to her task.

Never before had it caused her so much pain to write "Dear Lawrence" as to-night, and she was tempted to omit it, but Lilian was particular to have every word. "She never could remember, unless she saw it before her, whether the 'Dear' and the * Lawrence' occupied the same or separate lines," she said; so Mildred wrote it down at last, while half unconsciously to herself she repeated the words, "Dear Lawrence."

"You merely wish to invite him here?" she said to Lilian, who answered : "That's the main thing ; but you must write three pages at least, or he won't be satisfied. Tell him what a nice journey we had, and how pleasant Beechwood is. Tell him all about your new piano, and what a splendid girl you are,—how I wonder he never fell in love with you,—but I'm glad he didn't; tell him how much Oliver knows, and how much better he looks than I thought he did; that -if he was bigger and hadn't such funny feet he'd almost do for you ; tell him how dearly I like him,—Lawrence, I mean, not Oliver,—how glad I shall be when he comes, and Geraldine must send my coral ear-rings and bracelets, and "

" Stop, stop ! You drive me distracted ! " cried Mildred, who, from this confused jumble, was trying to make out a sensible letter.

Her task was finished at last, and she submitted it to Lilian's inspection.

"But you didn't tell him what a splendid girl you are,

HO LILIAN AND MILDRED.

nor how much I like him," said Lilian, her countenance falling at once. " Can't you add it in a postscript some how ? »

" Never mind, Lily," returned Mildred, lifting one of the long golden curls which had escaped from the lace cap. " He knows you like him, and when he comes you can tell him anything you please of me. It does not look well in me to be writing my own praises."

"But you used to," said Lilian. "You wrote to him once, ' I love Mildred Howell best of anybody in the world, don't you ? ' and he answered back, ' Yes, next to you, Fairy, I love Mildred best.' Don't you remember it, Milly ? "

Mildred did remember it, and remembered, too, how that answer had wrung from her bitter tears ; but she made no reply, and, as Lilian began to show signs of sleepiness, she arose cautiously and put aside the letter, which would be copied next morning in Lilian's delicate little hand and sent on its way to Boston.

CHAPTER VIII.
LAWRENCE AND HIS FATHER.

"LAWRENCE, step in here for a moment," said Mr. Thornton; and Lawrence, equipped for travelling, with carpet-bag, duster, and shawl, followed his father into the library, where all the family edicts were issued and all the family secrets told. "Lawrence, Geral-dine tells me you are going to Beechwood for three or four days."

"Why, yes," returned the son. "I received a letter from Lilian last night inviting me to come. I told you of it at the time, else my memory is very treacherous."

"It may be,—I don't remember," said the father; "but Geraldine has given me a new idea about your going there, and it is for this that I have called you in. Lawrence do you love Lilian Veille?"

"Why do you ask me that question, when you know that I have always loved her?" was the reply, and Mr. Thornton continued: "Yes, yes, but how do you love her,—as a sister,—as a cousin,—or as one whom you intend to make your wife?"

"I have been taught to think of her as one who was to be my wife, and I have tried to follow my instructions."

"Sit down, sit down," said Mr. Thornton, for Lawrence had risen to his feet. "I have not finished yet. Lilian has been with us for years, and I who have watched her carefully, know that in all the world there is not a purer, more innocent young girl. She is suited to you in every way. She has money,—her family is one of the first in the land, and more than all, she has been trained to believe that you would some day make her your bride."

"Please come to the point," interrupted Lawrence, consulting his watch. "What would you have me do?"

"I would have the matter settled while you are at Beechwood. She is eighteen now, you are twenty-three; I have made you my partner in business, and should like to see Lilian mistress of my house. So arrange it at once, instead of spending your time fooling with that girl, Mildred," and with this the whole secret was out, and Law rence knew why he had been called into the library and subjected to that lecture.

Mildred Howell was a formidable obstacle in the way of Lilian Veille's advancement. This the lynx-eyed Geral-dine had divined, and with her wits all sharpened, she guessed that not Lilian alone was taking the young man to Beechwood. So she dropped a note of warning mtc the father's ear, and now, outside the door, was listening to the conversation.

"I have never fooled with Mildred Howell," said Law rence, and his father rejoined quickly:

"How, then? Are you in earnest? Do you love her?"

"I am not bound to answer that," returned Lawrence; "though I will say that in some respects I think her far superior to Lilian."

"Superior!" repeated the father, pacing up and down the room. "Your superior women do not always make their husbands happy. Listen to me, boy,—I have been married twice. I surely ought to judge in these matters better than yourself. Your mother was a gentle, amiable creature, much like Lilian Veille. You inherit her disposition, though not her mind,—thank Heaven, not her mind! I was happy with her, but she died, and then I married one who was famed for her superior intellect quite as much as for the beauty of her person,—and what was the result? She never gave me a word or a look different from what she would have given to an entire stranger. Indeed, she seemed rather to avoid me, and, if I came near, she pretended always to be occupied either with a book or with you. And yet I was proud of her, Lawrence,— proud of my girlish bride, and when she died I shed bitter tears over her coffin."

Lawrence Thornton was older now than when he sat upon the river bank, and told little Mildred Hawkins of his beautiful young step-mother, and he knew why she had shrunk from his father's caresses and withered beneath his breath,—so he ventured at last to say:

"Mildred Howell was young enough to be your daughter, and should never have been your wife."

"It was not that,—it was not that," returned the father, stiffly. "There was no compulsion used; she was too intellectual,—too independent,—too high-tempered, I tell you, and this other one is like her in everything."

"How do you account for that?" asked Lawrence, who had his own private theory with regard to Mildred's parentage.

"I don't account for it," said Mr. Thornton. "I only know she is not at all connected with the Howells. She is the child of some poor wretch who will be claiming her one day. It would be vastly agreeable, wouldn't it, to see a ragged pauper, or maybe something worse, ringing at our door, and claiming Mrs. Lawrence Thornton for her daughter! Lawrence, that of itself is a sufficient reason why you must not marry Mildred, even if there were no Lilian, who has a prior claim."

"Father," said Lawrence, "you think to disgust me, but it cannot be done. I like Mildred Howell. I think her the most splendid creature I ever looked upon; and were I a little clearer as to her family, Lilian's interest might perhaps be jeopardized."

"Thank Heaven, then, that her family is shrouded in mystery!" said Mr. Thornton, while Lawrence sat for a moment intently thinking.

Then suddenly springing up and seizing his father's arm, he asked:

"Did you ever know for certain that the child of sister Helen died?"

"Know for certain? Yes. What put that idea into your head?" Mr. Thornton asked, and Lawrence replied:

"The idea was not really in there, for I know it is not so, though it might have been, I dare say; for, if I remember right, no one save an old nurse was with Helen when she died, while even that miserable Hawley, her husband, was in New Orleans."

"Yes," returned the father, "Hawley was away, and never, I think, came back to inquire after his wife or child, for he, too, died within the year."

"Then how do you know Mildred is not that child?" persisted Lawrence,—not because he had the most remote belief that she was, but because he wished to see how differently his father would speak of her if there was the slightest possibility of her belonging to the Thornton line.

"I know she isn't," said the father. "I went to No. 20 Street myself, and talked with Esther Bennett, the old woman who took care of Helen, and then of the child until it died. She was a weird, haggish-looking creature, but it was the truth she told. No, you can't impose that tale on me. This Mildred is not my grandchild."

"For which I fervently thank Heaven," was Lawrence's response; and in these words the black-eyed Geraldine, watching by the door, read how dear Mildred Howell was to the young man, and how the finding her to be his sister's child would be worse to him than death itself.

"He shall not win her, though," she muttered between her glittering teeth, "if I can prevent it, and I think I can. That last idea is a good one, and I'll jot it down in my book of memory for future use, if need be."

Geraldine Veille was a cold-hearted, unprincipled woman, whose early affections had been blighted, and now at thirty-one she was a treacherous, intriguing creature, void of heart or soul, except where Lilian was concerned. In all the world there was nothing half so dear to the proud woman as her young half-sister, and, as some fierce tigress keeps guard over its only remaining offspring, so she watched with jealous eye to see that nothing harmed her Lilian. For Mildred Howell she had conceived a violent aversion, because she knew that one of Lawrence Thornton's temperament could not fail to be more or less influenced by such glowing beauty and sparkling wit as Mildred possessed.

During the long vacation which Mildred spent in the family she had barely tolerated her, while Mildred's open defiance of her opinions and cool indifference to herself had only widened the gulf between them. She had at first opposed Lilian's visiting Beechwood, but when she

LAWRENCE AND HIS FATHER.

saw how her heart was bent upon it, she yielded the point, thinking the while that if Lawrence on his return showed signs of going, too, she would drop a hint into his father's ear. Lawrence was going, — she had dropped her hint, — and, standing outside the door, she had listened to the result, and received a suggestion on which to act in case it should be necessary.

Well satisfied with her morning's work, she glided up the stairs just as Lawrence came from the library and passed out into the street. His interview with his father had somewhat disturbed him, while at the same time it had helped to show him how strong a place Mildred had in his affections.

"And yet why should I think so much of her?" he said to himself, as he walked slowly on. "She never can be anything to me more than she is. I must marry Lilian, of course, just as I have always supposed I should. But I do wish she knew a little more. Only think of her saying, the other day, that New Orleans was in Kentucky. and Rome in Paris, she believed! How in the name of wonder did she manage to graduate?"

Mildred Howell, who sat next to Lilian at the examination, might perhaps have enlightened him somewhat, but as she was not there, he continued his cogitations.

"Yes, I do wonder how she happened to graduate, knowing as little of books as she does. She writes splendidly, though!" and, as by this time he had reached the

Worcester depot, he stepped into a car and prepared to read again the letter received the previous night from Lilian. "She has a most happy way of committing her ideas to paper," he thought. "There must be more in her head than her conversation indicates. Perhaps father is right, after all, in saying she will make a better wife than Mildred."

all
live,

CHAPTER IX.
LAWRENCE AT BEECHWOOD.

"OME, Milly,—do hurry!" said Lilian to Mildred on the afternoon of the day when Lawrence was expected. "It seems as though you never would get all that hair braided. Thirty strands, as I live, and here I am wanting you to fix my curls, you do it so much better than I can." Iff! " Plenty of time," returned Mildred ; " Law-$j| rence won't be here this hour." "But I'm going to the depot," returned Lilian; "and I saw Finn go out to harness just now. Oh, I am so anxious to see him! Why, Millie, you don't know a thing about it, for you never loved anybody like Lawrence Thornton."

"How do you know?" asked Mildred; and catching instantly at the possibility implied, Lilian exclaimed : " Do you, as true as you live, love somebody ? " "Yes, a great many somebodies," was the while Lilian persisted:

" Yes, yes; but I mean some man,—somebody like Lawrence Thornton. Tell me ! " and the little be began to pout quite becomingly at Mildred's want of con fidence in her.

"Yes, Lily," said Mildred at last, "I do love some body quite as well as you love Lawrence Thornton, it is useless to ask his name, as I shall not tell."

Lilian saw she was in earnest, and she forebore to question her, though she did so wish she knew; and dipping her brush in the marble basin, and letting water drip all over the light carpet, she stood puzzling weak brain to think " who it was Mildred Ho well loved."

The beautiful braid of thirty strands was finished . last, and then Mildred declared herself ready to attend to Lilian, who rattled on about Lawrence, saying, " she did not ask Mildred to go with her to the station bee: she always liked to be alone with him. That will dc she cried, just as the last curl was brushed ; and, lea^ Mildred to pick up the numerous articles of femii wear, which in dressing she had left just where stepped out of them, she tripped gracefully down the walk, and, entering the carriage, was driven to the dep;'.

" Two lovers, a body'd suppose by their actions," i a plain, out-spoken farmer, who chanced to be at ! station and witnessed the meeting; while Finn, who 1 been promoted to the office of coachman, rolled his e knowingly as he held the door for them to enter.

" Oh, I'm so glad youVe come!" said Lilian, leaning back upon the cushions, and throwing aside her hat the bet ter to display her curls, which Mildred had arranged with a great deal of taste. " I've been moped almost to death."

"Why, I thought you said in your letter you were having a most delightful time ! "

And Lawrence looked smilingly down upon the little lady, who replied:

" Did she I—did I? Well, then, I guess I am ; but it's a heap nicer, now you've come. Mildred seems to me a little bit sober. Lawrence," and Lilian spoke in a whis per, for they were now ascending a hill, and she did not care to have Finn hear,—" Lawrence, I know something about* Mildred, but you mustn't never tell,—will you? She's in love with a man / She told me so confidentially this morning, but wouldn't tell me his name. Why, how your face flushes up? It is awful hot,—ain't it?" and Lilian began to fan herself with her leghorn hat, while Lawrence, leaning from the window, and watching the wheels grinding into the gravelly sand, indulged himself in thoughts not wholly complimentary either to Lilian or the man whom Mildred Howell loved.

"What business had Lilian to betray Mildred's confix dence, even to him ? Had she no delicate sense of honor? Or what business had Mildred to be in love ?" and, by the time the carriage turned into the avenue, Lawrence was

about as uncomfortable in his mind as he well could be, 6

" There's Mildred ! Isn't she beautiful with those white flowers in her hair ? " cried Lilian ; and, looking up, Lawrence saw Mildred standing near a maple a little way in advance.

With that restlessness natural to people waiting the arrival of guests, she had left the Judge and Oliver, who were sitting in the parlor, and walked slowly down the avenue until she saw the carriage coming, when she stopped beneath the tree.

" Get in here, Milly,—get in," said Lilian ; and, hastily alighting, Lawrence offered her his hand, feeling strongly tempted to press the warm fingers, which he fancied trembled slightly in his own.

" She has been walking fast," he thought, and he was about to say so, when Lilian startled them with the exclamation :

"Why don't you kiss her, Lawrence, just as you do me?"

Lawrence thought of the man, and rather coolly replied :

" I never kissed Miss Howell in my life,—neither would she care to have me."

"Perhaps not," returned Lilian, while Mildred's cheeks flushed crimson,—" perhaps not, for she is a bit of a prude, I think ; and then, too, I heard her say she didn't like you as well as she did Clubs."

"Oh, Lilian, when did I say so?" and Mildred's eyes for an instant flashed with anger.

"You needn't be so mad," laughed Lilian. "You did say so, that first night I came here. Don't you remember that I surprised you telling Oliver how Uncle Thornton kept you looking over those old stones for fear you'd talk with Lawrence, and how you hated them all ? "

" Lilian," said Lawrence, sternly, " no true woman would ever wantonly divulge the secrets of another, particularly if that other be her chosen friend."

" S'pected they'd end in a row when I seen 'em so lovin'," muttered Finn; and, hurrying up his horses, he drew up at the gate just as Lilian began to pout, Mildred to cry, and Lawrence to wish he had stayed at home.

" Tears, Gipsy ? Yes, tears as true as I live," said the Judge, who had come down to meet them, and with his broad hand he wiped away the drops resting on Mildred's long eyelashes.

" Nothing but perspiration," she answered, laughingly, while the Judge rejoined :

" Hanged if I ever saw sweat look like that!"

"Telling him "he hadn't seen everything yet," she forced her old sunny smile to her face and ran up the walk, followed by Lawrence and Lilian, who ere they reached the portico were on the best of terms, Lilian having called him a " great hateful," while he in return had playfully pulled one of her long curls. The cloud, however, did not so soon pass from Mildred's heart, foi she knew Lawrence Thornton had received a wrong impression, and, what was worse than all, there was no means of rectifying it.

"What is it, Gipsy? What ails you?" asked the Judge, noticing her abstraction. " I thought you'd be in the seventh heaven when you got Lawrence Thornton here, and now he's come you are bluer than a whetstone."

Suddenly remembering that she must give some directions for supper, Mildred ran off to the kitchen, where she found Finn edifying his sister Lucy with an account of the meeting between Lawrence and Lilian.

" She stood there all ready," said he, " and the minute the cars stopped he made a dive and hugged her,—so," and Finn's long arms wound themselves round the shoulders of his portly mother, who repaid him with a cuff such as she had been wont to give him in his babyhood.

"Miss Lily didn't do that way, I tell you," said Finn, rubbing his ear; " she liked it, and stood as still. But who do you s'pect Miss Milly's in love with ? Miss Lily told Mr. Thornton how she 'fessed to her this morning that she loved a man."

" In course she'd love a man," put in Rachel. " She'd look well lovin' a gal, wouldn't she ? "

"There ain't no bad taste about that, nuther, let me tell you, old woman," and Finn's brawny feet began to cut his favorite pigeon wing as he thought of a certain yel low girl in the village. " I axes yer pardon, Miss Milly ! " he exclaimed, suddenly bringing his pigeon wing to a close as he caught sight of Mildred, who had over heard every word he said.

With a heart full almost to bursting she hastily issued her orders, and then ran up to her room, and, throwing herself upon the bed, did just what any girl would have done,—cried with all her might.

" To think Lily should have told him that! " she ex claimed, passionately. " I wish he had not come here."

" You don't wish so any more than I," chimed in a voice, which sounded much like that of Lilian Veille.

She knew that Mildred was offended, and, seeing her go up the stairs, she had followed her, to make peace, if possible, for Lilian, while occasionally transgressing, was constantly asking forgiveness.

"I'm always doing something silly," she said; "and then you did tell Clubs you didn't like Lawrence."

"It is not that," sobbed Mildred. " Finn says you told him I loved somebody."

" The hateful nigger !" exclaimed Lilian. " What busi ness had he to listen and then 'to blab ? If there's any thing I hate it's a tattler ! "

" Then why don't you quit it yourself? " asked Mildred, jerking away from the hand which was trying to smooth the braid of thirty strands.

" What an awful temper you have got, Milly !" said Lil ian, seating herself very composedly by the window, and looking out upon the lawn. I should suppose you'd try to control it this hot day. I'm almost melted now."

And thus showing how little she really cared for her foolish thoughtlessness, Lilian fanned herself compla cently, wondering why Mildred should feel so badly if Lawrence did know.

" Gipsy," called the Judge from the lower hall, " supper is on the table. Come down."

In the present condition of her face Mildred would not for the world show herself to Lawrence Thornton, and she said to Lilian:

"You make some excuse for me, won't you ? "

"I'll tell them you're mad," returned Lilian, and she did, adding by way of explanation : " Milly told me this morning that she was in love. I told Lawrence, Finn over heard me, and like a meddlesome fellow as he is, repeat ed it to Mildred, who is as spunky about it as you please."

"Mildred in love!" repeated the Judge. "Who in thunder is she in love with?"

In a different form Lawrence had asked himself that same question many a time within the last hour; but not caring to hear the subject discussed, he adroitly turned the conversation to other topics, and Mildred soon heard them talking pleasantly together, while Lilian's merry laughter told that her mind at least was quite at ease. Lilian could not be unhappy long, and was now quite de-

lighted to find herself the sole object of attraction to three of the male species.

Supper being over, she led the way to the back piazza, where, sitting close to Lawrence, she rattled on in her simple, childish way, never dreaming how, while seeming to listen, each of her auditors was thinking of Mildred and wishing she was there.

For a time Oliver lingered, hoping Mildred would join them again, but as she did not, he at last took his leave. From her window Mildred saw him going down the Cold Spring path, and with a restless desire to know if he thought she had acted very foolishly, she stole out of the back way, and, taking a circuitous route to avoid observation, reached the gable-roof and knocked at the door of Oliver's room just after he had entered it. " May I come in ? " she said.

"Certainly," he answered. " You are always welcome here."

And he pushed toward her the stool on which she sat, but pushed it too far from himself to suit Mildred's ideas.

She could not remember that she was no longer the little girl who used to lavish so many sisterly caresses upon the boy Oliver ; neither did she reflect that she was now a young lady of seventeen, and he a man of twenty-one, possessing a man's heart, even though the casket which enshrined that heart was blighted and deformed.

" I want to put my head in your lap just as I used to do." she said ; and, drawing the stool closer to him, she rested her burning cheek upon his knee, and then waited for him to speak.

" You have been crying, Milly," he said at last, and she replied :

"Yes, I've had an awful day. Lilian led me into confessing that I loved somebody, never dreaming that she would tell it to Lawrence; but she did, and she told him, too, that I said I hated all the Thorntons. Oh, Oliver, what must he think of me ? "

" For loving somebody or hating the Thorntons, which ?" Oliver asked, and Mildred replied :

" Both are bad enough, but I can't bear to have him think I hate him, for I don't. I,—oh, Oliver, can't you guess ? don't you know ? —though why should you when you have loved only me ? "

" Only you, Milly,—only you," said Oliver, while there came a mist before his eyes as he thought of the hopeless anguish the loving her had brought him.

But not for the worlc^ would he suffer her to know of the love which had became a part of his very life, and he was glad that it was growing dark, so she could not see the whiteness of his face, nor the effort that it cost him to say in his usually quiet tone :

" Milly, do you love Lawrence Thornton ? "

He knew she did, but he would rather she should tell him so, for he fancied that might help kill the pain which was gnawing at his heart.

"I have never kept anything from you, Oliver/' she said; "and, if you are willing to be troubled, I want to tell you all about it. Shall I ? "

1 Yes, tell me," he replied; and, nestling so close to him that she might have heard the beating of his heart, Mildred told him of her love, which was so hopeless because of Lilian Veille.

" I shall never be married," she said; " and when we are old we will live together, you and I, and I shall forget that I ever loved anybody better than you ; for I do,— forgive me, Oliver," and her little, soft, warm hand crept after the cold, clammy one, which moved farther away as hers approached, and at last hid itself behind the chair, while Mildred continued : " I do love him the best, though he has never been to me what you have. But I can't help it. You are my brother, you know, and it's all so different. I don't suppose you can understand it, but try to imagine that you are not lame, nor small, but tall and straight, and manly as Lawrence "Thornton, and that you loved somebody,—me, perhaps."

"Yes, you—say you, M.illy," and the poor, deformed Oliver felt a thrill of joy as he thought of himself "tall, and straight, and handsome, and loving Mildred HowelL"

"And suppose I did not love you in return," said Mil-6*

dred, " wouldn't your heart ache as it never has ached yet?"

Oliver could have told her of a heartache such as she had never known, but he dared not, and he was about framing some word of comfort, when Judge Ho well's voice was heard below, asking if his runaway were there.

" Oh, it's too bad ! " said Mildred. " I wanted to have such a nice long talk, and have not said a word I came to say ; but it can't be helped."

And kissing the lips which inwardly kissed her back a thousand times, though outwardly they did not move, she hurried down the stairs, where the Judge was waiting for her.

" I thought I should find you here," he said, adding that it was not polite in her to flare up at nothing, and run off from her guests.

Mildred made no reply, and knowing from past experi ence that it was not always safe to reprove her, the Judge walked on in silence until they reached the house, where Lilian greeted Mildred as if nothing had occurred, while Lawrence made himself so agreeable, that when at last they separated for the night the shadow was entirely gone from Mildred's face, and nearly so from her- heart.

CHAPTER X.

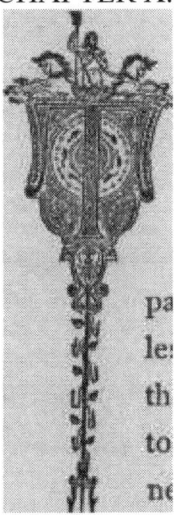

THE RIVER.

HE next day was excessively hot and sultry, confining the young people to the cool, dark parlor where Lilian fanned herself furiously, while Lawrence turned the pages of a book, and Mildred drummed list lessly upon the piano. Oliver did not join them, and Luce, who, before dinner went down to the Cold Spring for water, brought back the news that he was suffering from one of his ner vous headaches.

" He needs more exercise," said Lawrence. " I mean to take him with me this afternoon when I go down to bathe in the river."

Accordingly, about four o'clock, he called upon Oliver, who looked pale and haggard, as if years of suffering had passed over him since the previous night. Still, he was so much better, that Lawrence ventured to propose his going to the river.

"No matter if you can't swim," he said; "you can sit upon the grass and look at me."

Oliver knew that the fresh air would do him good, and he went at last with Lawrence to the quiet spot which the latter had selected, partly because it was remote from any dwelling, and partly because the water was deeper there than at the points higher up. Sitting down beneath a tree, which grew near to the bank, Oliver watched his companion, as he plunged boldly into the stream, and struck out for the opposite shore.

" Why am I not like him, instead of being thus femin ine and weak ? " was the bitter thought creeping into Oliver's heart, when suddenly a fearful cry rose on the air,—a cry of " Help! I'm cramped! oh, help me, Clubs! " and turning in the direction whence it came, Oliver saw a frightened face disappearing beneath the water, while the outstretched hand, which went down last, seemed imploring him for aid.

In an instant Oliver stood by the river bank, and when the face came up again, he saw that it was whiter than be fore, and the voice was fainter which uttered another name than that of Clubs. At first Oliver thought he was mistaken, but when it came a second time, he reeled as if smitten by a heavy blow, for he knew then that the drowning man had cried out:

" Milly ! dear Milly !" as if he thus would bid her fare well.

For a second Oliver stood spell-bound, while thought after thought traversed his whirling brain. Lawrence was

Ws rival, and yet not his rival, for, even had he never been, such as Oliver Hawkins could not hope to win the queenly Mildred, whose heart would break when they told her Lawrence was dead. She would come to him for comfort, as she always did, and how could he tell her he had looked silently on and seen him die ? There would be bitter reproach in the eyes which never yet had rested upon him save in love, and rather than meet that glance Oliver resolved at last to save Lawrence Thornton, even if he perished in the attempt.

" Nobody will mourn for the cripple," he said. " Nobody miss me but Mildred, and Lawrence will comfort her ;" and with one last, hurried glance at the world which had never seemed so bright as on that July afternoon, the he roic Oliver sprang into the river, and struck out for the spot where Lawrence last went down.

He forgot that he had never learned to swim,—nor knew that he was swimming,—for one thought alone was uppermost in his mind, and that a thought of Mildred. Hers was the name upon his lip,—hers the image before his mind as he struggled in the rolling river,—for her he ran that fearful risk,—and the mighty love he bore her buoyed him up, until he reached the spot where the waters were still in wild commotion. By what means he grasped the tangled hair,—held up the rigid form and took it back to the shore, he never knew, it passed so like a dream. With an almost superhuman effort, he

dragged the body up the bank, laid it upon the grass, and then his feeble voice, raised to its highest pitch, went echoing up the hill, but brought back no response. Through the soft summer haze he saw the chimneys of the Beechwood mansion, and the cupola on the roof where Mildred often sat, and where she was sitting now. But his voice did not reach her, or if it did she thought it was some insect's hum, and turned again to her book, un mindful of the dying Lawrence beneath the maple tree, or of the distracted Oliver, who knelt above him, feel ing for his pulse, and dropping tears like rain upon his face.

*' I must go for help, and leave him here alone," he said, at last, and he started on his way, slowly, painfully, for ere plunging into the river he had thrown aside his shoes, and his poor, tender feet had been cut upon a sharp-pointed rock.

But he kept on his way, while his knees shook beneath him, and in his ears there was a buzzing sound like the rush of many waters. Human strength could not endure much more, and by the time he reached his grandmother's gate he sunk to the ground, and crawled slowly to the door. In wild affright old Hepsy came out, asking what was the matter.

" Lawrence ! " he gaspedj—" he's drowned,—he's dead! "

Then from his mouth and nose the crimson blood gushed out, and Hepsy had just cause for screaming as she did :

" Help ! Murder ! Fire ! Mildred Howell! Oliver is dead, and Lawrence too ! "

From her seat in the cupola Mildred heard the cry, for Hepsy's voice was shrill and clear, and it rang out like an alarm-bell. Mildred heard her name and that Oliver was dead, and bounding down the stairs she went flying down the Cold Spring path, while close behind her came the wheezing Judge, with Lilian following slowly in the rear.

On the floor, just where he had fainted, Oliver was lying, and Mildred's heart stood still when she saw his dripping garments and the blood stains round his pallid lips.

" Poor, poor Oliver," she said, kneeling down beside him, and wringing his wet hair. " Where has he been ? " At the sound of her voice his eyes unclosed, and he whispered faintly:

" Lawrence, Milly. Lawrence is dead under that tree."

Then, for one brief instant, Mildred fancied herself dying, but the sight of Lilian, who had just come in, brought back her benumbed faculties, and going up to her, she said:

"Did you hear, Lily? Lawrence is dead,—drowned. Let us go to him together. He is mine, now, as much as yours."

" Oh, I carn't, I carn't!" sobbed Lilian, cowering back into a corner. " I'm afraid of dead folks! I'd rather stay here."

" Fool! dough-head ! " thundered the Judge, who thor oughly disliked her, and was now out of all kind of pa tience. " Go to the house, then, and see that his cham ber is ready for the body," and without waiting to see if his orders were obeyed, he hastened after Mildred, who was flying over the distant fields as if she sported a pair of unseen wings.

She saw the stains from Oliver's wounded feet, and knowing that she was right she ran on, and on until she reached the spot, whither other aid had preceded her, else Lawrence Thornton had surely floated down the deep, dark river of death.

Two villagers, returning from a neighboring wood, had found him lying there, and were doing for him what they could when Mildred came up begging of them to say if he were dead.

" Speak to him, Miss Howell," said one of the men. " That may bring him back—it sometimes does; " but Mil dred's voice, though all powerful to unlock Oliver's scat tered senses, could not penetrate the lethargy which had stolen over Lawrence, and, with an ominous shake of their heads, the two men lifted him between them, and bore him back to the house, where Lilian, in her own room, was sobbing as if her heart would break, and saying to Rachel's grandchild, who had toddled in and asked what was the matter :

" Oh, I don't know; I want to go home and see Geral-dine."

" Go home, then, and be hanged" the Judge finally added, speaking the last word very naturally, as if that were what he had all the time intended to say.

With one scornful glance at Lilian, who, as Lawrence was borne past her door, covered her face with her hands and moaned: "Oh, I carn't look at him," Mildred saw that everything was made comfortable, and then all through the anxious, exciting hour which followed, she stood bravely by, doing whatever was necessary for her to do, and once, at her own request, placing her warm lips next to the cold ones of the unconscious man, and send ing her life-breath far down into the lungs, which gave back only a gurgling sound, and Mildred, when she heard it, turned away, whispering :

" He is dead ! "

But Lawrence was not dead; and when the night shadows were stealing into the room, he gave signs that life was not extinct. Mildred was the first to discover it, and her cry of joy went ringing through the house, and pene trated to the room where Lilian still cowered upon the floor. But Lilian mistook the cry, and grasping the dress of the little child, who had started to leave her, she sobbed:

" Don't go,—don't leave me alone,—it's getting dark, and I'm afraid of ghosts ! "

ie Confounded fool!" muttered the Judge, who passed the door in time to hear the remark, and who felt strongly tempted to hurl at her head the brandy bottle he carried in his hand. " It wouldn't make any more impression though, than on a bat of cotton wool," he said, and he hurried on to the chamber where Lawrence Thornton was enduring all the pangs of a painful death.

But he was saved, and when at last the fierce struggle was over, and the throes of agony had ceased, he fell away to sleep, and the physician bade all leave the room except Mildred, who must watch him while he slept.

" Will he live ? Is he past all danger ? " she asked, and when the physician answered, "Yes," she said: "Then I must go to Oliver. Lilian will sit with Mr. Thornton."

" But is her face a familiar one ? Will he be pleased to see her here when he wakes ? " the doctor asked, and Mil dred answered sadly:

"Yes, far more pleased than to see me."

"Let her come, then," was the reply, and hurrying to Lilian, Mildred told her what was wanted.

" Oh, I carn't, I carn't! " and Lilian drew back. " I ain't used to sick folks ! I don't know what to do. You stay, Milly, that's a dear, good girl."

"But I can't," answered Mildred. "I must go to Oliver, I've neglected him too long," and seeing that

Lilian showed no signs of yielding, she took her by the arm, and led her into Lawrence's chamber.

" Sit there," she said, placing her in a chair by the bed side, "and when he wakes, give him this," pointing to something in a cup, which the doctor had prepared.

"Oh, it's so dark, and his face so white," sobbed Lilian, while Mildred, feeling strongly inclined to box her ears, bade her once more sit still, and then hurried away.

" There's grit for you," muttered the Judge, who in the next room had overheard the whole. "There's a girl worth having. Why, I'd give more for Milly's little finger than for that gutta perch a's whole body. Afraid of the dark,— little fool! How can he coo round her as he does! But I'll put a flea in his ear. I'll tell him that in Mildred Howell's face, when she thought that he was dead, I saw who it was she loved. I ain't blind," and the Judge paced up and down the room, while Mildred kept on her way, and soon reached the gable roof.

" A pretty time of day to get here," growled old Hepsy ; " after the worst is over, and he got well to bed. I'd save that city sprig for you again if I was Clubs."

" Grandmother, please go down," said Oliver, while Mildred, unmindful of old Hepsy's presence, wound her arms around his neck, and he could feel her hot tears dropping like rain upon his face, as she whispered:

"Darling Oliver, heaven bless you, even as I do. I

knew it must have been so ; but why did you risk youi life for him ? Say, did you ? "

" Grandmother, will you go down ? " Oliver said again ; and muttering something about " being glad to get rid of such sickishness," old Hepsy hobbled off.

When sure that she was gone, Oliver placed a hand on each side of the face bending over him, and said :

" Don't thank me, Mildred ; I don't deserve it, for my first wicked thought was to let him drown, but when I remembered how much you loved him, I said I'll save him for Milly, even though I die. It is far better that the poor cripple should be drowned than the handsome Lawrence. Do you love me more for saving him, Milly ?"

" Yes, yes,' answered Mildred ; " and so does Lilian, or she will when I tell her, for you know you saved him for her, not for me."

" Mildred," said Oliver, laying his clammy hand upon her hair, " When Lawrence Thornton was sinking in the river, whose name do you think he called ? "

" Lilian's !" and by the dim light of the candle burning on the stand, Oliver could see the quivering of her lips.

" No, darling, not Lilian, but ' Milly, dear Milly.' That was what he said; and there was a world of love in the way he said it."

Mildred's eyes were bright as diamonds, but Oliver's were dim with tears, and he could not see how they sparkled and flashed, while a smile of joy broke over the

face. He only knew that both Mildred's hands were laid upon his forehead as if she would doubly bless him for the words which he had spoken. There was silence a moment, and then Mildred's face came so near to his that he felt her breath and Mildred whispered timidly :

" Are you certain, Oliver, that you heard aright ? Wasn't it Lilian ? Tell me again just what he said."

" Milly, dear Milly," and Oliver's voice was full of yearning tenderness, as if the words welled up from the very depths of his own heart.

She looked so bright, so beautiful, sitting there beside him, that he would willingly have given his life, could he once have put his arms around her and told her how he loved her. But it must not be and with a mighty effort, which filled the blue veins on his forehead and forced out the drops of perspiration, he conquered the desire, but not until he closed his eyes to shut out her glowing beauty.

" You are tired," she said. " I am wearing you out," and arranging his pillows more comfortably, she made a movement to go.

He let her think he was tired, for he would rather she should leave him, and with a whispered " good-by, dear Oliver/' she glided from the room.

CHAPTER XI.
LAWRENCE DECEIVED AND UNDLCEIVED.

OR a time after Mildred left him, Lawrence slept on quietly, and Lilian gradually felt her fears subsiding, particularly as Rachel brought in a lamp and placed it on the mantel. Still she was very nervous and she sat sobbing behind her handkerchief, until Lawrence showed signs of waking; then remembering what Mildred had said of something in a cup, she held it to his lips, bidding him drink, but he would not, and setting it down she went back to her crying, thinking it mean in Mildred to leave her there so long when she wasn't a bit accus tomed to sick folks.

Suddenly she felt a hand laid upon her own, and start ing up she saw Lawrence Thornton looking at her. Instantly all her fortitude gave way, and laying her face on the pillow beside him she sobbed :

"Oh, Lawrence, Lawrence, I'm so glad you ain't dead, and have waked up at last, for it's dreadful sitting here alone."

Drawing her nearer to him the young man said :
"Poor child, have you been here long ?"
"Yes, ever since the doctor left," she answered. "Mildred is with Clubs. I don't believe she'd care a bit if you should die."
"Mildred—Mildred," Lawrence repeated, as if trying to recall something in the past. "Then it was you who were with me in all that dreadful agony, when my life came back again ? I fancied it was Mildred."

Lilian had not the courage to undeceive him, for there was no mistaking the feeling which prompted him to smooth her golden curls and call her "Fairy." Still she must say something, and so she said:
"I held the cup to your lips a little while ago."
"I know you did," he answered. "You are a dear girl, Lilian. Now tell me all about it and who saved my life."

"Waked up in the very nick of time," muttered the Judge, who all the while had been in the next room, and who had been awake just long enough to hear all that had passed between Lawrence and Lilian. "Yes, sir, just in the nick of time, and now we'll hear what soft-pate has to say ;" and moving nearer to the door he listened while Lilian told Lawrence how Oliver had taken him from the river and laid him under a tree, where he was found by two of the villagers, who brought him home.

"Then," said she, "they sent for the doctor, who did

144 DECEIVED AND UNDECEIVED.

all manner of cruel things, until you came to life and went to sleep."
"And Mildred wasn't here at all," said Lawrence sadly. "Why did she stay with Oliver? What ails him ?"
"He had the nose-bleed, I believe," answered Lilian. "You know he's weak, and getting you out of the water made him sick, I suppose. Mildred thinks more of Oliver than of you, I guess."
"The deuce she does," muttered the Judge, and he was about going in to charge Lilian with her duplicity, when Mildred herself appeared, and he resumed his seat to hear what next would occur.

"I am sorry I had to leave you," she said, going up to Lawrence, "but poor Oliver needed the care of some one besides old Hepsy, and I dare say you have found a competent nurse in Lilian."

"Yes, Fairy has been very kind," said Lawrence, taking the young girl's hand, " I should have been sadly off without her. But what of Oliver ? "

Mildred did not then know how severe a shock Oliver had received, and she replied that, " he was very weak, but would, she hoped, be better soon."

" I shall go down to-morrow and thank him for saving my life," was Lawrence's next remark, while Mildred asked some trivial question concerning himself.

"Why in thunder don't she tell him all about it? growled the Judge, beginning to grow impatient.

don't she tell him how she worked like an ox, while t'other one sat on the floor and snivelled ? " Then as he heard Mildred say that she must go and see which of the negroes would stay with him that night, he continued his mutterings : " Mildred's a fool,—Thornton's a fool,— and that Lilian is a consummate fool; but I'll fix 'em ; " and striding into the room, just as Mildred was leaving it, he said, " Gipsy, come back. Yon needn't go after a nigger. I'll stay with Lawrence myself."

It was in vain that both Lawrence and Mildred remonstrated against it. The Judge was in earnest. " Unless, indeed, you want to watch," and he turned to Lilian : * You are such a capital nurse,—-not a bit afraid of the lark, nor sick folks, you know," and he chucked her mder the chin, while she began to stammer out :

" Oh, I carn't! I carn't! it's too hard,—too hard."

" Of course, it's too hard," said Lawrence, amazed at the Judge's proposition. " Lilian is too delicate for that; she ought to be in bed this moment, poor child. She's been sadly tried to-day," and he looked pityingly at Lilian, who, feeling that in some way wholly unknown to herself, she had been terribly aggrieved, began to cry, and left the room.

" Look out that there don't something catch you in the 4 hall," the Judge called after her, shrugging his shoulders, and thinking that not many hours would elapse ere he iretty thoroughly undeceived Lawrence Thornton.

7 d

146 DECEIVED AND UNDECEIVED.

But in this he began to fancy he might be disappointed, for soon after Mildred left them, Lawrence fell away to sleep, resting so quietly that the Judge would not awake him, but sat listening to his loud breathings until he himself grew drowsy. But Lawrence disturbed him, and after a few short nods, he straightened up, exclaiming, " the confoundedest snorer I ever heard. I can hear him with my deaf ear. Just listen, will you!" and he frowned wrathfully at the curtained bed, where lay the unconscious object of his cogitations. " It's of no use," he said at last, as he heard the clock strike one. " No use to be sitting here. Nothing short of an earthquake could wake him, and sleep will do him more good than that slush in the cups. I ain't going to sit up all night either. 'Icarn't! I carn't ! it's too hard,—too hard !' Little fool!" and laughing to himself as he mimicked Lilian, he stalked into the adjoining chamber, and when at sunrise Mildred came in she found the medicines all untouched, and the Judge fairly outdoing Lawrence in the quantity and quality of his snores !

But the Judge was right in one conclusion,—sleep did Lawrence more good than medicine could possibly have done, and he awoke at last greatly refreshed. Smiling pleasantly upon Mildred, whom he found sitting by him, he asked her to open the shutters, so he could inhale the morning air, and see the sun shine on the eastern hills.

" My visit has had a sad commencement," he said, as she complied with his request, and went back to his side ; " and lest it should grow worse. I shall return home in a day or so. Do you think Lilian will be ready to accompany me ? "

Instantly the tears came to Mildred's eyes, but Lawrence thought they were induced by a dread of losing Lilian, and he hastened to say, " She need not go, of course, unless she chooses."

"But you,—why need you go?" asked Mildred. "I was anticipating so much pleasure from your visit, and that first night you came I was so rude and foolish. You must think me a strange girl, Mr. Thornton."

Whether he thought her strange or not, he thought her very beautiful, sitting there before him in her white morning wrapper, with her cheeks fresh as roses and her brown hair parted smoothly back from her open brow.

" It was wrong in Lilian to betray your confidence," he replied ; " but she did it thoughtlessly, and has apologized for it, I presume; she promised me she would."

Mildred did not tell him that she hadn't, and he continued. " It is very natural that a girl like you should have hosts of admirers, and quite as natural that you should give to some one of them the preference. I only hope he is worthy of you, Milly."

Mildred felt that she could not restrain her tears much longer, and she was glad when Lilian at last came in,

thus affording her a good excuse for stealing away. She did not hear what passed between the two, but when Lilian came down to breakfast she said, " Lawrence had suggested their going home," and as nothing could please her more, they would start the next day if he were able.

" I'll bet he won't go before he gets a piece of my mind," thought the Judge, as he watched for a favorable opportunity, but Lilian was always in fhe way, and when long after dinner he went to Lawrence's room, he found that he had gone down to visit Oliver, who was still confined to his bed and seemed to be utterly exhausted.

Lawrence had not expected to see him so pale and sick, and at first he could only press his hands in silence.

11 It was very kind in you, Clubs," he said at last, " to save my life at the risk of your own."

"You are mistaken," returned Oliver; "it was for Mildred I risked my life, far more than for you."

"For Mildred, Clubs,—for Mildred!" and all over]Lawrence Thornton's handsome face there broke a look of perplexity and delight, for Oliver's words implied a something to believe which would be happiness indeed.

" I can't tell you now," said Oliver, "I am too faint And weak. Come to me before you go and I will explain ; but first, Lawrence Thornton, answer me truly, as you hope for heaven, do you love Mildred Howell ? "

« Love Mildred Howell,—love Mildred Howell! " Lawrence repeated, in amazement. " Yes, Clubs, as I hope for heaven, I love hor better than my life, but she isn't for me, she loves somebody else," and he hurried down the stairs, never dreaming that the other was himself, for had it been, she would not have deserted him the previous day, when he was so near to death. " No, Oliver is deceived," he said, and he walked slowly back to Beech-wood, thinking how bright the future would look to him could he but possess sweet Mildred Howell's love. " I never receive any help, from Lilian," he unconsciously said aloud. " She lies like a weight upon rny faculties, while

Mildred has the most charming way of rubbing up one's ideas. Mildred is splendid," and his foot touched the lower step of the back piazza just as the Judge's voice chimed in :

" I'm glad you think so. That's what I've been trying to get at this whole day, so sit down here, Thornton, and we'll have a confidential chat. The girls are off riding, and there's no one to disturb us."

Lawrence took the offered seat, and the Judge con tinued :

" I don't know how to commence it, seeing there's no head nor tail, and I shall make an awful bungle, I pre sume, but what I want to say is this : You've got the wool pulled over your eyes good. I ain't blind, nor deaf either, if one of my ears is shut up tight as a drum. I heard her soft-soaping you last night, making you think nobody did anything but her. It's Lilian, I mean," he continued, as

he saw the mystified expression on Lawrence's face. " Now, honest, didn't she make you believe that she did about the whole ; that is, did what women would natur ally do in such a case ? "

Lawrence had received some such impression and as he had no reason for thinking Lilian would purposely de ceive him, he roused up at once in her defense.

" Everybody was kind, I presume," he said, " but I must say that for a little, nervous creature as she is, Lilian acted nobly, standing fearlessly by until the, worst was over, and then, when all the rest was gone, who was it sat watching me, but Lilian ? "

'* Lilian ! the devil! There, I have sworn, and I feel the better for it," said the Judge, growing red in the face, and kicking over one of Mildred's house plants with his heavy boot. " Thornton, you are a fool."

"Very likely," answered Lawrence; lt but I am cer tainly willing to be enlightened, and as you seem capable of doing it, pray continue."

" Never granted a request more willingly in my life," returned the Judge. " Thornton, you certainly have some sense, or your father never would have married my daugh ter."

Lawrence could not tell well what that had to do with his having sense, but he was too anxious to interrupt the Judge, who continued : " You see, when Clubs crawled back to his door and told how you were dead, and wheQ

Hepsy screamed for help like a panther as she is, Mildred was the first to hear it, and she went tearing down the hill, while I went wheezing after, with Lilian following like a snail. I was standing by when Clubs told Milly you were dead, and then, Thornton, then there was a look on her face which made my very toes tingle, old as I am. Somehow the girl has got an idea that you think Lilian a little angel, and turning to her, she said, ' Lilian, Law rence is dead. Let us go to him together. He is mine now as much as yours,' but do you think, boy, that she went ? "

"Yes, yes, I don't know. Go on," gasped Lawrence, whose face was white as ashes.

"Well, sir, she didn't, but shrank back in the corner, and snivelled out, ' I carn't, I carn't. I'm afraid of dead folks. I'd rather stay here.' I suppose I said some sav age things before I started after Milly, who was flying over the fields just as you have seen your hat fly in a strong March wind. When I got to the tree I found her with her arms around your neck, and as hard a wretch as I am, I shed tears to see again on her face that look, as if her heart were broken. When we reached home with you, we found Lilian crying in her room, and she never so much as lifted her finger, while Mildred stood bravely by, and once, Thornton, she put her lips to yours and blew her breath into your lungs, until her cheeks stuck out like two globe lamps. I think that did the business, for you soon

showed signs of life, and then Mildred cried out for joy while Lilian, who heard her, fancied you were dead, and wanted somebody to stay with her, because she was afraid of ghosts. Just as though you wouldn't have enough to do seeing what kind of a place you'd got into, without appearing to her ? When the danger was all over, and you were asleep, Mildred, of course, wanted to go to Clubs, so she asked Lilian to stay with you, but she had to bring her in by force, for Lilian said she was afraid of the dark. I was in the next room and heard the whole performance. I heard you, too, make a fool of yourself, when you woke up and Lilian gave you her version of the story. Of course, I was considerably riled up, for Mildred is the very apple of my eye. Lawrence, do you love Lilian Vielle ? "

Scarcely an hour before, Oliver had said to Lawrence, " Do you love Mildred Howell ? " and now the Judge asked, " Do you love Lilian Veille ? " To the first Law rence had answered " Yes." He could answer the same to the last, for he did love Lilian, though not as he loved Mildred, and so he said yes, asking in a faltering voice :

"What he was expected to infer from all he had heard ? "

" Infer ? " repeated the Judge. " Good thunder, you ain't to infer anything ! You are to take it for gospel truth. Mildred does love somebody, as that blabbing Lilian said she did, and the two first letters of his name

are LAWRENCE THORNTON ! But what the mischief, boy; are you sorry to know that the queen of all the girls that ever was born, or ever will be, is in love with you ? " he asked, as Lawrence sprang to his feet, and walked rapidly up and down the long piazza.

" Sorry,—no ; but glad ; so glad ; and may I talk with her to-night ?" answered Lawrence, forgetting his father's wrath, which was sure to fall upon him,—forgetting Lilian, —forgetting everything, save the fact that Mildred Howell loved him.

"Sit down here, boy," returned the Judge. "I have more to say before I answer that question. You have seen a gnarled, crabbed old oak, haven't you, with a green, beautiful vine creeping over and around it, putting out a broad leaf here, sending forth a tendril there, and covering up the deformity beneath, until people say of that tree, * It's not so ugly after all ? ' But tear the vine away, and the oak is uglier than ever. Well, that sour, crabbed tree is me; and that beautiful vine, bearing the broad leaves and the luxurious fruit, is Mildred, who has crept around and over, and into my very being, until there is not a throb of my heart which does not bear with it a thought of her. She's all the old man has to love. The other Mildred is dead long years ago, while Richard, Heaven only knows where my boy Richard is," and lean ing on his gold-headed cane, the Judge seemed to be wandering away back in the past, while Lawrence, who 7*

154 DECEIVED AND UNDECEIVED.

thought the comparison between the oak and the vine very fine, very appropriate, and all that, but couldn't, for the life of him, see what it had to do with his speaking to Mildred that night, ventured again to say:

" And I may tell Mildred of my love,—may I not ? " Then the Judge roused up and answered, " Only on condition that you both stay here with me. The oak withers when the vine is torn away, and I, too, should die if I knew Milly had left me forever. Man alive, you can't begin to guess how I love the vixen, nor how the sound of her voice makes the little laughing ripples break all over my old heart. There comes the gipsy now," and the little, laughing ripples, as he called them, broke all over his face, as he saw Mildred galloping to the door, her starry eyes looking archly out from beneath her riding hat, and her lips wreathed with smiles as she kissed her hand to the Judge. " Yes, boy, botheration, yes," whisper ed the latter, as Lawrence pulled his sleeve for an answer to his question, ere hastening to help the ladies alight. " Talk to her all night if you want to, I'll do my best to keep back * softening of the brain,' " and he nodded toward

Lilian, who was indulging herself in little bits of feminine screams as her horse showed signs of being frightened at a dog lying behind some bushes.

But the judge had promised more than he was capable of performing. All that evening he manoeuvred most skilfully to separate Lilian from Mildred, but the thing could not be done, for just so sure as he asked the former to go with him upon the piazza and tell him the names of the stars, just so sure she answered that " she didn't know as stars had names," suggesting the while that he take Mildred, who knew everything, and when at last he told her, jokingly as it were, that " it was time children and fools were in bed," she answered with more than her usual quickness :

" I would advise you to go then."

" Sharper than I s'posed," he thought, and turning to Lawrence, he whispered : " No use—no use. She sticks like shoemaker's wax, but I'll tell you what, when she is getting ready to go to-morrow I'll call Milly down, on the pretence of seeing her for something, and then you'll have a chance," and with this Lawrence was fain to be satisfied.

He did not need to go to Oliver for an explanation of his words,—he knew now what they meant,—knew that the beautiful Mildred did care for him, and when he at last laid his head upon his pillow, he could see in the future no cloud to darken his pathway, unless it were his father's anger, and even that did not seem very formi dable.

" He will change his mind when he sees how deter mined I am," he thought. "Mildred won the crusty Judge's heart,—she will win his as well. Lilian will shed some tears, I suppose, and Geraldine will scold, but after

156 DECEIVED AND UNDECEIVED.

knowing how Lilian deceived me, I could not marry her, even were there no Mildred' with the starry eyes and nut-brown hair.'"

He knew that people had applied these terms to his young step-mother, and it was thus that he loved to think of Mildred, whose eyes were as bright as stars and whose hair was a rich nut-brown. He did not care who her parents were, he said, though his mind upon that point was pretty well established, but should he be mistaken, it was all the same. Mildred, as his wife and the adopted daughter of Judge Howell, would be above all reproach, and thus, building pleasant castles of the future, he fell asleep.

CHAPTER XII.
THE PROPOSAL.

ISS VEILLE," said the Judge at the break fast-table next morning, " the carriage will be round in just an hour, and as, if you are at all like Milly, you have a thousand and one traps to pick up, you'd better be about it."

" Milly is going to help me. I never could do it alone," returned Lilian, sipping her coffee tvery leisurely and lingering in the dining-room to talk with Lawrence, even after breakfast was over.

Mildred, however, had gone upstairs, and thither Judge Howell followed, finding her, as he expected, folding up Lilian's clothes, and placing them in her trunk.

"That girl is too lazy to breathe," he said. "Why, don't she come and help you, when I've a particular rea son for wishing you to hurry," and by way of accelerating matters, he crumpled in a heap two of Lilian's muslin dresses, and ere Mildred could stop him, had jammed them into a band-box, containing the mite of a thing which Lilian called a bonnet.

A lace bertha next came under consideration, but Mildred snatched it from him just as he was tucking it away with a pair of India rubbers.

" You ruin the things ! " she cried. " What's the matter?"

" I'll tell you, gipsy," he answered, in a whisper, " I want to see you alone a few minutes before they go off. I tried last night till I sweat, but had to give it up."

"We are alone now," said Mildred, while the Judge replied:

"Hang it all, 'tain't me that wants to see you. Don't you understand ? "

Mildred confessed her ignorance, and he was about to explain, when Lilian came up with a letter just received from her sister.

" The Lord help me," groaned the Judge, while Lilian, thinking he spoke to her, said :

" What, sir ? "

" I was swearing to myself," he replied, and adding in an aside to Mildred : " Come down as quick as you can," he left the room.

Scavcely had he gone when Lilian began :

" Guess, Milly, what Geraldine has written. She says Lawrence was intending to propose to me while he was here, and she thinks I'd better manage—dear me, what was it she said," and opening the letter she read : " If he has not already offered himself, and a favorable opportunity should occur, you had better adroitly lead the conversation in that direction. A great deal can sometimes be accomplished by a little skilful management."

" There, that's what she wrote, and now, what does she mean for me to do ? Why, Mildred, you are putting my combs and brushes in my jewel-box ! What ails you ? "

"So I am," returned Mildred. "I am hardly myself this morning."

"It's because I'm going away, I suppose ; but say, how can I adroitly lead the conversation in that direction ? "

"I'm sure I don't know," answered Mildred, but Lilian persisted that she did, and at last, in sheer despair, Mildred said : " You might ask him if he ever intended to be married."

" Well then, what ? " said Lilian.

" Mercy, I don't know," returned Mildred. " It would depend altogether upon his answer. Perhaps he'll say he does—perhaps he'll say he don't."

This was enough to mystify Lilian completely; and, with a most doleful expression she began to change her dress, saying the while :

" I see you won't help me out; but I don't care. He most offered himself that night I sat with him when you were down with Clubs;" and she repeated, in an exagerated form, several

things which he had said to her,
while all the while poor Mildred's tears were dropping into the trunk which she was packing.

Ever since Oliver had told her of Lawrence's drowning cry there had been a warm, sunny spot in her heart, but Lilian's words had chilled it, and to herself she whispered sadly:

" Oliver did not hear aright. It was ' Lily ! dear Lily !' he said."

" Mildred !" screamed the Judge from the lower hall, " come down here, quick ; I want you for as much as fif teen minutes • and you, Miss Lilian, if that packing isn't done, hurry up, or Thornton will go off without you."

" I think it's right hateful in him," muttered Lilian, adding, in a coaxing tone, as Mildred was leaving the room, " won't you kind of be thinking how I can lead the conversation in that direction, for I shall have a splendid chance in the cars, and you can whisper it to me before I go."

"I wonder what he wants of her?" she continued to herself as Mildred ran down stairs. " I mean to hurry and see," and she so quickened her movements that scarcely ten minutes had elapsed ere her trunk was ready, and she had started in quest of Mildred.

" Go back, you filigree. You ain't wanted there;" and the Judge, who kept guard in the hall below, inter posed his cane between her and the door of the drawing-room, where Lawrence and Mildred sat together, his arm
round her waist, her hand in his own, and her eyes down cast, but shining like stars beneath their long-fringed lashes.

In answer to her question, " What do you want of me ?" the Judge had pointed to the drawing-room, and said :

" The one who wants you is in there."

" Who can it be ?" she thought, tripping through the hall, and crossing the threshold of the door, where she stopped suddenly, while an undefinable sensation swept over her, for at the farthest extremity of the room, and directly beneath the portrait of Richard Howell, Law rence stood waiting for her.

" Did you wish to speak with me, Mr. Thornton ? Do you want me ? " she asked, when a little recovefed from her astonishment.

"Yes, Milly, yes," Lawrence answered impetuously, "I want you for life,—want you forever," and advancing toward her, he wound his arm about her and led her back to the sofa, where she sank down utterly bewildered, and feeling as if she were laboring under some hallucination.

Could it be herself he wanted ? Wasn't it Lilian, who was even now puzzling her brain how " to lead the con versation " so as to produce a scene similar to this, save that she and not Mildred would be one of the actors ?

" Dear Mildred," the voice at her side began, and then she knew it was not Lilian he meant. .

She could not mistake her own name, and she listened breathlessly while he told her of the love conceived more than two years before, when she was a merry, hoydenish school-girl of fifteen, and had spent a few days at his father's house.

" It has always been my father's wish," he said, " that I must marry Lilian, and until quite recently I have myself fostered the belief that I should some time do so, even though I knew I could be happier with you ; but, Milly,—• Lilian can never be my wife."

" Oh, Lawrence, Lawrence, Lawrence !" and spite of the Judge's cane,—spite of the

Judge's boot,—spite of the Judge's burly figure, planted in the doorway to impede her ingress, Lilian Veille rushed headlong into the middle of the room, where she stood a moment, wringing her hands in mute despair, and then fell or rather crouched upon the floor, still crying : " Oh, Lawrence, Lawrence."

Wholly blinded by her sister, she had as much expected to be the future wife of Lawrence Thornton as to see the next day's sun, and had never thought it possible for him to choose another, so when she saw his position with Mildred and heard the words : " Lilian can never be my wife," the shock was overwhelming, and she sank upon the carpet, helpless, sick and fainting.

" Now, I'll be hanged," said the Judge, "if this ain't a little the greatest performance ; but go right on, boy, have your say out. I'll tend to her," and bursting into the

library, he caught up in his trepidation the ink-bottle in stead of the camphor. "A little thrown in her face will fetch her to. Camphor is good for the hysterics," he said, and hurrying back he would undoubtedly have deluged poor Lilian with ink, if Mildred had not pushed him away just as the first drop had fallen on her dress.

Whether Lawrence would have " had his say out" or not, was not prove 1, for Mildred sprang to Lilian's side, and lifting her head upon her lap asked if she were sick.

" No, no," moaned Lilian, covering her face with her harfds and crying a low, plaintive cry, which fell on Mil dred's heart like a reproachful sound, " no, not sick, but I wish that I were dead. Oh, Mildred, how could you serve me so, when you knew that he was mine ? Ain't you, Lawrence ? Oh, Lawrence ! " and burying her face in Mildred's lap, she sobbed passionately.

"Lilian," said Lawrence, drawing near to her, " Lilian, I have never intended to deceive you; I am not responsi ble for what my father and Geraldine have said "

"Stop, I won't hear," cried Lilian, putting her fingers to her ears. " Mildred coaxed you, I know she did, and that hateful old man, too. Let's go home, where Gerald ine is. You always loved me there."

She did not seem to blame him in the least; on the contrary, she charged all to Mildred, who could only an swer with her tears, for the whole had been so sudden,— so like a dream to herself.

"Carriage at the gate,—is the young lady's trunk ready ? " asked Finn in the hall, and consulting his watch Lawrence saw that if they went that day they had no time to lose.

" Hadn't we better stay till to-morrow ? " he suggested, unwilling to leave until Mildred had told him yes.

"No, no," Lilian fairly screamed. "We mustn't stay another minute;" and grasping his arm, she led him into the hall, while the Judge, with the ink-bottle still in his hand, slyly whispered:

" You can write, boy—you can write."

Yes, he could write, and comforted by this thought, Lawrence raised Mildred's hand to his lips, while Lilian's blue eyes flashed with far more spirit than was ever seen in them before. She would not say good-by, and she walked stiffly down to the carriage, holding fast to Law rence, lest by some means he should be spirited away.

It was a most dismally silent ride from Beechwood to the depot, for Lilian persisted in crying behind her vail, and as Lawrence knew of no consolation to offer, he wisely refrained from speaking, but employed himself the while in thinking how the little red spots came out all over Mildred's face and neck when she sat upon the sofa, and he called her :

" Dear Mildred."

When they entered the cars where Lilian had hoped for a splendid time provided Milly told her " how to lead the conversation," the little lady was still crying and con tinued so until Boston was in sight. Then, indeed, she cheered up, thinking to herself how " she'd tell Geraldine and have her see to it."

" Why, Lawrence,—Lilian,—who expected you to day?" Geraldine Veille exclaimed, when about four o'clock she met them in the hall.

In as few words as possible Lawrence explained to her that he had been nearly drowned, and as he did not feel much like visiting after that, he had come home and brought Lilian with him.

"But what ails her? She has not been drowned too," said Geraldine, alarmed at her sister's white face and swollen eyes.

Thinking that Lilian might explain, Lawrence hastened off leaving them alone.

" Oh, sister," cried Lilian, when he was gone. " Come upstairs to our room, where I can tell you all about it and how unhappy I am."

In a moment they entered their chamber, and throw ing her bonnet and shawl on the floor, Lilian threw her self into the middle of the bed, and half smothering her self with the pillows, began her story, to which Geraldine listened with flashing eyes and burning cheeks.

"The wretch! " she exclaimed, when Lilian had finished. " Of course she enticed him. It's like her; but don't dis« tress yourself, Lily dear. I can manage it, I think."

"It don't need any managing," sobbed Lilian, "now that we've got home. He always loves me best here, and he'll forget that hateful Mildred."

This was Lilian's conclusion. Geraldine's was differ ent. Much as she hated Mildred Ho well, she knew that having loved her once, Lawrence would not easily cease to love her, let him be where he would, and though from Lilian's story she inferred that he had not yet fully com mitted himself, she knew he would do so, and by letter, too, unless she devised some means of preventing it. Still she would not, for the world, that Lawrence should suspect her designs, and when at dinner she met him at the table, her smiling face told no tales of the storm within. Mr. Thornton was absent, and for that she was glad, as it gave her greater freedom of action.

" Where's Lily ? " Lawrence asked, a little anxious to hear what she had to say.

With a merry laugh, Geraldine replied : " Poor little chicken, she can't bear her grief at all, and it almost killed her to find that you preferred another to herself. But she'll get over it, I daresay. Mildred is a beautiful girl; and though I always hoped, and indeed expected, that you would marry Lilian, you are, of course, at liberty to choose for yourself; and I am glad you have made so good a choice. When is the happy day ? "

Lawrence was completely duped, for, manlike, he did not see how bitterly one woman could hate another, even while seeming to like her, and his heart warmed toward Geraldine for talking of this matter so coolly.

"I do not even know that the happy day will be at all," he replied; "for Lily came upon ns before I had half finished. She may refuse me yet."

" It's hardly probable," answered Geraldine, helping him to another cup of tea. " When Miss Howell was last here I suspected her of being in love with some one, and foolishly fancied it might be young Hudson, who called on her so often. But I see my mistake. You did not finish your proposal, you say. You'll write to her to-night, of course, and have the matter decided."

" That is my intention," returned Lawrence, begin ning to feel a little uneasy at having suffered Geraldine to draw so much from him.

Still he did not suspect her real design, though he did wonder at her being so very cordial when she had always looked upon him as her brother-in-law elect. " As long as there is no help for it she means to make the best of it, I presume," he thought, and wishing she might transfer some of her sense to Lilian, he went to his room to write the letter, which would tell Mildred Howell tiiat the words he said to her that morning were in earnest.

Could Geraldine have secured the letter and destroyed it, she would unhesitatingly have done so, but Lawrence did not leave his room until it was completed;' and when at last he went out, he carried it tc the office, and thus

placed it beyond her reach. But the wily woman had another plan, and going to Lilian, who had really made herself sick with weeping, she casually inquired what time Judge Howell usually received his Boston letters.

" At night if he sends to the office," said Lilian, " and in the morning if he don't."

"He will send to-morrow night," thought Geraldine, " for mademoiselle will be expecting a letter," and as she just then heard Mr. Thornton entering his room, she stepped across the hall and knocked cautiously at his door.

Mr. Thornton was not in a very amicable mood that night. Business was dull,—money scarce,—debts were constantly coming in with no means of canceling them, and in the dreaded future he fancied he saw the word " Insolvent," coupled with his own name. Froni this there was a way of escape. Lilian Veille had money, and if she were Lawrence's wife, Lawrence as his junior part ner could use the money for the benefit of the firm. This was a strong reason why he was so anxious for a speedy marriage between the two, and was also one cause of his professed aversion to Mildred Howell. Having i seen Judge Howell and Mildred together, he did not |cnow how strong was the love the old man bore the child of his < adoption, and he did not believe he would be foolish enough to give her much of his hoarded wealth. Thorn ton must marry Lilian, and that soon, he was thinking to himself as he entered his room, for his son's mar .:

is the burden of his thoughts, and having just heard of

s return, he was wondering whether he had engaged him-! If to Lilian, or fooled with Mildred as he told him not to do, when Geraldine came to the door.

Thinking it was Lawrence who knocked, he bade him

me in at once, but a frown flitted over his face when he saw that it was his niece.

: ' I supposed you were Lawrence," he said. "I heard he was at home. What brought him so soon? "

In a few words Geraldine told of the accident, and then, when the father's feeling of alarm had subsided, Mr. ;iornton asked :

*' Did he come to an understanding with Lilian ? "

" -Yes, I think she understands him perfectly," was Geraldine's reply, at which Mr. Thornton caught quickly.

; 'They are engaged, then? I am very glad," and the

word " Insolvent" passed from his mental horizon, leav-

there instead bonds and mortgages, bank stocks, city

;\<y ses, Western lands and ready money at his command.

But the golden vision faded quickly when Geraldine repeated to him what she knew of Lawrence and Mildred Howell.

Not engaged to her ? Oh, Heavens ! " and Mr. Thorn ton's face grew dark with passion ; " I won't have it so.

i break it up. I'll nip it in the bud," and he strode across the floor, foaming with fury and uttering bitter in-ves against the innocent cause of his wrath.

"Sit down, Uncle Robert," said Geraldine, when his wrath was somewhat expended. "The case isn't as hope less as you imagine. A little skill on my part, and a little firmness on yours, is all that is necessary. Lilian sur prised them before Lawrence had asked the question itself, but he has written to-night and the letter is in the office. Mildred will receive it, of course,—there's no helping that; but we can, I think, prevent her answering yes."

" How,—how ? " Mr. Thornton eagerly demanded, and Geraldine replied : " You know that if they are once en gaged, no power on earth can separate them, for Law rence has a strong will of his own, and what we have to do is to keep them from being engaged."

" No necessity for repeating that again," growled Mr. Thornton. " Tell me at once what to do."

* Simply this," answered Geraldine: " Do not awake Lawrence's suspicions, though if, when you meet him to night, he gives you his confidence, you can seem to be angry at first, but gradually grow calm, and tell him that what is done can't be helped."

" Well, then, what ? " interrupted Mr. Thornton, impa tient to hear the rest.

" Mildred will receive his letter to-morrow night," said Geraldine, " and as it is Saturday, she cannot answer until Monday, of course. In the meantime you must go to see her "

" Me ! " exclaimed Mr. Thornton. " I go to Beech-wood to rouse up that old lion ! It's as much as my life is worth. You don't know him, Geraldine. He has the most violent temper, and I do not wish to make him angry with me just at present."

"Perhaps you won't see him," returned Geraldine. " Lilian says he frequently takes a ride on horseback about sunset, as he thinks it keeps off the apoplexy, and he may be gone. At all events, you can ask to see Miss Howell alone. You must tell Lawrence you are going to Albany, and that will account for your taking the early train. You will thus reach Mayfield at the same time with the letter, but can stop at the hotel until it has been received and read."

" I begin to get your meaning," said Mr. Thornton, brightening up. " You wish me to see her before she has had time to answer it, and to give her some very weighty reason why she should refuse my son. I can do that, too. But will she listen ? She is as fiery as a pepper-pod herself."

" Perhaps not at first, but I think her high temper and foolish pride will materially aid you, particularly when you touch upon her parentage, and hint that you will be ashamed of her—besides, you are to take from me a lettei in which I shall appeal to her sympathy for Lilian, and that will go a great ways with her, for I do believe she loves Lilian."

A while longer they talked together, and Geraldine had

thoroughly succeeded in making Mr. Thornton understand what he was to do, when Lawrence himself came to the door, knocking for admittance. He seemed a little sur prised at finding Geraldine there, but her well-timed re mark to his father, " So you think I'd better try Bridget a week or two longer ? " convinced him that there was some trouble with the servants, a thing not of rare occurrence in their household.

Mr. Thornton looked up quickly, not quite comprehend ing her, but she was gone ere he had time to ask her what she meant, and he was alone with his son. Lawrence had come to tell his father everything, but his father did not wish to be told. He was not such an adept in cunning as Geraldine, and he feared lest he might betray himself either by word or manner, so he talked of indifferent sub jects, asking Lawrence about the accident,—and Beech-wood, and about Judge Howell, and finally coming to business, where he managed to drag in rather bunglingly, that he was going to Albany in the morning, aod should not return till Monday.

" I can tell him then," thought Lawrence, " and if she should refuse me, it would be as well for him not to know it."

Thus deciding, he bade his father good-night, and when next morning at a rather late hour he came down to breakfast, he was told by the smiling Geraldine that " Uncle Robert had started on the mail train for Albany."

CHAPTER XIII.
THE ANSWER.

OR a long time after the departure of Lawrence and Lilian, Mildred sat in a kind of maze, wondering whether the events of the last hour were real or whether they were all a dream, and that Lawrence Thornton had not called her " dear Mildred," as she thought he did. The Judge, who might have enlightened her, had been suddenly called away just as the carriage rolled down the avenue, and feeling a restless desire to talk with somebody, she at last ran off to Oliver. He would know whether Lawrence was in earnest, and he would be almost as happy as she was.

" Dear Oliver," she whispered softly as she tripped down the Cold Spring path, " how much he loses by not knowing what it is to love the way I do."

Deluded Milly ! How little she dreamed of the wild, absorbing love which burned in Oliver Hawkins' heart, and burned there the more fiercely that he must not let it be known. It was in vain he tried to quench it with his last dre cal Th bee tears; they were like oil poured upon the flame, and often in the midnight hour, when there was no one to hear, he cried in bitterness of spirit : " Will the Good Father forgive me if it is a sin to love her, for I cannot, cannot help it"

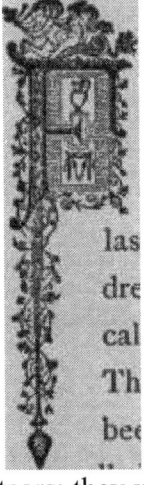

He was in bed this morning, but he welcomed Mildred with his accustomed smile; telling her how glad he was to see her, and how much sunshine she brought into his sick-room.

"The world would be very dark to me without you, Milly," he said, and his long, white fingers moved slowly over her shining hair.

It was a habit he had of caressing her hair, and Mildred, who expected it, bent her beautiful head to the familiar touch.

" Why did Lawrence go without coming to see me ? v he asked, and at the question Mildred's secret burst out. She could not keep it any longer, and with her usual impetuosity she told him all, and asked, if " as true as he Jived, he believed Lawrence would have offered himself to her if Lilian hadn't surprised them ? "

" I'm sure of it," he said ; adding, as he saw the sparkle in her eyes : " Does it make my little Milly very happy to know that Lawrence Thornton really loves her ? "

" Yes, Oliver. It makes me happier than I ever was before in my life. I wish you could, for just one minute, know the feeling of loving some one as I do him."

"Oh, Milly! Milly!"

It was a cry of anguish, wrung from a fainting heart, but Mildred thought it a cry of pain.

" What is it, Oliver ? " she said, and her soft hand was laid on his face. " Where is the pain ? Can I help it ? Can I cure it ? Oh, I wish I could. There, don't that make it better ? " and she kissed the pale lips where there was the shadow of a smile.

" Yes, I'm better," he answered. " Don't, Milly, please don't," and he drew back as he saw her about to repeat the kiss.

Mildred looked at him in surprise, saying :

" Why, Oliver, I thought you loved me."

There was reproach in her soft, lustrous eyes, and folding his feeble arms about her, Oliver replied:

" Heaven grant that you may never know how much I love you, darling."

She did not understand him even then, but satisfied that it was all well between them, she released herself from his embrace and continued: "Do you think he'll write and finish what he was going to say ? "

"Of course he will," answered Oliver, and Mildred was about to ask if he believed she'd get the letter the next night, when old Hepsy came up and said to her rather stiffly : " You've talked with him long enough. He's all beat out now. It's curis what little sense some folks has."

THE ANSWER.

" Grandmother," Oliver attempted to say, but Mildred's little hand was placed upon his lips, and Mildred herself said :

" She's right, Oily. I have worried you to death. I'm afraid I do you more hurt than good by coming to see you so often."

He knew she did, but he would not for that that she should stay away, even though her thoughtless words caused him many a bitter pang.

" Come again to-morrow," he said, as she went from his side, and telling him that she would, she bounded down the stairs, taking with her, as the poor, sick Oliver thought, all the brightness, all the sunshine, and leaving in its stead only weariness and pain.

Up the Cold Spring path she ran, blithe as a singing-bird, for she saw the Judge upon the back piazza, and knew he had returned.

" Come here, Gipsy," he cried, and in an instant Mildred was at his side. " Broke up in a row, didn't we ? " he said, parting back her hair, and tapping her rosy chin. " How far along had he got ? "

"He hadn't got along at all," answered Mildred, §< and I don't believe he was going to say anything, do you ? "

Much as he wished to tease her, the Judge could not resist the pleading of those eyes, and he told her all he knew of the matter, bidding her wait patiently until to morrow night, and see what the mail would bring her.

" Oh, I wish it were to-morrow now," sighed Mildred. 0 I'm afraid there's some mistake, and that he didn't mean me after all."

Laughing at what he called her nervousness, the Judge walked away to give some orders to his men, and Mildred tried various methods of killing time, and making the day seem shorter. Just before sunset she stole away again to Oliver, but Hepsy would not let her see him.

" He's allus wus after you've been up there," she said. " He's too weakly to stan' the way you rattle on, so you may as well go back," and Mildred went back, wondering how her presence could make Oliver worse, and thinking to herself that she would not go to see him once during the next day, unless, indeed, the letter came, and then she must show it to him,—he'd feel so badly if she didn't.

The to-morrow so much wished for came at last, and spite of Mildred's belief to the contrary, the hours did go on as usual, until it was five o'clock, and she heard the Judge tell Finn to saddle the horses, and ride with him to the village.

" I am going up the mountain a few miles," he said ; " and as Mildred will want to see the evening papers be fore my return, you muet bring them home."

The Judge knew it was not the papers she wanted, and Mildred knew so, too, but it answered quite as well for Finn, who, within half an hour after leaving the house, came galloping up the hill.

THE ANSWER.

" Was there anything for me ? " asked Mildred, meet ing him at the gate.

"Yes'm," he answered; "papers by the bushel. There's the Post, the Spy, the Traveler, and "

"Yes, yes," interrupted Mildred; "but the letter. Wasn't there a letter ? "

" Yes'm ;" and diving first into one pocket and then into another, Finn handed her the letter.

She knew it by its superscription, and leaving the papers Finn had tossed upon the grass, to be blown about the yard, untfl they finally fell into the little destructive hands of Rachel's grandbaby, she hurried to her room, and breaking the seal, saw that it was herself and not Lilian Veille whom Lawrence Thornton would have for his bride. Again and again she read the lines so fraught with love, lingering longest over the place where he called her " his beautiful, starry-eyed Mildred," telling her "how heavy his heart was when he feared she loved another, and how that heaviness was removed when the Judge explained the matter."

" Write to me at once, darling," he added in conclu sion, " and tell me yes, as I know you will, unless I have been most cruelly deceived."

" I will write to him this very night," she said, " but I will show this to Oliver first. I am sure he is anxious to know if it came," and pressing it to her lips she went fly ing down to the gable-roof.

Hepsy was riot this time on guard, and gliding up the stairs Mildred burst into the room where Oliver lay, par tially propped up in bed, so that he could see the fading sunlight shining on the river and on the hill-tops beyond.

" It's come, Oliver, it's come !" she exclaimed, holding the letter to view.

" I am glad for your sake, Milly," said Oliver, a deep flush stealing over his face, for he felt instinctively that he was about to be called upon to pass a painful ordeal.

" I wouldn't show it to anybody else," she continued: " and I can't even read it to you myself; neither can I stay here while you read it, for, somehow, I should blush, and grow so hot and fidgety, so I'll leave it with you a few minutes while I take a run down to the tree where Law rence found me sleeping that Sunday." and thrusting the letter into his hand, she hurried out, stumbling over and nearly upsetting Hepsy, who was shelling peas by the open door.

" Oh, the Lord !" groaned the old lady, " you've trod on my very biggest corn," and the lamentations she made over her aching toe, she forgot to go up and see " if the jade had worried Oliver," who was thus left to himself, as he wished to be.

He would not for the world have opened that letter. He could not read how much Mildred Howell was beloved by another than himself, and he let it lay just where it had dropped from his nerveless fingers.

"Why will she torture me so?" he cried. "Why does she come to me day after day with her bright face, and her words of love which sound so much like mockery, and yet 'tis far better thus than to have her know my wicked secret. She would hate me then,—would loathe me in my deformity just as I loathe myself. Oh, why didn't I die years ago, when we were children together, and I had not learned what it was to be a cripple!"

He held up in the sunlight the feet which his dead mother used to pity and kiss,—he turned them round,—• took them in his hands, and while his tears dropped fast upon them, he whispered mournfully : "This is the curse which stands between me and Mildred Howell. Were it not for this, I would have won her love ere Lawrence Thornton came with his handsome face and pleasant ways; but it cannot be. She will be his bride, and he will cherish her long years after the grass is growing green over poor, forgotten Clubs!"

There was a light step on the stairs ; Mildred was com ing up; and hastily covering his feet, he forced a smile upon his face, and handing her the letter, said : "It's just as I expected. You'll consent, of course?"

"Yes, but I shall write ever so much before I get to that, just to tantalize him," returned Mildred, adding that she'd bring her answer down for Oliver to see if it would do!"

A half-stifled moan escaped Oliver's lips, but Mildred

did not hear it, and she went dancing down the stairs singing to herself:

"Never morning smiled so gayly, Never sky such radiance wore, Never passed into the sunshine Such a merry queen before."

"A body'd s'pose you'd nothing to do but to sing and dance and trample on my corns," growled Hepsy, still busy with her peas and casting a rueful glance at her foot, encased in a most wonderful shoe of her own manufac ture.

"I am sorry, Aunt Hepsy," said Mildred, "but your feet are always in the way," and singing of the "sun shine," and the "merry queen of May," she went back to Beechwood, where a visitor was waiting for her, Mr. Robert Thornton!

He had followed Geraldine's instructions implicitly, and simultaneously with the May field mail-bag he entered the hotel where the Post-Office was kept. Seating himself in the sitting-room opposite, he watched the people as they came in for their evening papers, until, at last, looking from the window, he caught sight of the Judge and Finn. Moving back a little, so as not to be observed, he saw the former take the letter which he knew had been written by his son,—saw, too, the expression of the Judge's face as he glanced at the superscription, and then handed it to

Finn, bidding him hurry home, and saying he should not return for two hours or more.

"Everything works well thus far," thought Mr. Thorn ton ; "but I wish it was over," and with a gloomy, for bidding face, he walked the floor, wondering how he should approach Mildred, and feeling glad that the Judge at least was out of the way. "I'd rather stir up a whole menagerie of wild beasts than that old man," he said to himself, "though I don't apprehend much trouble from him either, for of course he'd take sides with his so-called son-in-law sooner than with a nameless girl. I wonder how long it takes to read a love-letter?"

"Supper, sir," cried the colored waiter, and thinking this as good a way of killing time as any, Mr. Thornton found his way to the dining-room.

But he was too excited to eat, and forcing down a cup of tea he started for Beechwood, the road to which was a familiar one, for years before he had traversed it often in quest of his young girl-wife. Now it was another Mildred he sought, and ringing the bell he inquired "if Miss

Howell was in ? "

"Down to Hepsy's. I'll go after her," said Luce, at the same time showing him into the drawing-room and asking his name.

" Mr. Thornton," was the reply, and hurrying off, Luce met Mildred coining up the garden walk.

" Mr. Thornton returned so soon ! " she exclaimed, and

without waiting to hear Luce's explanation that it was not Mr. Lawrence, but an old, sour-looking _ian, she sprang swiftly forward. " I wonder why he sent the letter if he intended coming himself? " she thought; " but I am so glad he's here," and she stole, before going to the par lor, up to her room to smooth her hair and take a look in the glass.

She might have spared herself the trouble, however, for the cold, haughty man, waiting impatiently her coming cared nothing for her hair, nothing for her beautiful face, and when he heard her light step in the hall he arose, and purposely stood with his back toward the door and his eyes fixed upon the portrait of her who, in that room, had been made his bride.

" Why, it isn't Lawrence. It's his father !' dropped involuntarily from Mildred's lips, and blushing like a guilty thing, she stopped upon the threshold, half trembling with fear as the cold gray eyes left the portrait and were fixed upon herself.

"So you thought it was Lawrence," he said, bowing rather stiffly, and offering her his hand. " I conclude then that I am a less welcome visitor. Sit down by me, Miss Howell," he continued, "I am here to talk with you, and as time hastens I may as well come to the point at once. You have just received a letter from my son ? "

" Yes, sir," Mildred answered faintly.

" And in that letter he asked you to be his wife ? " Mr

Thornton went on in the same hard, dry tone, as if it were nothing to him that he was cruelly torturing the young girl at his side. " He asked you to be his wife, I say. May I, as his father, know what answer you intend to give ? "

The answer was in Mildred's tears, which now gushed forth plenteously. Assuming a gentler tone, Mr. Thorn ton continued :

" Miss Howell, it must not be. I have other wishes for my son, and unless he obeys them, I am a ruined man. I do not blame you as much as Lawrence, for you do not know everything as he does."

" Why not go to him, then ? Why need you come here to trouble me ?" cried Mildred, burying her face in the cushions of the sofa.

"Because," answered Mr. Thornton, "it would be use less to go to him. He is infatuated,—blinded as it were, to his own interest. He thinks he loves you, Miss Howell, but he will get over that and wonder at his fancies."

Mildred's crying ceased at this point, and not the slight est agitation was visible, while Mr. Thornton continued :

" Lilian Veille has long been intended for my son. She knew it. He knew it. You knew it, and I leave you to iudge whether under these circumstances it was right for you to encourage him."

Mildred sat bolt upright now, and in the face turned to ward her tormentor there was that which made him quail for an instant, but soon recovering his composure he went on

" He never had a thought of doing otherwise than mar rying Lilian until quite recently, even though he may say to the contrary. I have talked with him. I know, and it astonished me greatly to hear from Geraldine that he had been coaxed into "

"Stop!" and like a young lioness Mildred sprang to her feet, her beautiful face pale with anger, which flashed like sparks of fire from her dark eyes.

Involuntarily Mr. Thornton turned to see if it was the portrait come down from the canvas, the attitude was so like what he once had seen in the Mildred of other days. But the picture still hung upon the wall, and it was an other Mildred, saying to him indignantly :

" He was not coaxed into it! I never dreamed of such a thing until Judge Howell hinted it to me, not twenty minutes before Lilian surprised us as she did."

" Judge Howell," Mr. Thornton repeated, beginning to get angry. " I suspected as much. I know him of old. Nineteen years ago, he was a poorer man than I, and he conceived the idea of marrying his only daughter to the wealthy Mr. Thornton, and though he counts his money now by hundreds of thousands, he knows there is power and influence in the name of Thornton still, and he does not think my son a bad match for the unknown foundling he took from the street, and has grown weary of keeping!"

"The deuce I have!" was hoarsely whispered in the adjoining room, where the old Judge sat, hearing every word of that strange conversation.

He had not gone up the mountain as he intended, and had reached Beechwood just as Mildred was coming down the stairs. Lucy told him Mr. Thornton was there, and, thinking it was Lawrence, he went into his library to put away some business papers ere joining his guest in the drawing-room. While there he heard the words, " You have just received a letter from my son ? "

" Bob Thornton, as I live ! " he exclaimed. " What brought him here ? I don't like the tone of his voice, and I wouldn't wonder if something was in the wind. Any way, I'll just wait and see, and if he insults Mildred, he'll find himself histed out of this house pretty quick ! "

So saying, the Judge sat down in a position where not a word escaped him, and, by holding on to his chair and swearing little bits of oaths to himself, he managed to keep tolerably quiet while the conversation went on.

" I will be plain with you, Miss Howell," Mr. Thornton said. " My heart is set upon Lawrence's marrying Lilian. It will kill her if he does not, and I am here to ask you, as a favor to me and to Lilian, to refuse his suit. Will you do it ? "

" No !" dropped involuntarily from Mildred's lips, and was responded to by a heavy blow of the fist upon Judge Howell's fat knee.

" Well done for Spitfire ! " he said. " She's enough for

-
-

THE ANSWER. 187

old Bobum yet. I'll wait a trifle longer before I fire my gun."

So he waited, growing very red in the face, as Mr. Thornton answered, indignantly :

" You will not, you say ? I think I can tell you that which may change your mind;" and he explained to her briefly how, unless Lilian Veille were Lawrence's wife, and that very soon, they would all be beggars. " Nothing but dire necessity could have wrung this confession from me," he said, "and now, Miss Howell, think again. Show yourself the brave, generous girl I am sure you are. Tell my son you cannot be his wife; but do not tell him why, else he might not give you up. Do not let him know that I have seen you. Do it for Lilian's sake, if for no other. You love her, and you surely would not wish to cause her death."

" No, no—oh, no ! " moaned Mildred, whose only weakness was loving Lilian Veille too well.

Mr. Thornton saw the wavering, and, taking from his pocket the letter Geraldine had prepared with so much care, he bade her read it, and then say if she could answer " Yes " to Lawrence Thornton.

Geraldine Veille knew what she was doing when she wrote a letter which appealed powerfully to every woman-ly tender feeling of Mildred's impulsive nature. Lilian was represented as being dangerously ill, and in her deli rium begging of Mildred not to take Lawrence from her.

" It would touch a heart of stone," wrote Geraldine, " to hear her plaintive pleadings, * Oh Miliy, dear Milly, don't take him from me—don't—for I loved him first, and he loved me ! Wait till I am dead, Milly. It won't be long. I can't live many years, and when I'm gone, he'll go back to you.' "

Then followed several strong arguments from Geraldine why Mildred should give him up and so save Lilian from dying, and Mildred, as she read, felt the defiant hardness which Mr. Thornton's first words had awakened slowly giving way. Covering her face with her hands, she sobbed:

" What must I do ? What shall I do ? "

"Write to Lawrence and tell him no," answered Mr. Thornton ; while Mildred moaned :

" But I love him so much, oh, so much."

" So does Lilian," returned Mr. Thornton, beginning to fear that the worst was not yet over. " So does Lilian, and her claim is best. Listen to me, Miss Howell—Law rence may prefer you now, but he would tire of you when the novelty wore off. Pardon me if I speak plainly. The Thorntons are a proud race, the proudest, perhaps, in Boston. Lawrence, too, is proud, and in a moment of cool reflection he would shrink from making one his wife whose parentage is as doubtful as your own."

Mildred shook now as with an ague chill. It had not occurred to her that Lawrence might sometimes blush when asked who his wife was, and with her bright

eyes fixed on Mr. Thornton's face she listened breath lessly, while he continued :

"Only the day that he came to Beechwood he gave me to understand that he could not think of marrying you un less the mystery of your birth were made clear. But when here, he was, I daresay, intoxicated with your beauty, for, excuse me, Miss Howell,you are beautiful; " and he bowed low, while he paid this compliment to the girl whose lip curled haughtily as if she would cast it from her in disdain.

" He forgot himself for a time, I presume, but his bet ter judgment will prevail at last. I know you have been adopted by the Judge, but that does not avail—that will not prevent some vile woman from calling you her child. You are not a Hovvell. You are not my son's equal, and if you would escape the bitter mortification of one day seeing your husband's relatives, aye, and your husband, too, ashamed to acknowledge you, refuse his suit at once, and seek a companion—one who would be satisfied with the few thousands the Judge will probably give you, and consider that a sufficient recompense for your family. Will you do it, Miss Howell ? "

Mildred was terribly excited. Even death itself seemed preferable to seeing Lawrence ashamed of her, and while object after object chased each other in rapid circles before her eyes, she answered :

" I will try to do your bidding, though it breaks my heart"

The next moment she lay among the cushions of the sofa, white and motionless save when a tremor shook her frame, showing what she suffered.

" The little gun, it seems, has given out, and now it's time for the cannon," came heaving up from the deep chest of the enraged Judge, and snatching from his private drawer a roll of paper, he strode into the drawing-room, and confronting the astonished Mr. Thornton, began : " Well, Bobum, are you through ? If so, you'd better be travelling if you don't want the print of my foot on your fine broadcloth coat," and he raised his heavy calfskin threateningly. "I heard you," he continued, as he saw Mr. Thornton about to speak. " I heard all about it. You don't wan't Mildred to marry Lawrence, and not satisfied with working upon her most unaccountable love for that little soft, putty-head dough-bake, you tell her that she ain't good enough for a Thornton, and bid her marry somebody who will be satisfied with the few thousands I shall probably give her. Thunder and Mars, Bob Thornton, what do you take me to be ? Just look here, will you ? Then tell me what you think about the few thousands," and he unrolled what was unquestionably the te Last Will and Testament of Jacob Howell." "You won't look, hey," he continued. " Listen, then. But first, how much do you imagine I'm worth? What do men in Boston say of old Howell when they want his name ? Don't they rate him at half

a million, and ain't every red of that willed on black and white to Mildred, the child of my adoption, except indeed ten thousand given to Oliver Hawkins, because I knew Gipsy* d raise a fuss if it wasn't, and twenty thousand more donated to some blasted Missionary societies, not because I believe in't, but because I thought maybe 'twould atone for my swearing once in a while, and sitting on the piazza so many Sundays in my easy-chair, instead of sliding down hill all day on those confounded hard cushions and high seats down at St. Luke's. The Apostle himself couldn't sit on 'em an hour without getting mighty fidgety. But that's nothing to do with my will. Just listen," and he read : " I give, bequeath and devise, —and so forth," while Mr. Thornton's face turned black, red, and white alternately.

He had no idea that the little bundle of muslin and lace now trembling so violently upon the sofa had so large a share of Judge Howell's heart and will, or he might have acted differently, for the Judge's money was as valuable as Lilian Veille's, and though Mildred's family might be a trifle exceptionable, four hundred thousand dollars, or thereabouts, would cover a multitude of sins. But it was now too late to retract. The Judge would see his motive at once, and resolving to brave the storm he had raised, he affected to answer with a sneer :

" Money will not make amends for everything. I think quite as much of family as of wealth."

" Now, by the Lord," resumed the Judge, growing p; pie in the face, " Bob Thornton, who do you think) be ? Didn't your grandfather make chip baskets all his life over in Wolf Swamp ? Wasn't one of your aunts r,o better than she should be ? Didn't your uncle die in tiie poor-house, and your cousin steal a sheep ? Answer me that, and then twit Mildred about her parentage. How do you know that she ain't my own child, hey ? Wou J you swear to it ? We are as nigh alike as two pe; -everybody says. I tell you, Bobum, you waked up the wrong passenger this time. I planned the marriage, did J« between you and my other Mildred? It's false, B Thornton, and you know it,—but I did approve Heaven forgive me, I did encourage her to barter 1-glorious beauty for money. But you didn't enjoy 1 long. She died, and now you would kill the other one, the little ewe-lamb that has slept in the old man's bosc so long."

The Judge's voice was gentler now in its tone, a drawing near to Mildred, he smoothed her nut-brov-. • hair tenderly, oh, so tenderly.

"I did not come seeking a quarrel with you," said M>, Thornton, who had his own private reasons for not wising to exasperate the Judge too much. " I came after a promise from Miss Howell. J have succeeded, ai knowing that she will keep her word, I will now take ri leave "

" No you won't," thundered the Judge, leaving Mildred

and advancing toward the door, so as effectually to cut off 11 means of escape. " No you won't till I've had my say ut. If Mildred ain't good enough for your son, your son rin't good enough for Mildred. Do you hear ? "

" I am not deaf, sir," was the cool answer, and the judge went on :

" " Ev^en if she hadn't promised to refuse him, she should <io so. I've had enough to do with the Thorntons. I hate the whole race, even if I did encourage the boy. I've nothing against him in particular except that he's a Thornton, and maybe I shall get over that in time. No, I won't, though, hanged if I do. Such a paltry puppy as he's got for a father. You may all go to the bad ; but be fore you go, pay me what you owe me, Bob Thornton,— pay me what you owe me."

" It isn't due yet," faltered Mr. Thornton, who had Veared some such demand as this, for the Judge was his lieaviest creditor.

"Ain't due, hey?" repeated the Judge. "It will be in just three weeks, and if the money ain't forthcoming the very day, hanged if I don't foreclose ! I'll teach you to i,ay Mildred ain't good enough for your son. Man alive ! she's good enough for the Emperor of France ! Get out of my house ! What are you waiting for ? " and, stand ing back, he made way for the discomfitted Mr. Thornton to pass out,

In the hall the latter paused and glanced toward Mil dred as if he would speak to her, while the Judge, divin ing his thoughts, thundered out :

" I'll see that she keeps her word. She never told a lie yet."

One bitter look of hatred Mr. Thornton cast upon him, and then moved slowly down the walk, hearing, even after he reached the gate, the words :

" Hanged if I don't foreclose ! "

"There! that's done with!" said the Judge, walking buck to the parlor, where Mildred still lay upon the sofa, stunned, and faint, and unable to move. " Poor little girl! " he began, lifting up her head and pillowing it upon his broad chest. " Are you almost killed, poor little Spit fire ? You fought bravely though a spell, till he began to twit you of your mother,—the dog ! Just as though you wasn't good enough for his boy! You did right, darling, to say you wouldn't have him. There I there ! " and he held her closer to him, as she moaned:

" Oh, Lawrence ! Lawrence ! how can I give you up ? "

"It will be hard at first, I reckon," returned the Judge.; " but you'll get over it in time. I'll take you over to Eng land next summer, and hunt up a nobleman for you ; then see what Bobum will say when he hears you are Lady Somebody."

But Mildred did not care for the nobleman. One thought alone distracted her thoughts. She had promised to re-

fuse Lawrence Thornton, and, more than all, she could give him no good reason for her refusal.

" Oh, I wish I could wake up and find it all a dream ! " she cried ; but, alas ! she could not; it was a stern reality ; and covering her face with her hands, she wept aloud as she pictured to herself Lawrence's grief and amazement when he received the letter which she must write.

" I wish to goodness I knew what to say !" thought the Judge, greatly moved at the sight of her distress.

" Then, as a new idea occurred to him, he said :

41 Hadn't you better go down and tell it all to Clubs,—he can comfort you, I guess. He's younger than I am, and his heart ain't all puckered up like a pickled plum."

Yes, Oliver could comfort her, Mildred believed ; for if there was a ray of hope he would be sure to see it; and although it then was nearly nine, she resolved to go to him at once. Hepsy would fret, she knew ; but she did not care for her,—she didn't care for anybody; and drying her tears, she was soon moving down the Cold Spring path, not lightly, joyously, as she was wont to do, but slowly, sadly, for the world was changed to her since she trod that path before, singing of the sunshine and the merry queen of May.

She found old Hepsy knitting by the door, and enjoying the bright moonlight, inasmuch as it precluded the necesity of wasting a tallow candle.

" Want to see Oliver ? " she growled. " You can't do it. There's no sense in your having so much whispering up there, and that's the end on't. Widder Simras says it don't look well for you, a big, grown-up girl, to be hangin' round Oliver."

" Widow Simrns is an old gossip! " returned Mildred, adding by way of gaining her point, that she was going to "buy a pair of new, large slippers for Hepsy's corns."

The old lady showed signs of relenting at once, and when Mildred threw in a box of black snuff with a bean in it, the victory was won. and she at liberty to join Oliver. He heard her well-known step, but he was not prepared for her white face and swollen eyes, and in much alarm he asked her what had happened.

" Oh, Oliver ! " she cried, burying her face in the pillow, " it's all over. I shall never marry Lawrence. I have promised to refuse him, and my heart is aching so hard that I most wish I were dead."

Very wonderingly he looked at her, as in a few words she told him of the exciting scene through which she had been passing since she left him so full of hope. Then laying her head a second time upon the pillow, she cried aloud, while Oliver, too, covering his face with the sheet, wept great burning tears of joy—joy at Mildred's pain. Poor, poor Oliver; he could not help it, and for one single moment he abandoned himself to the selfishness which whispered that the world would be the brighter and his life the happier if none ever had a better claim to Mildred than himself.

"Ain't you going to comfort me one bit? " came plaintively to his ear, but he did not answer.

The fierce struggle between duty and self was not over yet, and Mildred waited in vain for his reply.

" Are you crying, too ? " she asked, as her ear caught a low, gasping sob. " Yes, you are/' she continued, as removing the sheet she saw the tears on his face.

To see Oliver cry was in these day? a rare sight to Mildred, and partially forgetting her own sorrow in her grief at having caused him pain, she laid her arm across his neck, and in her sweetest accents said :

" Dear, dear Oily, I didn't think you would feel so badly for me. There—don't," and she brushed away the tears whioh only fell the faster. " I shall get over it, maybe ; Judge Howell says I will, and if I don't I sha'n't always feel as I do now—I couldn't and live. I shall be comfortably happy by-and-by, perhaps, and then if I never marry, you know you and I.are to live together. Up at Beech-wood, maybe. That is to be mine some day, and you shall have that pleasant chamber looking out upon the town and the mountains beyond. You'll read to me every morning, while I work for the children of some Dorcas Society, for I shall be a benevolent old maid, I guess. Won't it be splendid ? " and in her desire to comfort Oliver, who, she verily believed, was weeping because she

THE ANSWER.

was not going to marry Lawrence Thornton, Mildred half forgot her own grief.

Dear Milly! She had yet much to learn of love's great mystery, and she could not understand how great was the effort with which Oliver dried his tears, and smiling upon her, said:

"I trust the time you speak of will never come, for I would far rather Lawrence should do the reading while you work for children with eyes like yours, Milly," and he smiled pleasantly upon her.

He was beginning to comfort her now. His own feelings were under control, and he told her how, though it would be right for her to send the letter as she promised, Lawrence would not consent. He would come at once to seek an explanation, and by some means the truth would come out, and they be happy yet.

"You are my good angel, Oily," said Mildred. "You always know just what to say, and it is strange you do, seeing you never loved any one as I do Lawrence Thornton."

And Mildred's snowy fingers parted his light-brown hair, all unconscious that their very touch was torture to the young man.

"I am going now, and my heart is a great deal lighter than when I first came in," she said, and pressing her lips to his forehead she went down the stairs and out into the moonlight, not singing, not dancing, not running, but

with a quicker movement than when she came, for there was stealing over her a quiet hopelessness that, as Oliver had said, all would yet be well.

Monday morning came, and with a throbbing heart, and fingers which almost refused to do their office, she wrote to Lawrence Thornton:

"I cannot be your wife,—neither can I give you any reason.

MILDRED."

With swimming eyes she read the cold, brief lines, and then, as she reflected that in a moment of desperation Lawrence might offer himself to Lilian, and so be lost to her forever, she laid her head upon the table and moaned:

"I cannot, cannot send it."

"Yes you can, Gipsy, be brave," came from the Judge, who for a moment had been standing behind her. "Show Bobum that you have pluck."

But Mildred cared more for Lawrence Thornton than for pluck, and she continued weeping bitterly, while the Judge placed the letter in the envelope, thinking to himself:

"It's all-fired hard, I s'pose, but hanged if she shall have him, after Bob said what he did. I'll buy her a set of diamonds though, see if I don't, and next winter she shall have some five hundred dollar furs. I'll show Bob Thornton whether I mean to give her a few thousands or not, the reprobate!"

And finishing up his soliloquy with a thought of the mortgages he was going to foreclose, he sealed the letter, jammed it into his pocket, and passing his great hand caressingly over the bowed head upon the table, hurried away to the post-office.

CHAPTER XIV.
WHAT FOLLOWED.

"WONDER if the Western mail is in yet," and Geraldine Veille glanced carelessly up at the clock ticking upon the marble mantel, peered sideways at the young man reading upon the sofa, and then resumed her crocheting.

"I was just thinking the same," returned Lawrence, folding up his paper and consulting his watch. "I suppose father comes in this train. I wonder what took him to Albany ? "

"The same old story,—business, business," answered Geraldine. " He is very much embarrassed, he tells me, and unless he can procure money he is afraid he will have to fail. Lily might let him have hers, I suppose, if it were well secured."

Lawrence did not reply, for, truth to say, he was just then thinking more of his expected letter than of his father's failure, and taking his hat he walked rapidly to the office, already crowded with eager faces. There were several letters in the Thornton box that night, but Lawrence cared for only one, and that the one bearing the Mayfield post-mark. He knew it was from Mildred, for he had seen her plain, decided handwriting before, and he gave it a loving squeeze, just as he would have given the fair writer, if she had been there instead. Too impatient to wait until he reached his home, he tore the letter open in the street, and read it, three times, before he could believe that he read aright, and that he was rejected.

Crumpling the cruel lines in his hand, he hurried on through street after street, knowing nothing where he was going, and caring less, so suddenly and crushingly had the blow fallen upon him.

" I cannot be your wife,—I cannot be your wife ! " he heard it ringing in his ears, turn which way he would, and with it at last came the maddening thought that the reason why she could not be his wife was that she loved another. Oliver had been deceived, the Judge had been deceived, and he had been cruelly deceived.

But he exonerated Mildred from all blame. She had never encouraged him by a word or look, except indeed when she sat by him upon the sofa, and he thought he saw in her speaking face that she was not indifferent to him. But he was mistaken. He knew it now, and, with a wildly beating heart and whirling brain, he wandered on and on, until the evening shadows were beginning to fall, and he felt the night dew on his burning forehead.

Then he turned homeward, where more than one waited Anxiously his coming.

Mr. Thornton had returned, and, entering his house just after Lawrence left it, had communicated to Geral-dine the result of his late adventure, withholding in a measure the part which the old Judge had taken in the affair, and saying nothing of the will, which had so astonished him.

" Do you think she'll keep her promise ? " Geraldine asked.

But Mr. Thornton could not tell, and both watched nervously for Lawrence.

Geraldine was the first to see him ; she stood upon the stairs when he came into the hall.

The gas was already lighted, showing the ghastly whiteness of his face, and by that she knew that Mildred Howell had kept her word. An hour later when Geraldine knocked softly at his door, and heard his reply, " Engaged," she muttered, " Not to Mildred Howell though," and then went to her own room, where lay sleeping the Lilian for whose sake this suffering was caused. Assured by Geraldine that all would yet be well, she had dried her tears, and, as she never felt badly long upon any subject, she was to all appearances on the best of terms with Lawrence, who, grateful to her for behaving so sensibly, treated her with even more than his usual kindness.

The illness of which Geraldine had written to Mildred was of course a humbug, for Lilian was not one to die of a broken heart, and she lay there sleeping sweetly now, while Geraldine paced the floor, wondering what Mildred Hovvell had written and what the end would be.

The next morning Lawrence came down to breakfast looking so haggard and worn that his father involuntarily asked if he were sick.

"No, not sick," was Lawrence's hurried answer, as he picked at the snowy roll and affected to sip his coffee.

M'r. Thornton was in a hurry as usual, and immediately after breakfast went out, leaving Geraldine and Lawrence alone, for Lilian had not yet come down.

"You have had bad news, I'm sure," said Geraldine, throwing into her manner as much concern as possible.

Lawrence made no reply, except indeed to place his feet upon the back of a chair and fold his hands together over his head.

" I was a little fearful of some such denouement" Geraldine continued, " for, as I hinted to you on Friday, I was almost certain she fancied young Hudson. He called here last evening,— and seemed very conscious when I casually mentioned her name. What reason does she give for refusing you ? "

" None whatever," said Lawrence, shifting his position a little by upsetting the chair on which his feet were placed.

" That's strange," returned Geraldine, intently studying the pattern of the carpet as if she would there find a cause for the strangeness. " Never mind, coz," she added, laughingly, "don't let one disappointment break your heart. There are plenty of girls besides Mildred Howell; so let her have young Hudson, if she prefers him."

No answer from Lawrence, who was beginning to be dreadfully jealous of young Hudson.

" It may be. It may be," he thought, " but why couldn't she have told me so ? Why leave me entirely in the dark ? Does she fear the wrath of Hudson's mother in case I should betray her ? "

Yes, that was the reason, he believed, and in order to make the matter sure, he resolved to write again and ask her, and forgetting his father's request that he should " come down to the office as soon as convenient," he spent the morning in writing to Mildred a second time. He had intended to tell her that he guessed the reason of her refusal, but instead of that he poured out his whole soul in one passionate entreaty for her to think again, and reconsider her decision. No other one could love her as he did, he said, and he besought of her to give him one word of hope to cheer the despair which had fallen so darkly around him. This letter being sent, Lawrence sat down in a kind of apathetic despair to await the re sult.

" What, hey, the boy has written, has he ? " and adjust ing his gold specs, the old Judge looked to see if the eight pages Finn had just given to him were really from Lawrence Thornton.

"He's got good grit," said he, "and I like him for it, but hanged if I don't teach Bobum a lesson. I can feel big as well as he. Gipsy not good enough for his boy! I'll show him. She looks brighter to-day than she did. She ain't going to let it kill her, and as there's no use worrying her for nothing, I shan't let her see this. But I can't destroy it, nor read it neither. So I'll just put it where the old Nick himself couldn't find it," and touching the hidden spring of a secret drawer, he hid the letter which Mildred, encouraged by Oliver, had half expected to receive.

But he repented of the act when he saw how disappointed she seemed when he met her at the supper-table, and though he had no idea of giving her the letter, he thought to make amends some other way.

"I have it," he suddenly exclaimed, as he sat alone in his library, after Mildred had gone to bed. "I'll dock off five thousand from that missionary society and add it to Spitfire's portion. The letter ain't worth more than that," and satisfied that he was making the best possible reparation, he brought out his will and made the alteration, which took from a missionary society enough to feed and clothe several clergymen a year.

Four days more brought another letter from Lawrence Thornton—larger, heavier than the preceding one, crossed all over, as could be plainly seen through the envelope, and worth, as the Judge calculated, about ten thousand dollars. So he placed that amount to Mildred's credit, by way of quieting his conscience. One week more, and there came another.

"Great heaven!" groaned the Judge, as he gave Mildred the last five thousand dollars, and left the missionaries nothing. "Great heaven, what will I do next?" and he glanced ruefully at the clause commencing with "I give and bequeath to Oliver Hawkins," etc. "'Twon't do to meddle with that," said he. "I might as well touch Gipsy's eyes as to harm the reel-footed boy," and in his despair the Judge began to consider the expediency of praying that no more letters should come from Lawrence Thornton.

Remembering, however, that in the prayer-book there was nothing suited to that emergency, he gave up that wild project and concluded that if Lawrence wrote again he would answer it himself; but this he was not compelled to do, for Lawrence grew weary at last, and calling his pride to his aid resolved to leave Mildred to herself, and neither write again nor seek an interview with her, as he had thought of doing. No more letters came from him, but on the day when his father's mortgages were due, the Judge received one from Mr. Thornton begging for a little longer time, and saying that unless it were granted he was a ruined man.

"Ruined or not, I shall foreclose," muttered the Judge. "I'll teach him to come into my house and say Gipsy isn't good enough for his boy."

Looking a little further, he read that Lawrence was going to Europe.

"What for, nobody knows," wrote Mr. Thornton. "He will not listen to reason or anything else, and I suppose he will sail in a few days. I did not imagine he loved your Mildred so much, and sometimes I have regretted my interference, but it is too late now, I daresay."

This last was thrown out as a bait, at which Mr. Thornton hoped the Judge might catch. The fact that Mildred was an heiress had produced a slight change in his opinion of her, and he would not now greatly object to receiving her as his daughter-in-law. But he was far too proud to say so,—he would rather the first concession should come from the Judge, who, while understanding perfectly the hint, swore he would not take it.

"If anybody comes round it'll be himself," he said. "I'll teach him what's what, and I won't extend the time either. I'll see Lawyer Monroe this very day, but first I'll tell Gipsy that the boy is off for Eirope. Ho, Gipsy!" he called, as he heard her in the hall, and in a moment Mildred was at his side.

She saw the letter in his hand, and hope whispered that it came from Lawrence. But the Judge soon undeceived her.

"Spitfire," said he, "Bobum writes that Lawrence is going to Europe to get over his love-sickness. He sails in a few days. But what the deuce, girl, are you going to faint?"

And he wound his arm around her to prevent her falling to the floor.

The last hope was swept away, and while the Judge tried in vain to soothe her, asking what difference it made whether he were in Halifax or Canada, inasmuch as she had pledged herself not to marry him, she answered:

"None, none, and yet I guess I thought he'd come to see me, or write, or something. Oliver said he would, and the days are so dreary without him."

The Judge glanced at the hidden drawer, feeling strongly tempted to give her the letters it contained, but his temper rose up in time to prevent it, and muttering to himself: "Hanged if I do," he proceeded to tell her how by and by the days would not be so dreary, for she would forget Lawrence and find some one else to love, and then he added, suddenly brightening up, "there'll be some fun in seeing me plague Bobum. The mortgages are due to day, and the dog has written asking for more time, saying he's a ruined man unless I give it to him. Let him be ruined then. I'd like to see him taken down a peg or two. Maybe then he'll think you good enough for his boy. There, darling, sit on the lounge, while I hunt up the papers. I'm going up this very day to see my lawyer," and he pushed her gently from him.

Mildred knew comparatively nothing of business, but she understood that Judge Howell had it in his power to ruin Mr. Thornton or not just as he pleased, and though she had no cause for liking the latter, he was Lawrence's father, and she resolved to do what she could in his behalf. Returning to the Judge she seated herself upon his knee and asked him to tell her exactly how matters stood between himself and Mr. Thornton.

He complied with her request, and when he had finished, she said:

"If you choose, then, you can give him more time and so save him from a failure. Is that it?"

"Yes, yes, that's it," returned the Judge, a little petulantly. "But I ain't a mind to. I'll humble him, the wretch!"

Mildred never called Judge Howell father except on special occasions, although he had often wished her so to do, but she called him "father" now, and asked if "he loved her very much."

"Yes, love you a heap more than you deserve, but 'tain't no use to beg off for Bob Thornton, for I shall foreclose,—hanged if I don't."

"No, no. You mustn't," and Mildred's arms closed tightly around his neck. "Listen to me, father. Give him more time, for Milly's sake. My heart is almost broken now, and it will kill me quite to have him ruined, for Lawrence, you know, would suffer too. Lawrence would suffer most. Won't you write to him that he can have all the time he wants? You don't need the money, and you'll feel so much better, for the Bible says they shall be blessed who forgive their enemies. Won't you forgive Mr. Thornton?" \

She kissed his forehead and kissed his lips,—she caressed his rough, bearded cheek, while all the while her arms pressed tighter around his neck, until at last he gasped:

"Heavens and earth, Gipsy, you are choking me to death."

Then she released him, but continued her gentle pleading until the Judge was fairly softened, and he answered:

" Good thunder, what can a fellow do with such eyes looking into his, and such a face close to his own. Yes, I'll give Bobum a hundred years if you say so, though no body else under heaven could have coaxed me into it."

And in this the Judge was right, for none save Mildred could have induced him to give up his cherished scheme.

" 'Tisn't none of my doings though," he wrote in his letter to Mr. Thornton. " It's all Gipsy's work. She clambered into my lap, and coaxed, and teased, and cried, till I finally had to give in, though it went against the grain, I tell you, Bobum. Hadn't you better twit her again with being low and mean. Ugh, you dog !"

This letter the Judge would not send for a week or more, as he wished to torment Mr. Thornton as long as possible, never once thinking that by withholding it he was doing a wrong to Mildred. Mr. Thornton was not without kindly feelings, and had the letter been received before Lawrence's departure he might perhaps have ex plained the whole to his son, for Mildred's generous interference in his behalf touched his heart. But when the letter came Lawrence was already on the ocean, and as the days went on, his feelings of gratitude gradually-subsided, particularly as Geraldine, who knew nothing of the circumstances, often talked to him of a marriage between Lawrence and Lilian as something sure to take place.

" Only give him a little time to overcome his foolish fancy," she said, " and all will yet be right."

So Mr. Thornton, over whom Geraldine possessed an almost unbounded influence, satisfied his conscience by writing to Mildred a letter of thanks, in which he made an attempt at an apology for anything he might have said derogatory to her birth and parentage.

With a proud look upon her face, Mildred burned the letter, which seemed to her so much like an insult, and then, with a dull, heavy pain at her heart, she went about her accustomed duties, while the Judge followed her lan guid movements with watchful and sometimes tearful eyes, whispering often to himself:

"I didn't suppose she loved the boy so well. Poor Milly ! Poor Milly ! "

Oliver too said, " Poor, poor Milly," more than once when he saw how the color faded from her cheeks and the brightness from her eyes. His own health, on the contrary, improved, and in the autumn he went back to college, leaving Mildred more desolate than ever, for now there was no one to comfort her but the Judge, and he usually pained her more than he did her good. All through the long, dreary New England winter she was alone in her sorrow. Lilian never wrote, Oliver but sel dom, for he dared not trust himself, while, worse than all, there came no news from the loved one over the sea, ex cept, indeed, toward spring, when a Boston lady who was visiting in Mayfield brought the rumor that he was ex pected back before long to marry Lilian Veille; that some of the bridal dresses were selected, she believed, and that the young couple would remain at home, as Mr. Thornton wished his son to live with him.

The woman who repeated this to Mildred wondered at her indifference, for she scarcely seemed to hear, certainly not to care, but the storm within was terrible, and when alone in the privacy of her chamber it burst forth with all its force, and kneeling by her bedside she asked that she might die before another than herself was the bride of Law rence Thornton. Poor, poor little Milly 1

CHAPTER XV.
THE SUN SHINING THROUGH THE CLOUD.

HE dreary winter had passed away, the warm April sun shone brightly upon the college walls, and stealing through the muslin-shaded window looked smilingly into the room where two young men were sitting, one handsome, manly and tall, the other deformed, effeminate and slight, but with a face which showed that the suffering endured so long and patiently had purified the heart within and made it tenfold better than it might otherwise have been. The latter was Oliver Hawkins, and he sat talking with Law rence Thornton, who had landed in New York the pre vious day, and had surprised him half an hour before by coming suddenly into his room when he supposed him far away.

During the entire period of his absence Lawrence had heard nothing of Mildred, for in his letters he had never mentioned her name, and it was to seek some information of her that had turned out of his way and called on Oliver. After the first words of greeting were over, he said *

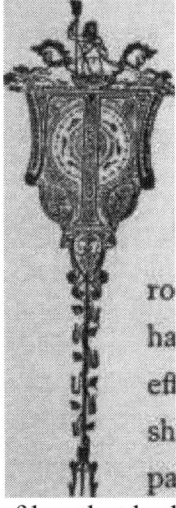

"You hear from Beech wood, I suppose ? "

" Occasionally," returned Oliver. " Mildred does not write as often as she used to do."

" Then she's there yet ? " and Lawre.nce waited anxiously for the answer.

" There !" of course she is. Where did you suppose she was ? "

Lawrence had in his mind a handsome dwelling looking out on Boston Common, with "T. HUDSON," engraved upon its silver plate, and he fancied Mildred might be there, but he did not say so ; and to Oliver's question, he rather abruptly replied :

" Clubs, I've come home to be married ! "

" To be married ! " and in Oliver's blue eyes there was a startled look. " Married to whom ! Surely not to Lilian Veille ? You would not marry her ? "

" Why not ? " Lawrence asked, and before Oliver could answer, he continued : " I must talk to some one, Clubs, and I may as well make you my father confessor. You know I proposed to Mildred Howell ? You know that she refused me ? "

Oliver bowed his head, and Lawrence continued :

" She gave me no reason for her refusal, neither did she deign to answer either of the three letters I sent to her,

216 THE SUN THROUGH THE CLOUD.

begging of her to think again, or at least to tell me why I was rejected."

"Three letters,—she never told me of that. There is surely a mistake," said Oliver, more to himself than to Lawrence, who rejoined :

" There could be no mistake. She must have received some one of them, but she answered none, and in despair I went away, believing, as I now do, that we were all de prived and she loved another. Wait,—listen," he said, as he saw Oliver about to interrupt him. " Father and Ger-aldine always wished me to marry Lilian, and until I learned how much I loved Mildred Howell, I thought it very likely I should do so."

There was a hard, defiant expression on his face as he said this, and, as if anxious to have the story off his mind, he hastened on :

" Mildred refused me, and now, though I have not said positively that I would marry Lilian, I have given Geral-dine encouragement to think I would, and have made up my mind that I shall do so. She is a gentle, amiable creature, and though not quite as intellectual as I could wish, she will make me a faithful, loving wife. Poor little thing. Do you know Geraldine thinks that her mind has been somewhat affected by my proposing to Mildred. then going away ? "

Had it been Judge Howell listening, instead of Oliver, ha would undoubtedly have said :

" Thornton, you're a fool! " but as it was, Oliver mildly interposed :

" If I remember right, her mind was never very sound."

Lawrence did not seem at all angry, but replied :

" I know she is not brilliant, but something certainly has affected her within the past few months. She used to write such splendid letters as to astonish me, but since I've been in Europe there's a very perceptible difference. Indeed, the change was so great that I could not recon cile it until Geraldine suggested that her ill-health and shattered nerves were probably the cause, and then I pitied her so much. There's not a very wide step between pity and love, you know."

Lawrence paused, and sat intently watching the sun light on the floor, while Oliver was communing with him self.

" Shall I undeceive him, or shall I suffer him to rush on blindfolded, as it were? No, I will not. I saved him once for Mildred, and I'll save him for her again."

Thus deciding, Oliver moved his chair nearer to Law rence's side, and said :

"Did it ever occur to you that another than Lilian wrote her letters,—her old letters I mean, when she was in Charlestown, and at school at Beechwood ? "

" Clubs!" and Lawrence looked him fixedly in the face. "Who should write Lilian's letters but herself?

What would you insinuate ? " 10

218 THE SUN THROUGH THE CLOUD.

-a

" Nothing but what I know to be true," returned Oliver. " Mildred Howell always wrote Lilian's letters for her,—always. Lilian copied them, 'tis true, but the words were Mildred's."

" Deceived me again," Lawrence hoarsely whispered. " I forgave the first as a sudden impulse, but this system atic, long-continued deception, never. Oh, is there no faith in women ? "

" Yes, Lawrence. There is faith and truth in Mildred Howell ;" and Oliver's voice trembled as he said it, for he knew that of his own free will he was putting from him that which for the last few months had made the world seem brighter, had kindled a glow of ambition in his heart, and brought the semblance of health to his pale cheek.

Mildred free was a source of greater happiness to him than Mildred married would be,— but not for this did he waver, and lest his resolution should give way, he told rapidly all that he knew of Lilian's intercourse with Mildred,—all that he knew of Mr. Thornton's visit to Beech wood,—of the promise wrung from Mildred by cruel insults, and by working upon her love for Lilian,—, of Mildred's hopeless anguish at first,—of her watching day by day for some word from Lawrence, until her starry eyes were dim with tears, which washed the roses from her cheek, and the hope from out her heart,—of her noble interference to save Mr. Thornton from ruin,—of her desolate condition now, and of the agony it would cause her to hear of Lawrence's marrying another.

For several minutes Lawrence seemed like one in a dream. It had come upon him so suddenly as to suspend his power to move, and he sat staring blankly at Oliver, who at last brought him back to reality by saying:

"You will go to Beech wood at once ? "

" Yes, yes," he answered ; " this very day, if possible. Clubs, I owe you more than I can ever repay. You saved me once from a watery grave, and now you have made me the happiest of men. I can understand much which seemed mysterious in father's manner. I always knew he was ambitious, but I did not think him equal to this cowardly act. Marry Lilian! Why, I wouldn't marry her were there no other girl in the wide, wide world ! God bless you, Clubs, as you deserve ! I hear the whistle, and if I would see Mildred before I sleep, I must be oft". Good-by ! " and wringing Oliver's hand, he hurried away.

The night train for Albany had just gone from the Mayfield depot, and Judge Howell, who had come down to see a friend, was buttoning his overcoat preparatory to returning home, when a hand was laid upon his shoulder, and £ familiar voice called his name.

" Lawrence Thornton ! Thunder, boy ! " he exclaimed. " Where did you drop from ? " And remembering how

he had set his heart against the boy, as he called him, he tried to frown.

But it was all lost on Lawrence, who was too supremely happy to think of an old man's expression. Mildred alone was uppermost in his thoughts, and following the Judge to his carriage, he whispered :

"I've seen Clubs; I know the whole of father's das tardly act, and I'm going home with you to see Mildred. I shall marry her, too. A thousand fathers can't hinder me now! "

" Pluck ! " exclaimed the Judge, disarmed at once of all prejudice by Lawrence's fearless manner of speaking. "Boy, there's nothing pleases me like pluck! Give us your hand!" and in that hearty squeeze by-gones were forgotten and Lawrence fully restored to favor. " Now, drive home like lightning !" he said to Finn, as they entered the carriage ; and as far as possible, Finn com plied with his master's orders.

But during that rapid ride there was sufficient time for questions and explanations, and before Beechwood was reached the Judge had confessed to the letters withheld and his reason for withholding them.

" But I made amends," said he ; "I docked the mis sionaries five thousand at one time, ten at another, and five at another. If you don't believe it I can show you the codicils, witnessed and acknowledged, so there'll be no mistake."

But Lawrence had no wish to discredit it. Indeed, he scarcely heard what the Judge was saying, for the Beech-wood windows were in view, and from one a light was shining, showing him where Mildred sat, thinking of him, perhaps, but not dreaming how near he was to her."

" You let me manage," said the Judge, as they ran up the steps. " If Milly's sitting with her back to the door, I'll go in first, while you follow me on tiptoe. Then I'll break it to her as gently as possible, and when she screeches, as women always do, I'll be off; for you know an old dud like me would only be in the way."

Mildred was sitting with her back to the door, and gazing fixedly into the fire. She was thinking of Law rence, too, and was so absorbed in her own thoughts as not to hear the Judge until he had a hand on either shoulder and called her by name.

" Did I scare you, Gipsy ? " he asked, as she started suddenly. " I reckon I did a little^ for your heart beats like a trip-hammer ; but never mind, I've brought you something that's warranted to cure the heart disorder. What do you guess it is ? "

Mildred did not know^and the Judge continued :

"It's a heap nicer than diamonds; and I shouldn't wonder if it hugged you tighter than furs. It stands six feet in its boots and has raised a pair of the confounded-est whiskers "

He did not need to tell her more, for directly opposite

and over the marble mantel a mirror was hanging, and glancing upward, Mildred saw what it was that would "hug her tighter than fur," and the screech the Judge had predicted burst forth in a wild, joyous cry of " Lawrence, Lawrence,—'tis Lawrence !"

In an instant the Judge disappeared, just as he said he would, leaving Lawrence and Mildred alone, and free to tell each other of the long, long dreary days and nights which had intervened since they sat together before, just as they were sitting now. Much Lawrence blamed her for having yielded to his father in a matter which so nearly concerned her own life's happiness, and at the mention of Mr. Thornton, Mildred lifted up her head from its natural resting-place, and parting Lawrence's dark hair, said:

" But won't it be wicked for me to be your wife. Didn't my letter mean that I would never marry you ? "

" No, it didn't," answered Lawrence, kissing the little fingers which came down from his hair. " You said you would refuse me and you did, but you never promised not to make up. / think the making up is splendid, don't you, darling ? "

Whether she thought so or not, she took it very quietl\'7d', and whenever the Judge looked in, as he did more than once, he whispered to himself:

" Guy, don't he snug up to her good, and don't she act as if she liked it!"

Ten, eleven, twelve, and even one the clock struck before that blissful interview was ended, and Lawrence had completed the arrangements, which he next morning submitted to the Judge for his approval. He would go to Boston that day, and would tell his father that Mildred was to be his wife on the 2oth of June, that being his birthday. After their bridal tour they would return to Beechwood, and remain with the Judge until he consented to part with Mildred,—then they would go to Boston and settle down into the happiest couple in the whole world. To all this the Judge assented, thinking the while that it would be some time before he would be willing to part with Mildred.

Breakfast being over, he gave Mildred the letters so long withheld, but she did not care to read them then. She preferred joining Lawrence in the parlor, where there was another whispered conference, which ended in her looking very red in the face, and running away up-stairs, to avoid the quizzical glance of the Judge, who, neverthe less, called after her, asking " what that wet spot was on her cheek."

" You are a happy dog," he said to Lawrence, as he went with him to the carriage, adding as he bade him good-by, " Give my regrets to Bobum, and tell him that what I said to him last fall are my sentiments still."

Lawrence promised compliance, and glancing up at the window, from which a bright face had just disappeared, he said good-by again, and was driven to the depot.

Contrary to Lawrence's expectation, his father seemed neither surprised nor offended when told what he had done.

"l Miss Howell was a nice girl/' he said, " and he had more than once been on the point of confessing to his son how he had influenced her decision."

Tjie will had wrought a great change in Mr. Thornton's opinion, and even the beggar who was some day to claim Mildred as her daughter, did not seem very formidable when viewed through a golden setting. Geraldine, on the contrary, was terribly disappointed, and when alone fairly gnashed her teeth with rage, while Lilian aban doned herself again to tears and hysterics. Not long, however, did Geraldine give way. She knew that Law rence did not suspect her of having anything to do with Mildred's refusal, further than to ask her for Lilian's sake to give him up, and as it was for her interest to keep him wholly blinded, she affected to congratulate him a second time, saying, laughingly, " The Fates have decreed that you should marry Mildred, so I may as well give it up and act like a sensible woman." But when alone with Mr. Thornton she assumed a new phase of character, fiercely demanding of him if he intended to sit quietly down and see Lawrence throw himself away. Mr. Thorn ton had never told her of the will, neither did he do so now, but he answered her that it was useless further to oppose Lawrence,—that he was sorry for Lilian, but hoped her disappointment would in time wear off. " Law rence will marry Miss Howell, of course," he said, in con clusion, " and won't it be better for us to make the best of it, and treat her with a show of friendship at least."

" Perhaps it will," returned Geraldine, whose thoughts no one could fathom. " I was indignant at first that he should treat Lilian so shamefully, but I will try to feel kindly toward this girl who is to be my cousin, and by way of making a commencement, I will write her a letter of congratulation."

Mr. Thornton was deceived, so was Lawrence, and so, indeed, was Mildred, when two days after Lawrence's de parture, she received a letter from Geraldine Veille, couched in the kindest of terms and written apparently in all sincerity:

" I was much vexed with you once, I'll confess," the wily woman wrote, "for I had so set my heart upon Lawrence's marrying Lilian that it was hard to give it up. But I have considered the matter soberly, and concluded that whether I am willing or not, Lawrence will do as he pleases, so pray forgive me, dear cousin that is to be, for anything you may heretofore have disliked in my conduct toward you. We shall, I know, be the best of friends, and I anticipate much pleasure in having you with us. I shall coax Lawrence to let me superintend the fitting-up your rooms, and here let me offer you my services in selecting any part of your bridal trousseau. Don't be afraid to trouble me, for do what I may, I shall consider it merely

as atoning for the ill-natured feelings I have cherished toward you. It you like, I will come out to Beechwood a few weeks before the wedding. I have given quite a number of lasge parties, and may be of some use to you. In short, call upon me as much as you please, and whatever you may have thought of me before, please consider me now as Your sincere friend,

GERALDINE VEILLE."

"She is a good woman after all," thought Mildred, as she carried the letter to the Judge, who read it over twice and then handed it back, saying, "There's bedevilment behind all that. Mark my words. I don't like those Veilles. I knew their father,—as sneaky a dog as ever drew breath."

But Mildred thought he was prejudiced, and after an swering Lawrence's letter of twelve pages, she wrote a note to Geraldine, thanking her for her kind offers, and saying that very likely she might wish for her services in the matter of selecting dresses, as Boston furnished so much greater variety than Mayfield.

Swimmingly now the matters progressed. Every week found Lawrence at Mayfield, while there seemed no end to the thick letters which passed between himself and Mildred, when he was not with her. Lilian, by some most unaccountable means, had been quieted, and wrote to Mildred as of old. Geraldine, too, was all amiability, and having been deputed to select the bridal dress, and having failed to find anything in Boston worth looking at, went

all the way alone to New York, remaining there several days, and returning home at last perfectly elated with her success! Such a splendid piece of satin as she had found at Stewart's,—such a love of a veil and wreath as she had purchased elsewhere, and such an exquisite point-lace collar as she had bought for herself at cost, having en listed in her behalf one of the firm of Blank & Co., who had written for her notes of introduction to clerks of different houses, and had sometimes gone with her himself to see that she wasn't cheated 1

CHAPTER XVI.
THE EBBING OF THE TIDE.

'HE fiishing sntroke was given to the hand some suite of rooms intended for the bride, which Geraldine pronounced per fect, while even Lilian went into ecstasies over them. Her taste had been consulted in everything, and a stranger would have easily mistaken her for the future occupant, so care ful was Geraldine that she should be suited. And now nothing was wanting to complete the furnishing except Mildred's beautiful piano, which was to come when she did, and with a self-satisfied expression upon her face, Geraldine locked the door, and giving the key to Lawrence said something pleasant to him of the day when Mrs. Lawrence Thornton would first cross the threshold of her future home.

Two dressmakers, one with her scissors fastened to her belt with a steel chain, and the other with a silken cord, were hired at an enormous expense and sent to Beech-wood, whither the

Lady Geraldine followed them to super-intend in person the making of the dresses and the ar rangements for the wedding. With an unsparing hand the Judge opened his purse, bidding Mildred take all she wanted, and authorizing Geraldine to buy whatever a bride like her was supposed to need. In the village everybody was more or less engaged in talking of the party,—wondering who would be invited and what they would wear. Mothers went to Springfield in quest of suitable garments for the daughters, who sneered at the dry-goods to be found at home. Husbands were bidden to be measured for new coats. White kids rose in value, and the Mayfield merchants felt their business steadily in creasing as the preparations progressed. Even Mildred became an object of uncommon interest, and those who had seen her all her life, now ran to the window if by chance she appeared in the street, a thing she finally ceased to do, inasmuch as Geraldine told her it wasn't quite genteel.

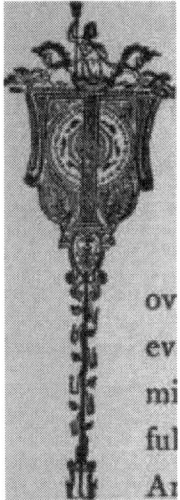

So Mildred stayed at home, where chairs and tables, piano and beds, literally groaned with finery, and where a dozen times a day the two dressmakers from Boston gave her fits^ with Geraldine standing by and suggesting another whalebone here and a little more cotton there, while Miss Steel-chain declared that "Miss HowelFs was a perfect form and didn't need such things at all."

" She's as free from deformity as most people," I'll ad mit," Geraldine would say, " but one shoulder is a trifle higher than the other, white she had a bad school-girl habit of standing on one foot, which naturally makes her waist wrinkle on one side."

So Mildred was tortured after the most approved fash ion, wondering if they supposed she was never to have a single thing after she was married, and so were making up a most unheard-of quantity of clothes to be hung away in the closet until they were entirely out of date.

Now, as of old, Oliver was her refuge when weary or low spirited. On the day of Lawrence's visit to him, he had been found by one of his companions lying upon the floor in a kind of fainting-fit, which left him so weak that he was unable longer to pursue his studies, and at last came home to Hepsy, who declared him to be in " a gal loping consumption." Mildred was sorry for his ill health, but she was glad to have him home again ; it seemed so nice to steal away from laces, silks, satins and flowers, and sit alone with him in his quiet room. She wondered greatly at the change one short month had produced in him, but she was too happy herself to think very much of it, and she failed to see how he shrank from talking with her of the future, even though he knew nothing could interest her more. '

I ain't a bit anxious to be married," she said to him one night, when making him her usual visit, " but I do want to be with Lawrence. I think it real mean in his father to send him West just now. Did I tell you he's gone to Minnesota, and I shan't see him for two whole weeks. Then he'll stay with me all the time till the very day \ but it seems so long to wait. To think I must eat breakfast, and dinner, and supper fourteen times before he comes ! It's terrible, Oliver, and then I've got a fidget in my brain that something is going to happen, either to him or to me,—him, most likely. Maybe he'll be killed. I do wish he hadn't gone ; " and Mildred's eyes filled with tears as she thought of Lawrence dying on the distant praries, the victim of some horrible railroad disaster. " But I am not going to borrow trouble," she said. "It comes fast enough," and asking Oliver if he should be very, very sorry when she was Mildred Thornton, she tripped back to the house, still bearing with her the harrow ing presentiment that " something was going to happen."

"I mean to write to Lawrence," she said, "and tell him to be careful; tell him not to ride in the front car, nor the last car, nor the middle car, nor over the wheels, nor in the night, and to be sure and walk across Suspen sion Bridge when he comes back."

Satisfied that, if he followed the directions implicitly he would return to her alive, she ran up to her room, where she could be alone whiJe she wrote the important letter. Groping about in the dark until she found the matches, she struck a light, and finding her portfolio, took it to the table, where lay a singular looking note, sealed with a wafer, and directed to " Miss Mildred Howell."

" What in the world !" she exclaimed, taking up the soiled bit of foolscap. " Where did this come from, and what can it be ? "

As a sure means of solving the mystery, she broke the seal at once, and with a beating heart read as follows :

" Forgive me, Miss Howell. If I keep still any longer I shall be awful wicked. I or'to have told you who you be long ago, but bein' I didn't I must tell you now. I've been hangin' 'round a good while to see you alone, but couldn't. I came to the door a day or two ago and asked for a drink of water, but that woman with the big black eyes was in the kitchen, and acted as if she mis trusted I wanted to steal, for she staid by watching me till I got tired, and went off without seeing you at all. You know that old hut across the river where there don't nobody live. Come there to-morrow just as it is getting dark, and I will tell you who you be. I know, for I'm the very one that brungyou to the door. You ain't low-lived, so don't go to worryin' about that; and if you are afraid to come alone, let that Judge come with you, and stay a little ways off. Now don't fail to be there, for it is important for you to know.

"E. B."

For a time after reading this Mildred sat in a kind of maze. She had been so happy of late that she had ceased to wonder who she was. Indeed she scarcely cared to know, particularly if the information must come through as ignorant a channel as this letter would seem to indi cate.

11 What ought I to do ? " she said, one moment half re-solving to keep the appointment at the deserted hut, as it was called, and the next shrinking from doing so with an undefinable presentiment that some great evil would re sult. " I wish Lawrence was here to go with me," she thought, but as that could not be, she determined at last to show the note to the Judge and ask him his advice.

" What the plague," exclaimed the Judge, reading the note a second time. " Somebody knows who you are ? Brought you herself in the basket? Ain't from a low lived family ? What does the old hag mean ? No, no, gipsy. Let her go to grass. We don't care who you are. It's enough that I've taken you for my daughter, and that in little more than three weeks, Lawrence will take you for his wife. No, no. Let E. B. sit in the deserted hut till she's sick of it."

And this he said because he, too, experienced a most unaccountable sensation of dread, as if a cloud were hovering over Mildred, darker, far darker than the one from under which she had so recently passed.

" But," persisted Mildred, " maybe I ought to know. I wonder who this woman is. She says she stopped here once for a drink, and was frightened off by the woman with .the big black eyes. That must have been Geraldine."

" Did you speak to me ? " asked the lady in question, who was passing through the hall, and had heard her name.

"Don't tell her of the note. Simply ask about the woman," whispered the Judge, feeling that if anything about Mildred should prove to be wrong, he would rather no one but themselves should know it.

Mildred comprehended his meaning at once, and in reply to Geraldine, said: " I have a reason for wishing to know if you remember an old woman's coming into the kitchen and asking for water, a day or two ago."

"Yes, I remember her well," answered Geraldine, "for she reminded me so much of the city thieves. She asked several questions, too, about the girl who was to be married,—which was your room, and all that. Why ? What of her ? "

" Nothing much," returned Mildred. " How did she look ? "

"Like a witch," answered Geraldine. "Tall, spare, angular, with a pock-marked face, a single long tooth projecting over her under lip, and a poking black bonnet. I thought I saw her going down the road just at dusk to night, ut might have been mistaken."

Mildred turned pale at the very idea of having ever been associated with such a creature, or of meeting her alone at the deserted hut, and she was trying to think of some excuse to render Geraldine for having thus questioned her, when one of the dressmakers came to the rescue, and called Miss Veille away.

"What do you think now?" Mildred asked of the Judge, when they were alone.

" Think as I did before," he replied. " We won't go near the hag. We don't want to know who you are."

"But," and drawing nearer to him, Mildred looked wistfully in his face ; " but what if I am somebody whom Lawrence mustn't marry? Wouldn't it be better to know it before it's too late ? "

" Heavens and earth, child," returned the Judge. " Do you think anything can induce him to give you up. Wouldn't you marry him if he was anything short of a nigger ? "

This remark was suggestive, and Mildred chimed in :

" I'll ask Rachel about that woman. She saw her, too."

Hurrying off to the kitchen she found the old negress, whose story agreed exactly with Geraldine's, except, indeed, that she described the stranger as worse-looking even than Miss Veille had done.

"I saw such a person in the avenue to-night," said Luce, who was present, while her little child six years old testified stoutly to having seen a woman with a big bonnet in the lower hall.

" Thinks she'll get some money," growled the Judge, when Mildred repeated this to him ; " but we'll cheat her. If she knows who you are, let her come boldly and tell, and not entice you into the woods. There's bedevilment somewhere."

But all his efforts were fruitless to convince Mildred.

The more she thought of it, the more excited she grew, and the more anxious she became to meet a person who could tell her of her parentage,—of her mother, maybe ; the mother she had never known, but had dreamed of many and many a time.

" Go to bed," the Judge said at last. " You'll feel differently in the morning."

Mildred obeyed so far as going to bed was concerned, but the morning found her more impatient than she had been the previous night, and not even Oliver, to whom she confided the story, had the power to quiet her. Go to the deserted hut she would, and if the Judge would not accompany her she would go alone, she said.

So it was at last decided that both the Judge and Oliver should act as her escort, by means of insuring her greater safety, and then, with a feverish restlessness, Mildred counted the lagging hours, taking no interest in anything, not even in the bridal dress, which was this day finished and tried on.

Very, very beautiful she looked in it, with the orange blossoms resting amid the braids of her nut-brown hair, but she scarcely heeded it for the terrible something which whispered to her continually :

" You will never wear it,—never."

Then as her vivid imagination pictured to her the possibility that that toothless hag might prove to be her mother, and herself lying dead in the deserted hut just as

THE EBBING OF THE TIDE.

she surely should do, her face grew so white that Geraldine asked in alarm what was the matter.

" Nothing much," she answered, as she threw off the bridal dress. " I am low-spirited to-day, I guess."

"You'll have a letter to-night, maybe, and that will make you feel better,' ' suggested Geraldine.

"I hope so," returned Milly, and fearful lest Geraldine, whom all the day she had tried to avoid, should speak again of the woman, she ran off upstairs, and indulged in a good, hearty cry, glancing often over her shoulder as if afraid there was some goblin there come to rob her of happiness.

Never once, however, did she waver in her resolution of going to the hut, and just after the sun went down she presented herself to the Judge, asking if he were ready.

" Ready for what ? Oh, I know, that wild-goose chase. Yes., I'm ready."

And getting his hat and cane, they started, stopping for Oliver, who even then tried to dissuade Mildred from going.

But he could not, and in almost unbroken silence the three went on their way, Mildred a little in advance, with a white, stony look upon her face, as if she had made up her mind to bear the worst, whatever it might be.

CHAPTER XVII.
THE DESERTED HUT.

T was a tumble-down old shanty, which for many years had been uninhabited save by the bats and the swallows, which darted through the wide chinks in the crumbling wall, or plunged down the dilapidated chimney, filling the weird ruin with strange, unearthly sounds, and procuring for it the reputation of being haunted ground. The path leading to it was long and tedious, for after leaving the river bridge, it wound around the base of a hill, beneath the huge forest trees, which now in the dusky twilight threw their grim shadows over every near object, and insensibly affected the spirits of the three who came each moment nearer and nearer to the hut.

"There, Clubs and I will stay here, I guess," said the Judge, stopping beneath a tall hemlock, which grew within a dozen rods of the building.

Mildred made no answer, but moved resolutely on until she had crossed the threshold of the hut, where she involuntarily paused, while a nameless feeling of terror crept over her, everything around her was so gloomy and so still.

In the farthest extremity of the apartment a single spot of moonlight, shining through the rafters above, fell upon the old-fashioned cupboard, from which two rats, startled by Mildred's steps, sprang out, and, running across the floor, disappeared in the vicinity of the broad stone hearth. Aside from this there was no sign of life, and Mildred was beginning to think of turning back, when a voice, between a whisper and a hiss, came to her ear from the dark corner where the shadows lay deepest, and where a human form crouched upon the floor.

"Mildred Ho well," the voice said, "is that you?"

Instantly Mildred grasped the oaken mantel to keep herself from falling; for, with that question, the human form arose and came so near to her that the haggish face and projecting tooth were plainly visible.

"You tremble," the figure said; "but you need not be afraid. I am not here to hurt you. I loved your mother too well for that."

There was magic in that word, and it unlocked at once the daughter's heart and divested it of all fear. Just then the moon passed from under a cloud, and through a pane-less window, shone full upon the eager, expectant face of the beautiful young girl, who, grasping the hand of the strange old woman, said, imploringly:

11 Did you really know my mother,—my own moth er?"

"Yes," returned the woman; "I knew her w< was with her when she died. I laid her in the coffin. I followed her to the grave, carrying you in my arms, and then I did with you what she bade me do,—I laid you at Judge Howell's door, and stood watching in the rain until he took you in."

She spoke rapidly, and, to Oliver, who had drawn so near that he could distinctly hear the whole, it seemed as if she were repeating some lesson learned by rote; but Mildred had no such thought, and, pressing the bony arm, she asked:

"But who am I? What is my name? Who was my father? and am I like my mother?"

"That's what I've been trying to make out," returned the woman, peering closer into her face, and adding, after a minute survey: "Not like her at all. You are more like the Howells; and well you may be, for your poor mother wore her knees almost to the bone praying that you might resemble them."

" Then I am a Howell!—I am a Howell! and Richard was my father ! Oh, joy, joy!" and the wild, glad cry w.ent ringing through the ghostly ruin, as Mildred thus gave vent to what she had so long and secretly cherished in her heart.

"Mildred"—and in the old woman's voice there was something which made the young girl shudder—" there is
not a drop of Howell blood in all your veins ; but look ! "
:• >:d drawing from her skinny bosom a worn, soiled letter,
i ; held it up in the moonlight, saying : " This your mother
Dte two days before she died. It does not belong to
i, for it is intended for your grandfather. I promised
give it to him, should it ever be necessary for him to
, ' >w; but you may read it, girl. It will explain the
whole better than I can."

How can I read it here ?" Mildred asked, and her ipanion replied by striking a match across the hearth, : lighting a bit of candle, which she brought from the depths of her pocket.

; folding it between her thumb and finger, she said : s? You see I've come prepared; but sit down, child. Yc '.'11 need to, maybe, before you get through," and she •..-lied a block of wood toward Mildred, who sat down, while all through her frame the icy chills were running, as if she saw the fearful gulf her feet were treading.

Tell me first one thing," she said, grasping the .. - tan's dress. "Tell me, am I greatly inferior to Law-
e Thornton ? "

Oh, that horrid, horrid smile, which broke over the old hag's face, and made the one long tooth seem starting from the shrivelled gums, as she replied :

"You are fully Lawrence Thornton's equal." Then I can bear anything," said Mildred; and open-he letter she pressed to her lips the delicate, though ii
rather uneven handwriting, said to have been her mother's.
It was dated in New York, nearly eighteen years before, and its contents were as follows :

"DEAR, DEAR FATHER: —Though you cast me off and turned me from your door, you are very dear to me; and should these lines ever come to you, pray think kindly of the erring child, whose fault was loving one so unworthy of her, for I did love Charlie, and I love him yet, although he has cruelly deserted me just when I need his care the most. Father, I am dying; dying all alone in this great city. Charlie is in New Orleans, gambling, drinking, and utterly forgetting me, who gave up everything for him.

"On the pillow beside me lies my little girl-baby; and when I look at her I wish that I might live, but, as that cannot be, I must do for her the best I can. Charlie said to me when he went away, that after baby was born he should come back and take her from me, so as to extort money from you, and he would do it, too, if he had an opportunity, but I'd rather see her dead than under his wicked influence; so I shall put her where he cannot find her..

" Once, father, I thought to send her to you, but the remembrance of your words : ' May you be cursed, and your children,' was ringing in my ears, and I said, ' he shall not have a chance to wreak his ven geance on my child. Strangers will be kinder far than my own flesh and blood,' so I have resolved to send her to Judge Howell. 'Tis a queer place, but I can think of nothing better. He is alone in his great house, and who knows but he may adopt her as his own.

"I have called her Mildred, too, praying earnestly that she may look like Mildred of the starry eyes and nut-brown hair, for that would soften the old Judge's heart toward her. I have written to him an anonymous letter asking him to take her, and when I am dead, faithful Esther Bennett, who is nursing me, will take it and my baby to in Maine, where her sister lives. There she will mail the letter, and whether the Judge answers it or not, she will in a short time secretly convey Milly to his door, watching until some one takes her in.

" Then she will look after my child, and if in coming years circumstances arise which seem to make it necessary for Mildred to know her parentage, she will seek her out, tell her who she is and carry you this letter. You may think me crazy to adopt this plan, and so, perhaps, I am. But my husband, who is her lawful protector, shall not have her, and as I do not care to burden you with Ifawley's brats, as you once termed any children which I might have, I shall send it to Beechwood.

" My strength is failing me, father, and in a day or so I shall be dead. I wish I could see you all once more, particularly Lawrence, my darling little brother Lawrence. Baby looks some like him, I think, and should she ever come to you, bid him love his little niece for his dead sister Helen's sake "

Mildred could not read another line—there was a sound like the fall of many waters in her ears,—the blood seemed curdling in her veins, and her very finger-tips tingled with one horrid, maddening thought.

"Lawrence,—Lawrence,—little niece," she moaned, and with eyes black as midnight, and face of a marble hue, she turned to the superscription, which she had not observed before, reading as she expected :

" ROBERT THORNTON, Esq.,
BOSTON, MASS."

<e Oh, Heaven ! " she cried, rocking to and fro. " Isn't it a dream. Isn't there some mistake ? Tell me, dear, good woman, tell me, is it true ? " and in her unutterable agony she knelt abjectly before the witch-like creature, who answered back:

" Poor, poor Milly. It is true. All true, or I would not come here to save you from a marriage with your mother's brother,—your own uncle, girl."

" Stop ! " and Mildred screamed with anguish ; "I will not know that name. Oh, Lawrence, Lawrence, you are surely lost to me for ever and ever !"

There was a rustling movement, and then Mildred lay with her face upon the threshold of the door.

" Hurry up, Clubs, for Heaven's sake. I've stuck a confounded stub through my boot," cried the Judge, limping with pain, as he went wheezing to the spot which Oliver had reached long before him.

From his position beneath the window, Oliver had heard the entire conversation, but not knowing the contents of the letter, he was at a loss to comprehend how Lawrence Thornton could be Mildred's uncle. Something, however, had affected her terribly, he knew, for there was no mistaking the look of hopeless suffering stamped upon the rigid face he lifted gently up and rested on his arm.

"What is it, Clubs? What's the row? Let me take her," and the panting Judge relieved Oliver of the fainting girl, whom he held carefully in his arms, talking to her the while in his own peculiar way.

" There, there, honey. What is it ? Come to a little, can't you ? Open your eyes, won't you ? and don't look so much as though you were dead." Then feeling for her pulse, he screamed : " She is dead, Clubs ! She is dead ! and you, old long-toothed madame," shaking his fist at the old hag Esther Bennett, " you killed her with some blasted lie, and I'll have you hung up by the heels on the first good tree I find. Do you hear ? "

Having thus relieved his mind, the excited Judge car ried Mildred into the open air, which roused her for a moment, but when she saw Esther Bennett she sank back again into the same death-like swoon, moaning faintly :

" Oh, Lawrence, Lawrence, lost forever ! "

" No he ain't,—no he ain't," said the Judge, but his words fell on deaf ears, and turning to Oliver, who had been hastily reading the letter, he asked what it was.

" Listen," and in a voice which trembled with strong emotion, Oliver read it through, while the Judge's face dropped lower and lower until it rested upon the cold, white forehead of Mildred, who lay so helpless in his arms.

" Bob Thornton's grandchild," he whispered. " Bob Thornton's grandchild ! Must I then lose my little Milly ?" and great tears, such as Judge Ho well only could shed, fell like rain on Mildred's face.

" There may be some mistake," suggested Oliver, and catching at once the idea, the Judge swore roundly that there was a mistake. "Needn't tell him ; blamed if he'd believe that 'twa'n't some big lie got up by somebody for something," and turning to the woman he demanded of her savagely to confess the fraud.

But Esther Bennett answered him :

" It is all true, sir; true ! I am sorry now that I kept it so long, for I never wanted to harm Miss Helen's child. Sure she has a bonny face, but she'll die, sir, lying so long in that faint."

This turned the channel of the Judge's thoughts, and, remembering that not far away there was a little stream, he arose, and, forgetting his wounded foot, walked swiftly on, bidding Esther follow, as he wished to question her further on the subject. To this she did not seem at all averse, but went with him willingly, answering readily all the questions which Oliver put to her, and appearing through the whole to be sincere in what she said. The cold water which they sprinkled copiously on Mildred's face and neck restored her for a moment, but, with a shudder, she again lay back in the arms of the Judge, who, declaring her as light as a feather, hobbled on, giving her occasionally a loving hug, and whispering, as he did so : " Hanged if they make me believe it. Bobum don't get her after I've made my will, and all that."

By the drawing-room window Geraldine was sitting, and

when, by the moonlight, she saw the strange procession moving up the Cold Spring path, she went out to meet it, asking anxiously what had happened.

" Clubs can tell you," returned the Judge, hurrying on with Mildred, while Oliver explained to Geraldine what he knew, and then referred her to Esther Bennett for any further information.

" Is it possible!" exclaimed Geraldine, while in her eyes there was a glitter of delight, as she fell back with Esther, and began a most earnest conversation.

Carrying Mildred to her room, Judge Howell laid her upon the bed as gently as if she had been an infant, and then bent over her until she came fully back to conscious ness and asked him where she was.

" Oh, I remember now !" she said. "A horrid thing came to me down in the hut, and Lawrence is lost for ever and ever!"

"No, he ain't; it's all a blasted lie!" said the Judge, and instantly on Mildred's face there broke a smile of such joy that Oliver, who had entered the room, cried out:

"It's cruel to deceive her so, Judge Howell, until we know for certain that the woman's story is false."

Like a hunted deer Mildred's eyes turned from one to the other, reading everywhere a confirmation of her fears, and, with a low piercing cry, she moaned:

"It's true, it's true! he is lost forever! Oh, Oliver! can't you comfort me a little? You never failed me before; don't leave me now when I need it the most!" and she wound her arms convulsively round his neck.

Oliver had his suspicions, but as he could give no reason for them he would not rouse hopes which might never be realized, and he only answered through his tears:

"I would like to comfort you, Milly, if I could; but I can't,—I can't!"

"Mildred!" It was Geraldine who spoke, and Mildred involuntarily shuddered as she heard the voice. "Uncle Robert once saw the woman who took care of Cousin Helen, and talked with her of his daughter and the baby, both of whom she declared to be dead. Had we not better send for him at once, and see if he remembers this creature," nodding toward Esther Bennett, who had also entered the room.. "He surely cannot mistake her if he ever saw her once."

Oliver looked to see the hag make some objections, but, to his surprise, she said eagerly:

"Yes, send for him. He will remember me, for he came to New York just three days after I left the baby at this door. He is a tall man, slightly bald, with black eyes, and coarse black hair, then beginning to be gray."

Mildred groaned as did Oliver, for the description was accurate, while even the Judge brought his fist down upon the table, saying:

"Bob to a dot! but hanged if I believe it! We'll telegraph though in the morning."

The result of the telegram was that at a late hour the next night Mr. Thornton rang the bell at Beechwood, asking anxiously why he had been sent for in such haste.

"Because," answered the Judge, who met him first, "maybe you've a grandchild upstairs, and maybe you hain't!"

"A grandchild!" gasped Mr. Thornton, all manner of strange fancies flitting through his brain. ".What can you mean?"

By this time Geraldine appeared, and hastily explaining to him what had occurred, she asked "if he could identify the woman who took care of Helen in New York?"

"Yes, tell her from a thousand, but not now, not now," and motioning her away, Mr. Thornton covered his face with his hand, and whispered faintly, "My grandchild! My Mildred! That beautiful creature Helen's child!" and with all his softer feelings awakened, the heart of the cold, stern man yearned toward the young girl he had once affected to despise. "Poor boy," he said, as he thought of Lawrence, "'twill be terrible to him, for his whole soul was bound up in her. Where is this woman? There may be some mistake. I trust there is, for the young people's sake," and the generous feeling thus displayed swept away at once all animosity from the Judge's heart.

IX*

"Describe her first as nearly as you can," said Geraldine, and after thinking a moment Mr. Thornton replied:

"Tall, grizzly; badly marked with small-pox, and had then one or more long teeth in front, which gave her a most haggish appearance."

"The same, the same!" dropped from Oliver's lips, while the Judge, too, responded:

" It's all almighty queer, but blasted if I believe it!"

At Mr. Thornton's request, Esther Bennett came in, and the moment his eyes fell upon her, he said :

"' Tis the woman I saw eighteen years ago ; I cannot be mistaken in that."

"Question her," whispered Geraldine, who seemed quite excited in the matter, and Mr, Thornton did ques tion her, but if she were deceiving them she had learned her legson well, for no amount of cross-questioning could induce her to commit herself.

Indeed she seemed, in spite of her looks, to be a sensi ble, straightforward woman, who was doing what she felt to be her duty.

" She had never lost sight of Mildred," she said; " and knowing that Judge Howell had adopted her, she had concluded not to divulge the secret until she heard that she was to marry Lawrence. But have you read the letter?" she asked. "That will prove that I am not lying."

"Surely," chimed in Geraldine. "I had forgotten that," and she handed to Mr. Thornton his daughter's letter, which he read through, saying, when he had fin ished :

" It is Helen's handwriting, and it must be true." Then passing it to the Judge he asked if it resembled the letter he received from the Maine woman.

" Good thunder, how do I know," returned the Judge. "I tore that into giblets. I can't remember eighteen years; besides that, I'm bound not to believe it, hanged if I do. I've made up my mind latterly that Gipsy belonged to Dick, and I'll be blamed if I don't stick to that through thick and thin."

But,whatever the Judge might wish to believe, he was obliged to confess that the evidence was against him, and when at an early hour the next morning the four assembled again for consultation, he said to Mr. Thorn ton :

" You want to see your granddaughter, I suppose ? " "I'd like to, yes," was the reply, to which the Judge responded:

"Well, come along, though hanged if I believe it." From Geraldine, Mildred had learned what Mr. Thorn ton said, and that he would probably wish to see her in the morning. This swept away the last lingering hope, and with a kind of nervous terror she awaited his visit, trembling when she heard him in the hall, and looking fearfully round for some means of escape.

l< Here, Milly," said the Judge, bustling up to her and forcing a levity he did not feel, " here's your grandfather come to see you."

" No, no, no^' sobbed Mildred, creeping closer to the Judge and hiding her white face in her hands.

"There, Bobum," said the Judge, smoothing her disor dered hair and dropping a tear upon it. " You see she don't take kindly to her new grandad. Better give it up, for I tell you it's a big lie."

"Mildred," said Mr. Thornton, seating himself upon the side of the bed, and taking one of the little feverish hands in his, " there can be no doubt that what we have heard is true, and if so, you are my child, and as such very dear to me. You are young yet, darling, and though your disappointment, as far as Lawrence is concerned, is terrible, you will overcome it in time. The knowing he is your uncle will help you so to do, and you will be happy with us yet. Don't you think so, dear ? "

"Bobum, you've made a splendid speech," returned the Judge, when he had finished. " Couldn't have done bet ter myself, but it fell on stony ground, for look," and lift ing up the beautiful head, he showed him that Mildred had fainted.

" Poor girl, poor girl," whispered Mr. Thornton; and the tears of both of those hard old men dropped on Mildred's face, as they bent anxiously over her.

It was, indeed, a dreadful blow to Mildred, for turn which way she would, there shone no ray of hope. Even Oliver deserted her as far as comfort was concerned, foi he had none to offer.

A day or so brought Lilian to Beech wood,—all love, all sweetness, all sympathy for Mildred, whom she cousined twenty times an hour, and who shrunk from her caresses just as she did from both Geraldine and Mr. Thornton.

"Oh, if I could go away from here for a time," she thought, " I might get over it, perhaps; but it will kill me to see Lawrence when he comes. I can't, I can't; oh, isn't there somewhere to go ? "

Then suddenly remembering that not long before she had received an invitation to visit a favorite teacher, who was now married and lived in a hotel among the New Hampshire hills, she resolved to accept it, and go for a few weeks,, until Lawrence returned and had learned the whole.

" I shall feel better there," she said to the Judge and Oliver, to whom she communicated her plan. "Mrs. Miller will be kind to me, and when it's all over here, and they are gone, you must write, and I'll come back to stay with you forever, for I won't live with Mr. Thornton, were he one hundred times my grandfather!"

This last pleased the Judge so much that he consented at once for Mildred to go, saying it possibly would do her good. Then, repeating to himself the name of the place where Mrs. Miller lived, he continued :

" What do / know of Dresden ? Oh, I remember, Hetty Kirby is buried there. Hetty Kirby; Hetty Kirby." He looked as if there was something more he would say of Hetty Kirby, but he merely added : " Maybe I'll come for you myself. I'd go with you if it wasn't for my confounded toe." Once he glanced at his swollen foot, which had been badly hurt on the night of his visit to the hut, and was now so sore that in walking he was obliged to use a crutch.

"I'd rather go alone," said Mildred, and after a little further conversation it was arranged that in two days' time she should set off for Dresden, first apprising Mrs. Miller by letter of all that had occurred, and asking her to say nothing of the matter, but speak of her as Miss Hawley, that being the name to which she supposed herself entitled.

This being satisfactorily settled, Mr. Thornton and Geraldine were both informed of Mildred's intentions.

" A good idea," said Geraldine. " Change of place will do her good, but I think Lily and I had better remain here until Lawrence arrives. A letter will not find him now, and as he intends stopping at Beechwood on his return, he will know nothing of it until he reaches here."

The Judge would rather have been left alone, but he was polite enough not to say so, though he did suggest that Esther Bennett, at least, should leave, a hint upon which she acted at once, going back to New York that very day.

Mildred would rather that Geraldine and Lilian too should have gone, but as this could not be she stipulated in their presence that Oliver and no other should break the news to Lawrence,—"he would do it so gently," she said, and she bade him say to Lawrence that " though she never could forget him, she did not wish to see him. She could not bear it, and he must not come after her."

Oliver promised compliance with her request, and the next morning she left Beechwood, accompanied by Mr. Thornton, who insisted upon going with her as far as the station, where she must leave the cars and take the stage to Dresden, a distance of ten miles. Here he bade her good-by, with many assurances of affection and good-will, to none of which Mildred listened. Her heart was too full of grief to respond at once to this new claimant for her love, and she was glad when he was gone and she alone with her sorrow.

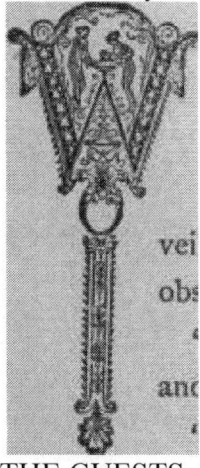

CHAPTER XVIII.
THE GUESTS AT THE HOTEL.

"HERE will you be left, miss?" asked the good-humored driver, thrusting his head in at the window of the coach, in one corner of which Mildred sat, closely veiled and shrinking as far as possible from observation.

"At the Stevens Hotel," she answered, and the driver returned:

"Oh, yes, Stevens Hotel. I have another passenger who stops there. Here he comes," and he held open the door for a remarkably fine-looking man, who, taking the seat opposite Mildred, drew out a book in which for a time he seemed wholly absorbed, never looking up, except once indeed when a fat old woman entered and sat down beside him, saying, as she sank puffing among the cushions, that "she shouldn't pester him long, — she was only going a mile or so to visit her daughter-in-law, who had twins."

Involuntarily Mildred glanced at the gentleman, who, showing a very handsome set of teeth, again resumed his book, while she scanned his features curiously, they seemed to her so familiar, so like something she had seen before.

"Who is he?" she kept asking herself, and she was about concluding that she must have seen him in Boston, when the stage stopped again before one of those low-roofed buildings so common in New England, and the fat old lady alighted, thanking the gentleman for holding the paper of anise-seed and catnip, which all the way had been her special care.

Again the handsome teeth were visible, while the stranger hoped she would find the twins in a prosperous condition. On the green in front of the house a little child was waiting to welcome grandma; and Mildred, who was fond of children, threw back her thick brown veil to look at it, nor did she drop it again, for the road now wound through a mountainous district, and in her delight at the wild, picturesque scenery which met her view at every turn, she forgot that she was not alone, and when at last they reached the summit of a long, steep hill/she involun tarily exclaimed :

" Isn't it grand?"

" You are not accustomed to mountainous views, per haps," said the stranger, and then for the first time Mil dred became conscious that a pair of soft, dark eyes were bent upon her with a searching, burning gaze, from which she intuitively shrank.

Ever since her veil had been removed that same look had been fixed upon her, and to himself the stranger more than once had said, " If it were possible; but no, it can not be;" and yet those starry eyes and that nut-brown hair, how they carried him back to the long ago. Could there be two individuals so much alike, and yet nothing to each other ? Some such idea passed through his mind as he sat watching her beautiful face, and determined at last to question her, he addressed her as we have seen.

"Yes, I am accustomed to mountain scenery," she re plied, " though not as grand as this."

" Were you born among the New England hills ?" was the next question put to her, and the answer waited for, oh, so eagerly.

For an instant Mildred hesitated, while the hot blood stained her face and neck, and then she replied :

u I was born in New York City," while over" the fine features of the gentleman opposite there fell a shade of disappointment.

Mildred had interested him strangely; and with a rest-

less deswe to know more of her history, he continued: " Pardon me, miss; but you so strongly resemble a

friend I have lost that I would like to know your name ? ' Again Mildred hesitated, while the name of Howell

trembled on her lips, but reflecting that she had no longer

a right to it, she answered :

"My name, sir, is Miss Hawley."

Something in her manner led the stranger to think she did not care to be questioned further, and bowing slightly he resumed his book. Still his mind was constantly dwelling upon the young girl, who met his curious glance so often that she began to feel uneasy, and was glad when they stopped at last at the Stevens Hotel. The stranger helped her out, holding her dimpled hand in his for a sin gle moment, and looking down again into the dark bright eyes, as if he fain would read there that what he had so long believed was false. He knew that he annoyed her, but he could not help it. Every movement which she made mystified him more and more, and he looked after her until she disappeared through the hall and was ad mitted to the chamber of her friend and former teacher.

Unfortunately Mrs. Miller was sick, but she welcomed Mildred kindly as Miss Hawley, and talked freely with her of the discovery that had been made.

"You will feel better after a time," she said, as she saw how fast Mildred's tears came at the mention of Lawrence Thornton. " Your secret is safe with me and my husband, and no one else knows that you ever had claim to another name than Hawley. I am sorry that I am iE. just at this time, but I shall be well in a few days, I hope. Meantime you must amuse yourself in any way you choose. I have given orders for you to have the large front chamber looking out upon the village. The room adjoining is occupied by a gentleman who came

here yesterday morning, intending to stop for a few days. He is very agreeable, they say, and quite a favorite in the house."

Mildred thought of her companion in the stage, and was about to ask his name, when a servant appeared, offering to show her to her room. It was one of those warm, languid days in early June, and Mildred soon began to feel the effects of her recent excitement and wearisome ride in the racking headache which came on so fast as to prevent her going down to dinner, and at last confined her to the bed, where she lay the entire afternoon, falling away at last into a deep, quiet sleep, from which about sunset she awoke greatly refreshed and almost free from pain. Observing that her door was open, she was wondering who had been there, when her ear caught a sound as of some child breathing heavily, and turning in the direction whence it came, she saw a most beautiful little girl, apparently four or five years old, perched upon a chair near the window, her soft auburn curls falling over her forehead, and her face very red with the exertions she was making to unclasp Mildred's reticule, which she had found upon the table.

As a carriage rolled down the street, she raised her eyes, and to Mildred it seemed as if she were looking once more upon the face which had so often met her view when she brushed her own hair before the cracked glass hanging on the rude walls of the gable roof.

"Is it my other self?" she thought, passing her hand before her eyes to clear away the mist, if mist there was. " Isn't it I as I used to be ? "

Just then the snapping apart of the steel clasp, and the child's satisfied exclamation of " There, I did do it," convinced her that 'twas not herself as she used to be, but a veritable mass of flesh and blood, embodied in as sweet a face and perfect a form as she ever looked upon.

"I will speak to her," Mildred thought, and involuntarily from her lips the word " Sister " came, causing the child to start suddenly and drop the reticule, with which she knew she had been meddling.

Shaking back her sunny curls, which now lay in rings about her forehead, and flashing upon Mildred a pair of eyes very much like her own, she said :

"How you did stare me ! Be you waked up ? "

"Come here, won't you ? " said Mildred, holding out her hand; and won by the pleasant voice, the little girl went to her, and winding her chubby arms around her neck, said :

"Is you most well, pretty lady?"

Mildred answered by kissing her velvety cheek and hugging her closer to her bosom, while over her there swept a most delicious feeling, as if the beautiful creature, nestling so lovingly to her side, were very near to her.

"Where do you live ?" she asked; and the child replied :

" Oh, in the ship, and in the railroad, and everything."

"But where's your mother?" continued Mildred, and over the little girl's face there flitted a shadow, as she replied :

" Ma's in heaven, and pa's down stairs smoking a cigar. He ties awful hard sometimes."

" Have you any sisters ? " was the next interrogatory ; and the answer was :

" I've got one in heaven, and a brother, too,—so pa says. I never seen the sister, but when ma died, and they lifted me up to look at her in the box, there lay on her arm a little teenty baby, not so big as dolly, and they put them both under the grass, over the sea, ever and ever and ever so ways off," and she pointed toward the setting sun, as if she thus would indicate the vast distance between herself and her buried mother.

"You came from over the sea, then?" returned Mildred. "Will you tell me what your name is ? "

" Edith Howell. What is yours ? " and Edith looked inquiringly at Mildred, who started suddenly, repeating:

"Edith Howell! Edith Howell! and did your father come in the stage this morning?"

"Yes," returned the child. " He went off in it before I was up, and brought me Old Mother Hubbard. Don't you want to see her ? " and Edith ran to her own room, while Mildred clasped her hands to her head, which

seemed almost bursting with the conviction which the name of Edith Howell had forced upon her.

She knew now where she had seen a face like that of her stage companion. She had seen it in the pleasant drawing-room at Beechwood, and the eyes which had so puzzled her that morning had many and many a time looked down upon her from the portrait of Richard Howell.

" Tis he, 'tis he," she whispered. " But why is he here instead of going to his father ? "

Then, as she remembered having heard how Richard Howell had cared for her, shielding her from the Judge's wrath, and how once she had dared to hope that she might be his child, she buried her face in the pillow and wept aloud, for the world seemed so dark,—so dreary.

" What you tie for, pretty lady ? " asked little Edith, returning to her side, laden with dolls and toys, and Old Mother Hubbard, which last Mildred did not fully appre ciate. " What is your name ? " Edith said again, as, mounting upon the bed, she prepared to display her trea sures.

" Milly Hawley;" and Mildred's voice trembled so that the child very easily mistook the word for Minnie.

11 Minnie," she repeated. " That's pretty. I love you, Minnie Hawley," and putting up her waxen hand, she brushed the tears from Mildred's eyes, asking again why she cried.

At first Mildred thought to correct her with regan her name. Then, thinking it was just as well to be Minnie as anything else, she let it pass, for without any tangible reason save that it was a sudden fancy, she had determii that if the handsome stranger were Richard Howell, he should not know from her that she was the foundling u'fl at his father's door. She had always shrank from hearing the subject discussed, and it seemed more distasteful to her now than ever; so on the whole she was glad Ed had misunderstood her, for Milly might have led to soi inquiries on the part of Richard, if it were he, inasmuch as his mother and sister had borne that rather unusual name; so, instead of replying directly to the child, she said, "Let us go over by the window where the co<.<' breeze comes in," and gathering up her playthings, EdL> went with her to the sofa, and climbing into her lap asked, " Where's your ma, Minnie ? "

" She's dead," was the reply.

" And is your pa dead, too ? "

Ere Mildred could answer this a voice from the hail, called out:

" Edith ! Edith ! where are you ? "

" Here, pa, here with Minnie. Come and see her,' and bounding across the floor, the active child seized her father's hand and pulled him into Mildred's room.

* Excuse me, Miss Hawley," he said. " Edith is very sociable ; and I am afraid you find her troublesome."

" Not in the least. I am fond of children," returned Mildred, taking the little girl again upon her lap, while Mr. Howell sat down by the other window.

He was a very handsome man, and at first appearance seemed to be scarcely thirty. A closer observation, how ever, showed that he was several years older, for his rich brown hair was slightly tinged with gray, and there were the marks of time or sorrow about his eyes and forehead. In manner he was uncommonly prepossessing, and a few minutes sufficed to put Mildred entirely at her ease, with one who had evidently been accustomed to the society of high-bred, cultivated people.

" Edith tells me you corne from England," she said at last, by way of ascertaining whether he really were Rich ard Howell or not.

" Yes," he replied, " I have lived in England for several years, though I am a native American and born in Bos ton. When six years old, however, my father removed to Mayfield, where he is living now."

" What for you jump ? " asked Edith, as Mildred started involuntarily when her suspicions were thus confirmed.

Mr. Howell's eyes seemed to ask the same question, and bowing her face over the curly head of the child, so as to conceal her tears, Mildred answered :

" I have been in Mayfield several times, and know an old gentleman whose son went off many years ago, and

has never been heard of since." 12

" What makes you ty ? " persisted Edith, who felt the drops upon her hair.

" I was thinking," returned Mildred, " how glad that old man will be if your father is the son he has so long considered dead."

Mr. Howell was gazing fixedly at her.

"Miss Hawley,' 5 he said, when she had finished speak ing, " who are you ?—that is, who are your parents, and why have you been in Mayfield ? "

Mildred knew that her resemblance to his sister puz zled him just as it did every one, and for a moment she was tempted to tell him everything ; then, thinking he would learn it fast enough when he went to Beechwood., she replied:

" My mother was Helen Thornton, of Boston, and my father, her music teacher, Charles Hawley, who died in New Orleans soon after I was born."

Mr. Howell seemed disappointed, but he replied :

" Helen Thornton your mother ? I remember her well, and her marriage with Mr. Hawley. You do not resemble her one-half so much as you do my sister Mildred, for I am that old man's son. I am Richard Howell."

" Every one who ever saw your sister speaks of the re semblance," returned Mildred. te Indeed, my old nurse says my mother was very anxious that I should look like her, and even used to pray that I might. This may, pei haps, account for it."

" It may,—it may," Richard answered abstractively, pacing up and down the room ; then suddenly turning to Mildred he asked : " When were you in Mayfield, and how is my father now ? Does he look very old ? "

Mildred did not tell him when she was in Mayfield, but merely replied that " his father was well, and that for a man nearly sixty-five he was looking remarkably young."

" And the negroes ? " said Richard; " though, of course, you know nothing of them, nor of those people who used to live in that gable-roofed house down the hill. Thomp son was the name."

Here was a chance for explanation, but Mildred cast it from her by simply answering :

" Old Mrs. Thompson lives there yet with her club-footed grandson, Oliver Hawkins, whose mother was probably living when you went away."

Spite of her resolution, Mildred hoped he would ask for the baby next, but he did not. He merely walked faster and faster across the floor, while she sighed mentally : " He has forgotten me, and I will not thrust myself upon his remembrance."

At last the rapid walking ceased, and coming up before her, Mr. Howell said :

" It seems strange to you, no doubt, that I have pur posely absented myself from home so long, and in looking back upon the past, it seems strange to me. I was very unhappy when I went away, and at the last I quarrelled

with my father, who, for a farewell, gave to me his curse, bidding me never come into his presence again. If you know him at all, you know he has a fiery temper. To a certain extent I inherit the same, and with my passions roused I said it would be many years before he saw my face again. Still, I should have returned had not circum stances occurred which rendered it unnecessary. I wrote to my father twice, but he never answered me, and I said * I will write no more.' For three years I remained among the South Sea Islands, and tfren found my way to India, where, in the excitement of amassing wealth, I gradually ceased to care for anything in America. At last I made the acquaintance of a fair young English girl, and making her my wife, removed with her to England, where, little more than a year since, she died, leaving me nothing to love but Edith. Then my thoughts turned homeward, for I promised Lucy, when dying, that I would seek a reconciliation with my father. So I crossed the ocean again, coming first to Dresden, for this wild, out-of-the-way place is connected with some of the sweetest and saddest memories of my life. In a few days, however, I go to Beechwood, but I shall not apprise my father of my return, for I wish to test the instincts of the parental heart, and see if he will know me.

" I have told you so much, Miss Hawley, because I know you must think strangely of my long absence, and then there is something about you which prompts me to

wish for your good opinion. I might tell you much more of my life,—tell you of an error committed in boyhood, as it were, and in manhood bitterly regretted,—not the deed itself, but the concealment of it, but the subject would not nterest you."

Mildred could not help fancying that the subject would interest her, but she did not say so, and as Mr. Howell just then observed that Edith had fallen asleep in her arms, he ceased speaking and hastened to relieve her. The movement awakened Edith, who insisted upon sleep ing with Minnie, as she called her.

11 Yes, let her stay with me," said Mildred; " she is such an affectionate little thing that she seems almost as near to me as a sister."

" You are enough alike to be sisters. Did you know that ?" Mr. Howell asked, and Mildred blushed painfully as she met the admiring gaze fixed upon her so intently.

He was thinking what a beautiful picture they made,— the rose just bursting into perfect loveliness, and the bud so like the rose that they might both have come from the same parent stem.

" Yes, Edith has your eyes," he continued, " your mouth and your expression, but otherwise she is like her English mother."

He bent down to kiss the child, who had fallen asleep again, and had Mildred been a little younger he might perhaps have kissed her, too, for he was an enthusiastic

admirer of girlish beauty, but as it was, he merely bade her good-night and left the room.

The next morning Mildred was roused by a pair of the softest, fattest, chubbiest hands patting her round cheeks, and opening her eyes, she saw Edith sitting up in bed, her auburn curls falling from beneath her cap and herself play ful as a kitten. Oh, how near and dear she seemed to Mildred, who hugged her to her bosom, calling her "little sister," and wishing in her heart that somewhere in the world she had a sister as gentle, and pretty, and sweet, as Edith Howell.

That afternoon, as Mildred sat reading in her room, she saw a carriage drive up to the door, and heard Edith's voice in the hall, saying to her father :

" Yes, Minnie must go,—Minnie must go."

A moment after Mr. Howell appeared, saying to her:

" We are going to ride, Miss Howell, and on Edith's account, as well as my own, shall be glad of your company. I shall visit the cemetery for one place, and that may not be agreeable, but the remainder of the trip I think you will enjoy."

Mildred knew she should, and hurrying on her bonnet and shawl, she was soon seated with Mr. Howell and Edith in the only decent carriage the village afforded.

"To the graveyard," said Mr. Howell, in answer tc the driver's question. " Where shall I drive you first ? " and after a rapid ride of a mile or more they stopped before the gate of the enclosure where slept the Dresden dead.

Holding Edith's hand in hers. Mildred followed whither Richard led, and soon stood by a sunken grave, unmarked by a single token of love, save the handsome stone, on which was inscribed

"HETTY K. Ho WELL, Aged 19."

" Hetty Howell!" repeated Mildred. " Who was she?" and she turned inquiringly towards Richard.

He was standing with folded arms and a most touch-ingly sad expression upon his face, but at her question he started, and unhesitatingly answered, " Hetty Kirby was my wife"

Mildred had incidentally heard of Hetty Kirby at Beech-wood, but never that she was Richard's wife, and she ex claimed, in some astonishment :

"Your wife, Mr. Howell? Were you then married when you went away ? "

"Yes," he answered; "and the concealment of it is one of my boyhood's errors which I regret. I married Hetty without my father's knowledge and against his wishes. He knew I loved her, and for that he turned her from his door and bade me forget her. But I did not. With the help of a college friend I went with her over the Bay State line into New York, where we were soon made cne. After a week or so she came to Dres den, where her grandmother lived, while I returned to college. I saw her as often as possible after that, until at last " here he paused, and seemed to be thinking of something far back in the past; then he suddenly added, " she sickened and died, and I buried her here."

" And did you not tell your father ? " asked Mildred.

" No, not then," he answered; " but I told him on the night I went away, and it was for this he cursed me."

There were tears in his eyes, and they came also to Mildred's, as she thought of poor Hetty, and how much she must have loved her handsome boy-husband. Insen sibly, too, there crept over her a strange affection for that grassy mound, as if it covered something which she had known and loved.

" There are no flowers here," she said, wishing to break the painful silence; and when Richard answered, sadly, " There has been no one to plant them," she continued, " I shall remain in Dresden some time, perhaps, and I will put some rose trees here and cover the sods with rnoss."

" Heaven bless you, Miss Hawley," and in that silent graveyard, standing by Hetty Kirby's grave, Richard Howell took the hand of Mildred and pressed it to his lip S) —modestly, gently, as if he had been her father.

" Tome, pa. Less doe,' Edith had said a dozen times, and yielding to her importunities, Mr. Howell now walked slowly away, but Mildred lingered still, chained to the spot by a nameless fascination.

" Tome, Minnie,—tome," called Edith, and roused thus from her reverie of the unknown Hetty Kirby, Mildred followed on to the carriage, where Mr. Howell was wait ing for her.

Down the hill, up another, round a curve, over a stream of water and down the second long, steep hill they went, and then they stopped again, but this time at a deserted old brown building, whose slanting roof had partially tumbled in, and whose doors were open to the weather, being destitute of latch or bolt. Through a gate half off the hinges they went, and going up a grass-grown path, they passed into a narrow entry, and then into a side room, where the western sun came pouring in. Here Mr. Howell stopped, and with his hand upon his fore head, stood leaning against the window, while the great tears dropped through his fingers and fell upon the old oak floor. Mildred saw all this, and needed nothing more to tell her that they stood in the room where Hetty Kirby died.

Oh, Mildred, Mildred,— if she could have known, but she did not. She only felt stealing over her a second time the same sensation which had come to her at Hetty's grave,—a feeling as if every spot once hallowed by Hetty Kirby's presence were sacred to her, and when at last they left the ruinous old house, she looked about for

some memento of the place, but everything had run to waste, save one thrifty cedar growing in a corner of the yard. From this she broke a twig and was think ing how she would preserve it, when Richard touched her arm, and said :

" I planted that tree myself and Hetty held it up while I put the earth about it."

The cedar bough was dearer far to Mildred now, and she stood long by the evergreen thinking how little Hetty dreamed that such as she would ever be there with Richard at her side, and a fairy creature frolicking over the grass, the child of another than herself.

" If she had left a daughter how Richard would have loved it," she thought, and through her mind there flitted the wild fancy that it would be happiness indeed to call him father and say sister to young Edith, who was now pulling at her dress, telling her to come away from that old place. "It isn't as pretty," she said, "as ma's home over the sea, for there were fountains and trees and flowers there."

Mildred could not forbear smiling as the little girl rattled on, while in listening to her prattle even Mr. Ho well forgot his sadness, and by the time they reached the hotel he was apparently as cheerful as ever.

The next morning he was slightly indisposed, and Mil dred kept Edith with her the entire day. The morning following he was still worse, and for two weeks he kept

his rooun, while Mildred took charge of Edith, going occasionally to his bedside, and reading to him from books which he selected. Never for a moment, however, did she forget her gnawing pain, which, as the days advanced, seemed harder and harder to bear, and when at last the morning came on which she was to have been a bride, she buried her face in her pillows, refusing to be comforted, even by little Edith, who, alarmed at her distress, begged of her father to come and cure Minnie, " who did ty so hard."

A severe headache was the result of this passionate weeping, and all the morning she lay upon the bed or sofa, almost blinded with pain, while Edith's little soft hands smoothed her aching head or brushed her beautiful hair. Once Richard, who was better now, came to the door, offering to do something for her, and suggesting many remedies for headache. Very gratefully Mildred smiled upon him, but she could not tell him how the heart was aching tenfold harder than the head, or how her thoughts were turning continually toward Beechwood, from which she had received no news, she having bidden them not to write until Lawrence, Geraldine, Lilian and all were gone ; then Oliver was to tell her the whole.

As he had not written, they, of course, had not gone, and fearful that something terrible had happened, her anxiety and excitement seemed greater than she could bear.

CHAPTER XIX

LAWRENCE AND OLIVER.

'ONTRARY to Mildred's expectations, Lawrence had reached Beechwood earlier than the time appointed. And on the very day when she in Dresden was standing with Richard Howell by Hetty Kirby's grave, he in Mayfield was listening with a breaking heart to the story Oliver had to tell. Flushed with hope and eager anticipation, as the happy bridegroom goes to meet his bride, he had come, thinking all the way of Mildred's joy of seeing him so many days before he had promised to be with her. Purposely he chose the back entrance to the house, coming through the garden, and casting about him many anxious glances for the flutter of a pink muslin robe, or the swinging of a brown straw flat. But he looked in vain, for Mildred was not there. Hoping to find her in the library alone, he kept on, until he reached the little room, where instead of Mildred, the Judge and Oliver sat together, talking sadly of her. At the sight of Lawrence both turned pale, while the former involuntarily exclaimed, " Oh, my boy, my boy."

In an instant Lawrence knew that something terrible had happened, and grasping the Judge's hand, he cried:' " She isn't dead. In pity tell me, is she dead ? "

" No, not dead," answered the Judge ; " but listen to Clubs. He promised to break it to you." And going from the room, he left the two alone, while Oliver told to Lawrence Thornton that Mildred never could be his wife, because she was his niece, the child of his own sister.

Every particular of the disclosure was minutely related, and every hope swept away from the horror-stricken man, who listened in mute despair, until the tale was finished, and then with one piercing cry of anguish fell upon his faee, moaning faintly : " I would rather she had died,— I would rather she had died."

In great alarm, Geraldine, who had heard the cry, hastened to the room, followed by Lilian ; but Lawrence scarcely noticed them, otherwise than to shudder and turn away from Geraldine when she tried to comfort him. Once, Lilian, touched at the sight of his distress, knelt before him, and folding her arms upon his lap, begged -of him " not to look so white,—so terrible." \

But he motioned her off, saying to her : " Don't try to comfort me unless you give me back my Mildred. Take me, Clubs, where I can breathe. I am dying in this stifled room."

Then into the open air Oliver led the fainting man, while Ji.dge Howell bustled after, the great tears rolling down his face, as he whispered: " They do have the all-firedest luck. Poor boy, poor boy,—he takes it harder even than Gipsy did."

And in this the Judge was right, for the blow had well-nigh crushed out Lawrence's very life, and before the sun went down they carried him to what was to have been the bridal chamber, a broken-hearted, delirious man, talking continually of Mildred, who he always said was dead, but never that she was his niece. For many days the fever raged with fearful violence, and Mr. Thornton, who was summoned in haste from Boston, wept bitterly as he gazed upon the flushed face and wild eyes of his son, and felt that he would die. From the very first Lawrence refused to let either Geralcline or Lilian come into the room, while Oliver, on the contrary, was kept constantly at his side, and made to sing continually of Mildred with the starry eyes and nut-brown hair.

"Sing, Clubs, sing," he would say, tossing from side to side; " sing of the maid with the nut-brown hair."

And all through the silent watches of the night could that feeble voice be heard, sweet as an ancient harp and plaintive as a broken lute, for it welled up from the depths of an aching heart, and he who sang that song knew that each note was wearing his life away.

Thrice Judge Howell, touched with compassion by his pale, suffering face, offered to take his place, bidding Oliver lie down while he sang of Milly's eyes and hair; but Lawrence detected the fraud in an instant. He knew the shaking, tremulous tones, raised sometimes to a screech and then dying away in a whisper, came from another than Oliver Hawkins, and his lip curled with supreme disdain as, raising himself upon his elbow, he said:

"You can't cheat me, old fellow, and you may as well send Clubs back again."

So poor Clubs went back, staying by him night and day, until human strength could endure no more ; and he' one morning fell forward upon the bed, deluging it with the blood which gushed from his mouth and nose.

With an almost superhuman effort, Judge Howell took him in his arms,—gently, tenderly, for Mildred's sake,— and carrying him down the Cold Spring path, laid him away in the little room beneath the gable-roof, where there was none to sing to him of Mildred, none to comfort him save Hepsy, whose homely attempts were worse than failures, and who did him more hurt than good by constantly accusing Lawrence Thornton of being the cause of his illness. Indeed, she seemed rather to enjoy it when she heard, as she did, how Lawrence moaned for '' Clubs," growing daily worse until at last the physician feared that he would die. ' This, however, she kept from Oliver, who lay all the day on his low bed, never seeing but one person from Beechwood, and that the Judge, who came at his request, and was in close consultation with him for more than an hour..

The result of this interview was a determination on the part of Judge Howell and Mr. Thornton to sift the matter of Mildred's parentage more thoroughly and see if there were not some mistake.

" Certainly," said Geraldine, when the subject was mentioned to her. " I would leave no stone unturned to test the truth of Esther Bennett's assertion. Only this morning it occurred to me that possibly Hannah Hawkins might have received some hint from that old witch ; for I have heard that when she was dying she tried to speak of Mildred, and pointed toward Beechwood. I'll go down to night and question Mrs. Thompson."

Accordingly that evening found Geraldine seated in Hep-sy's kitchen and so wonderfully gracious that the old lady mentally styled her a right nice girl, and wondered how she could ever have called her " nippin' " and " stuck-up."

Warily, cautiously, little by little, step by step, did Geraldine approach the object of her visit, throwing out a hint here and a bait there, until, feeling sure of her subject, she came out openly, and asked old Hepsy " if she had any objections to telling a lie provided she were well paid for it."

" But, mercy ! Is there any one who can hear us ? " she added, drawing near to Hepsy, who replied : " Not

a soul," forgetting the while the stove-pipe hole cut through the floor of the chamber above, where Oliver was listening eagerly to the conversation.

Not one word escaped him, and when it was finished he knew as well as Hepsy that for fifty dollars and a half-worn black silk dress, she was to stain her soul with a wicked lie,—was to say that in rummaging Hannah's things she came across a little box, which had not been opened since her daughter's death, and which when opened was found to contain a letter from Esther Bennett, telling her who the child of her adoption was, but bidding her to keep it a secret from everybody.

" I have written to New York to-day," said Geraldine, " giving to Esther a copy of what she is to write and send to me by return of mail. As I cannot get the New York post-mark I shall tear off the half sheet where the superscription naturally would be, leaving only the body of the letter. This I shall rub and smoke until it looks old and worn, and then bring it to you, who the day following must find it,—in Oliver's presence, if possible; of course your glasses will not be handy and you will ask him to read it. He'll probably tell of it at Beechwood, or if he does not, you can, which will answer quite as well. I can't explain all about the matter, though I may some time do so, and I assure you, dear Mrs. Thompson, that if my end is secured, I shall be willing to pay you something extra for your assistance."

Geraldine had spoken so rapidly that Hepsy had not quite comprehended the whole, and clutching her dress she said :

" Yes, yes, but one thing I want to know. Is Mildred Helen Thornton's child, or is that all a humbug, got up to stop her marriage ? "

Geraldine had not intended to confide the whole in Hepsy, but to a certain extent she was rather compelled to do so, and she answered hastily :

"Yes, all a humbug, and I'll give you twenty-five dollars a year as long as you do not tell."

Hepsy was bought, and offered to swear on a " stack of Bibles high as the house " that she'd be silent as the dead, but Geraldine declined the pleasure of receiving the oath, and after a few more remarks, took her leave.

For a time after she was gone, Oliver sat completely stunned by what he had heard. Then the thought burst upon him, " How delighted Milly will be," and he determined to be himself the bearer of the joyful news. He could write it, he knew, but there might be some delay in the mails and he would rather go himself. Geraldine could not receive an answer from Esther Bennett until the second day, and on the third Hepsy would probably take to Beechwood this new proof of Mildred's parentage. By that time he could find Mildred and bringing her home could confront the wicked plotters and render their plotting of no avail. Once he thought to tell the Judge, but knowing he could not keep it, he decided not to do so. Lawrence was better that day,—the crisis was past, the physicians said, and having no fears for him, he resolved to keep his secret from every one. By going to Springfield that night he could take the early train and so reach Dresden the next day, a thing he greatly desired to do, as it was the day once appointed for Mildred's bridal. He glanced at his gold watch, Mildred's gift, and saw that it wanted but half an hour of the time when the last train was due. Hastily changing his clothes, and forgetting all about his feeble health, he went down-stairs and astonished his grandmother by saying he was going to Springfield.

" To Springfield ! " she screamed, " when you can scarcely set up all day. Are you crazy, boy ? What are you going there for ? "

" Oh, I know," he returned, affecting to laugh. " It's just occurred to me that I must be there early to-morrow morning, and in order to do that, I must go to-night."

He did not wait for further comment from old Hepsy, who, perfectly confounded, watched him till he disappeared in the moonlight, muttering to herself:

" I've mistrusted all along that he was gettjn' light headed."

But Oliver's mind was never clearer in his life, and he hastened on, reaching the depot just in time for the downward train, which carried him in safety to Springfield, and when next morning Geraldine before her glass was brushing her jet-black hair, and thinking within herself how nicely her plans were working, he was on his way to Mildred.

He did not reach the terminus of his railroad route until the Dresden stage had been gone several hours, and to his inquiries for some other mode of conveyance, he invariably received the same answer :

" Every hoss and every wagon has gone to the big camp-meetin' up in the north woods."

" How far is it to Dresden ? " he asked.

" A little short of ten mile," returned the ticket agent. " You can walk it easy; though I don't know 'bout that," and he glanced at Oliver's crippled feet. •* Mebby you'll get a ride. There's allus somebody goin' that way."

Oliver felt sure he should, and though the June sun was pouring down a scorching heat, and the road to Dresden, as far as his eye could trace it, wound over hill after hill where no shade-trees were growing, he resolved to go, and quenching his thirst from the tempting-looking gourd hanging near a pail of delicious ice-water, he started on his way.

CHAPTER XX.
OLIVER AND MILDRED.

H, what a weary, weary road it was, winding up and up, and up, and seeming to the tired and heated Oliver as if it could never end, or Dresden be much nearer. Walking was always to him a slow process, and nothing but the thought of what lay beyond could have kept him up and moving on until his poor crippled feet were blistered and his head was throbbing with pain. Not once during that tedious journey did a single person pass him ; all were going the other way, and the heroic Oliver was ^almost fainting from exhaustion when, from the brow of a steep hill, he saw the Dresden spire flashing in the sunlight, and knew he was almost there.

Mildred was alone in her chamber her head resting upon the soft pillows which little Edith had arranged, her hands clasped over her forehead, and her thoughts with Lawrence Thornton, when a servant entered, bearing a card, and saying that the gentleman who sent it was in the parlor below.

"Oliver Hawkins!" and Mildred almost screamed as she read the name. "Dear, dear Oliver! show him up at once."

The servant departed, and in a moment the well-known step was heard upon the stairs, and darting forward, Mildred passed her arm round him, or he would have fallen, for he was very weak and faint.

"Mildred, dear Mildred!" was all he could, at first, articulate, and sinking upon the sofa, he motioned her to remove his shoes from his swollen feet.

"Did you walk from the station?" she asked, in much surprise.

"Yes," he whispered. "There was no one to bring me."

"What made you? What made you?" she continued, and he replied:

"I couldn't wait, for I have come to bring you joyful news; to tell you that you are free to marry Lawrence,—• that you are not his father's grandchild. It was all a wicked fraud got up by Geraldine Veille, who would have Lawrence marry her sister. I heard her telling grandmother last night, and hiring her to say she found a paper among my mother's things confirming Esther Bennett's story. Oh, Milly, Milly, you hurt," he cried, as in he* excitement she pressed hard upon his blistered feet.

Those poor feet! How Mildred loved them then! How she pitied and caressed them, holding them carefully in her lap, and dropping tears upon them, as she thought of the weary way they had come to bring her this great joy,—this joy too good to be believed until Oliver related every particular, beginning with the time when Lawrence first came back to Beechwood. He did not, however, tell her how, day and night, until his own brain grew dizzy, he had sung to the maniac of the maid with the nut-brown hair, nor did he tell her of anything that he had done, except to overhear what Geraldine had said; but Mildred could guess it all,—could understand just how noble and self-denying he had been, and the blessings she breathed upon him came from a sincere heart.

"Oh, Oily, darling Oily," she said, still caressing his wounded feet, "the news is too good to be true. I dare not hope again lest I be cruelly disappointed, and I could not bear another shock. I have suffered so much that my heart is almost numb; and though you tell me I am free to marry Lawrence, I'm afraid there's some mistake, and that I am his sister Helen's daughter after all. If I am not, Oily, who am I? Who was my mother?—where is she now? and where is my father?"

There were tears in Mildred's eyes,—once they choked her utterance as she said these last words, which, neverthe less, were distinctly heard in the adjoining room where Richard Howell sat, his face as white as ashes, his eyes un

naturally bright, and a compressed look about the mouth as if he had received some dreadful shock,—something which shook his heart-strings as they never were shaken before. He was reading by his window when Mildred met Oliver in the hall, and through the open door he heard dis tinctly the name " Mildred, dear Mildred !" and heard the girl he knew as Minnie answer to that name. Then the let tered page before him was one solid blur, the room around him was enveloped in darkness, and with his hearing quickened he sat like a block of stone listening, listening, listening, till every uncertainty was swept away, and from the depths of his inmost soul came heaving up " My child ! my Mildred ! " But though his heart uttered the words his lips gave forth no sound, and he sat there immovable, while the great drops of perspiration trickled down his face and fell upon his nerveless hands, folded so kelplessly together. Then he attempted to rise, but as often sank back exhausted, for the shock had deprived him of his strength and made him weak as a little child.

But when Mildred asked, "Where is my father now?" he rose with wondrous effort, and tottering to her door, stood gazing at her with a look in which the tender love of eighteen years was all embodied. Oliver saw him first, for Mildred's back was toward him. and to her he softly whispered, " Turn your head, Milly. There's some one at the door."

Then Mildred looked, but started quickly when she saw

Richard Hovvell, every feature convulsed with the emo tions he could not express, and his arms stretched implor ingly toward her, as if beseeching her to come to their embrace.

" My daughter, my daughter I" he said, at last, and though it was but a whisper it reached the ear of Mildred, and with a scream of unutterable joy she went forward to an embrace such as she had never known before.

Oh, it was strange to see that strong man weep as he did over his beautiful daughter, but tears did him good, and he wept on until the fountain was dried up, murmur ing, " My Mildred,—my darling,—my first-born,—my baby, Hetty's and mine. The Lord be praised who brought me to see your face when I believed you dead !" and all the while he said this he was smoothing her shiny hair, looking into her eyes, and kissing her girlish face, so much like his own as it used to be, save that it was softer and more feminine.

Wonderingly Oliver looked at them, seeking in vain for a clew with which to unravel the mystery, but when Mil dred, remembering him, at last said :

" Oliver, this is Richard Hovvell," he needed nothing more to tell him that he had witnessed the meeting be tween a father and his child.

To Mildred the truth came suddenly with the words, " My daughter." Like a flash of light it broke on her,— the secret marriage with Hetty Kirby,—her strong resem-13

OLIVER AND MILDRED.

blance to the Howells, and all the circumstances con nected with her first arrival at Beechwood. There could be no mistake, and with a cry of joy she sprang to meet her father as we have described.

"I heard what he told you," Richard said at last, mo tioning to Oliver. " I* heard him call you Mildred, and from your conversation knew you were the child once left at my father's door. You were my darling baby then ; you are my beautiful Mildred now," and he hugged her closer in his arms.

Very willingly Mildred suffered her fair head to rest upon his shoulder, for it gave to her a feeling of security she had never before experienced, for never before had she known what it was to feel a father's heart throbbing in unison with her own. Suddenly a new thought occurred to her, and starting up, she exclaimed :

11 Edith, father, Edith ! "

" I'me tomein', with lots of fowers," answered a child ish voice, and Oliver heard the patter of little feet in the hall.

In a moment she was with them, her curls blown over her face, and her white apron full of the flowers she had gathered for Minnie, ** 'cause she was so sick."

" Precious little sister," and Mildred's arms closed con vulsively around the wondering child, whose flowers were scattered over the carpet, and who thought more of gath ering them up than of paying very close attention to what her father told her of Minnie's being Mildred, her sister, who they thought was dead.

At last Edith began to understand, and rubbing her fat, round cheek against Mildred's, she said :

" I so glad you be my sister, and have come back to us from heaven. Why didn't you bring mamma and the baby with you ? "

It was in vain they tried to explain; Edith was rather too young to comprehend exactly what they meant, and when there was a lull in the conversation, she whispered to Mildred :

" I knew most you was an angel, and some time mayn't I see your wings and how you fly ? "

The interview between Mildred and Edith helped to restore Richard's scattered senses, and when the wing business was settled, he said to Mildred :

" Has my daughter no curiosity to know why I left her as I did, and why I have never been to inquire for her ? "

" Yes, father," answered Mildred, " I want so much to hear,—but I thought it might disturb you. Will you tell us now ? " and nestling closer to his side, with Edith on her lap, she listened breathlessly, while he repeated to her what she did not already know.

" I have told you," he said, "of my father's bitterness toward Hetty Kirby, and how, with the help of a compan ion, whom I could trust, I took her to New York, and was married, but I did not tell you how, after the lapse of time, there was born to the beardless college boy a smiling little infant. As soon as possible I hastened to Hetty's bedside, but the shadow of death was there before me, and one glance at her sweet young face assured me that she would die. 'Twas then that I regretted having kept our marriage a secret from my father, for I felt that I should need his sympathy in the dark hour coming Something, too, must be done with you, so soon to be made motherless. Hetty was the first to suggest dispos ing of you as I did. She knew my education was not yet completed, and laying her soft hand on my head, she said : ' My boy-husband wants to go through college, and if it becomes known that he has been married, those stern men may expel him. Your father, too, will turn you off, as soon as he learns that I have been your wife. I know how strong his prejudices are when once they have been roused, and if he knew our baby had in it a drop of Hetty's blood, he would spurn it from him, and so he must not know it. My grandmother will not last long, and when we are both dead, send baby to him secretly. Don't let him know who she is, or whence she came, until he has learned to love her. Then tell him she is yours."

" This is what Hetty said; and in an unguarded moment I promised to do her bidding, for I was young and dreaded my father's wrath. Not long after this Hetty died, with her baby folded to her bosom, and her lips murmuring a prayer that God would move the heart of the stern old Judge to care for her little waif.

" Her grandmother also died in a few days, and then, with the exception of the nurse, I was alone with you, my daughter, in that low brown house you visited with me, I little dreaming that the baby who in that west room first opened its eyes to the light of day was standing there beside me, a beautiful young maiden. Dresden is thinly populated now; it was far more so then, and of the few neighbors near, none seemed to be curious at all, and when told that I should take the child to my own home in Massachusetts, they made no particular comments. The same friend, Tom Chesebro, who had helped me in my marriage, now came to my aid again, planning and arranging the affair, even to the writing that letter, pur porting to have come from Maine. He had relatives liv ing in that vicinity, and as it was necessary for him to visit them, he left me a few days, and taking the letter with him, mailed it at one of the inland towns. When he re turned we started together to Mayfield, and tolerably well skilled in the matters to which I was a novice, I found him of invaluable service in taking care of you, whom I carried in my arms. At Springfield he left me, taking you with him in a basket which he procured there, and giving you, as he afterward told me, something to make you sleep. I never could understand exactly how he contrived to avoid observation as he did, but it was dusk when he left

Springfield, and the darkness favored him. He did not leave the cars at Mayfield, but at the next station got off on the side remote from the depot and striking across the fields to Beechwood, a distance of two miles. He had once spent a vacation there with me, and hence his familiarity with the localities. After placing you on the steps, he waited at a little distance until my father, or rather Tiger, took you in, and then, when it was time, went to the depot, where I met him as I was stepping from the car. In a whisper he assured me that all was safe, and with a somewhat lightened heart I hurried on.

" To a certain extent you know what followed ; know that Hannah Hawkins took care of you for a time, while the villagers gossiped as villagers will, and my father swore lustily at them all. Several times I attempted to tell him, but his determined hatred of you decided me to wait until time and your growing beauty had somewhat softened his heart. At last my failing health made a change of climate necessary for me, and as Tom Chesebro was going on a voyage to the South Sea Islands, I decided to accompany him, and then, for the first time, confided my secret to Hannah Hawkins, bidding her put you in father's way as much as possible, and, in case I died, to tell him who you were. Then I visited Hetty's grave, -de termining while there to tell my father myself; and this, on my return, I endeavored to do, but the moment I con fessed to him my marriage, he flew into a most violent

rage, cursing me bitterly and ordering me to leave the room and never come into his presence again. Then when I suggested that there was more to tell, he said he had heard enough, and, with a hard, defiant feeling, I left him, resolving that it should be long before he saw my face again.

" We had a pleasant voyage, but remorse was gnawing at my heart, and when we reached our destined port, none thought the boy, as they called me, would ever cross the sea again. But I grew daily better, and when at last poor Tom died of a prevailing fever, I was able to do for him the very office he had expected to do for me.

" After a time I went to India, having heard nothing from home, although I had written to my father twice and to Hannah once. I am ashamed to confess it, my dar ling, but it is nevertheless the truth, that continued absence and the new scenes amid which I found myself in India, made me somewhat indifferent to you,—less anxious to see your face ; and still when I had been gone from you nearly eight years, I resolved upon coming home, and was making my plans to do so when accident threw in my way a sick, worn-out sailor, just arrived from New York. He was suffering and I cared for him, learning by this means that he had friends in the vicinity of Beech wood, and that he had visited them just before his last voyage. Very adroitly I questioned him to see if he knew aught of the gable-roof, or the child adopted by Hannah Hawkins.

He must have been misinformed, for he said that Hannah Hawkins and the little girl both were dead, and that one was buried while he was in Mayfield."

" Oh, I can explain that," interrupted Mildred ; " I was very sick with scarlet fever when Hannah died. The' doctor said I would not live; while Widow Simms, a won derful gossip, reported that I was dead."

"That must have been the cause of the misunderstand ing," returned Richard, " for the sailor told me you died of scarlet fever, and crediting his statement, I had no longer a desire to return, but remained in India, amass ing wealth until I met with Edith's mother. Owing to her blessed influence I became, as I trust, a better man, though I obstinately refused to write to my father, as she often wished me to do. On her death-bed, however, I promised that I would come home and comfort his old age. I knew he was alive, for I sometimes saw his name in the American papers which came in my way, but I had no conception of the joyful surprise awaiting me in Dres den," and he fondly kissed Mildred's glowing cheek.

" The moment I saw your face I was struck with its resemblance to my sister's ; and to myself I said : ' If it were possible I should say that is my daughter.' Then the thought came over me, ' The sailor was perhaps mis taken,' and I managed to learn your name, which swept away all hope, especially when afterwards you told me that your mother was Helen Thornton. There has evi-

dently been some deep-laid scheme to rob you both of your birth-right and of a husband, and, as I do not quite understand it, will you please explain to me what it is about this Geraldine Veille and Esther Ben nett. Who is the latter, and why is she interested in you ?"

Briefly as possible, Mildred told him of all that had come to her during his absence, of the fraud imposed upon her by Geraldine; of Oliver's unfailing kindness, and how but for the wicked deception she would that night have been a bride.

" You only deferred the marriage until your father came," said Mr. Howell, kissing her again, and telling her how, on the morrow, they would go together to Beech-wood, and confronting the sinful Geraldine, overthrow her plans. " And you, young man," he continued, turning to Oliver, "you, it seems, have been the truest friend my Milly ever had. For this I owe you a life-long debt of gratitude; and though I am perhaps too young to have been your father, you shall be to me henceforth a brother. My home shall be your home, and if money can repay you for your kindness, it shall be yours even to tens of thousands."

With a choking voice, Oliver thanked the generous man, thinking to himself the while, that a home far more glori ous than any Richard Howell could oifer to his acceptance would ere long be his. But he did not say so, and when '3*

Mildred, in her old, impulsive way, wound her arms around his neck and said :

<f Father cannot have you, Oily, for you will stay with me and be my own darling brother," he gently put her from him saying :

" Yes, Milly, as long as I live I will be your Brother/ 1

It was very late when they separated, for Mr. Howell was loath to leave his newly-recovered treasure, while Oli ver was never weary of feasting his eyes upon Mildred's beautiful, and now perfectly happy face. But they said good-night at last, Richard taking Oliver to his own room, where he could nurse his poor, bruised feet, while Mildred kept Edith with her, hugging her closer to her bosom as she thought: " She is my sister."

At an early hour next morning the three assembled to gether again, and when the lumbering old stage rattled down the one long street, it carried Richard and Oliver, Mildred and Edith, the first two silent and thoughtful, the last two merry and glad as singing-birds, for the heart of one was full of "danfather Howell," while the other thought only of Lawrence Thornton, and the blissful meeting awaiting her.

CHAPTER XXI.
THE MEETING.

: ARK night had closed in upon Beechwood, but in the sick-room a light was dimly burn ing, showing the white face of the invalid, who was sleeping quietly now. The crisis was passed, and weak as a little child he lay, power less and helpless beneath the mighty weight of sorrow which had fallen upon him. Geraldine had been sitting with him, but when she saw that it was nine, she cautiously left the room, and stealing down the stairs, joined the Judge and Mr. Thorn ton in the parlor. Sinking into a chair and leaning her head upon it, she did not seem to hear the hasty step in the hall; but when Hepsy's shrill voice said, "Good evenin', gentle folks," she looked up, apparently sur prised to see the old lady there at that hour of the night. "Have you heard from Oliver?" she asked; and Hepsy answered:

"Not a word. I'm gettin' awful consarned ; but that ain't what brung me here. Feelin' lonesome-like without Clubs, thinks to me, I'll look over the chest where I keep Hannah's things."

" An all-fired good way to get rid of the blues," said the Judge, while Hepsy continued :

" Amongst the things was a box, which must have been put away unopened, for I found in it this letter concern ing Mildred," and she held up the bit of paper which, having been nicely rubbed and smoked by Geraldine, looked old and rather soiled.

" Let me see it," said the Judge, and adjusting his spec tacles, he real aloud a letter from Esther Bennett, telling Hannah Hawkins that Mildred was the child of Helen Thornton, and bidding her keep it a secret. " This con firms it," he said. "There is no need now of your sifting the matter as we intended to do," and he handed the half-sheet to Mr. Thornton just as the sound of many feet was heard in the hall without.

Richard, Oliver, Mildred and Edith had come! The latter being fast asleep, was deposited upon the floor, with Mildred's satchel for a pillow, and while Mildred stole off upstairs, promising her father only to look into Lawrence's room, and not to show herself to him, Richard and Oliver advanced into the parlor.

" Clubs ! Clubs ! " screamed Hepsy, catching him round the neck. " Where have you been ? "

Oliver did not answer, but sat watching Richard, who was gazing at his father with an expression upon his face

something like what it wore when first he recognized his daughter. Every eye in the room was turned toward him, but none scanned his features so curiously as did the old Judge.

" Who is it, Bobum ? " he whispered, while his cheek turned pale. " Who is it standing there, and what makes him stare so at me ? " f

But Bobum could not tell, and he was about to question the stranger, when Richard advanced toward his father, and laying a hand on either shoulder, looked wistfully into the old man's eyes; then pointing to his own por trait hanging just beyond, he said :

" Have I changed so greatly that there is no resemblance between us ? "

" Oh, heaven ! it's Richard !—it's Richard ! Bobum, do you hear? 'Tis my boy ! 'Tis Dick come back to me again !"

The Judge could say no more, but sank upon the sofa faint with surprise, and tenderly supported by his son.

Half beside herself with fear, Geraldine came forward, demanding haughtily :

" Who are you, sir, and why are you here ! "

" I am Richard Howell, madame, and have come to expose your villanous plot," was the stranger's low-spoken answer, and Geraldine cowered back into the farthest cor ner, while the Judge, rallying a little, said mournfully :

" You told me, Dick, of lonesome years when I should

wish I hadn't said those bitter things to you, and after you were gone I was lonesome, oh, so lonesome, till I took little Mildred. Richard" and the old man sprang to his feet electrified, as it were, with the wild hope which had burst upon him, "Richard, WHO is MIL DRED ? "

" My own daughter, father. Mine and Hetty Kirbfs" was the answer deliberately spoken, while Richard cast a withering glance at the corner, where Geraldine still sat, overwhelmed with guilt and shame, for she knew now that exposure was inevitable.

With a sudden, hateful impulse, she muttered :

" An unlawful child, hey. A fit wife, truly, for Law rence Thornton."

The words caught Judge Ho well's ear, and springing like lightning across the floor, he exclaimed :

" Now, by the Lord, Geraldine Veille, if you hint such a thing again, I'll shake you into shoe-strings," and, by way of demonstration, he seized the guilty woman's shoulder and shook her lustily. " Mildred had as good a right to be born as you, for Dick was married to Hetty. I always knew that," and he tottered back to the sofa, just as Edith, frightened at finding herself in a strange place, began to cry.

Stepping into the hall for a moment, Richard soon re turned, bringing her in his arms, and advancing toward the Judge, he said :

'* I've brought you another grandchild, father,—one born of an English mother. Is there room in your heart for little Edith ? "

The eyes, which looked wonderingly at the Judge, were very much like Mildred's, and they touched a chord at once.

"Yes, Dick, there's room for Edith," returned the Judge ; "not because of that English mother, for I don't believe in marrying twice, but because she's like Gipsy," and he offered to take the little girl, who, not quite cer tain whether she liked her new grandpa or not, clung closer to her father, and began to cry for " Sister Milly."

" Here, Edith, come to me," said Oliver, and taking her back into the hall, he whispered: " Mildred is up stairs ; go and find her."

The upper hall was lighted, and following Oliver's directions, Edith ascended the stairs, while her father, thus relieved of her, began to make some explanations, having first greeted Mr. Thornton, whom he remembered well.

" Where have you been, Dick ? Where have you been all these years ? " asked the Judge, in a hoarse voice ; and holding his father's trembling hands in his, Richard repeated, in substance, what the reader has already heard, asking if neither of his letters were received.

" Yes, one ; telling me you were going to India," returned the Judge ; " but I hadn't forgiven you then for

marrying Hetty Kirby, and I would not answer it; but I've forgiven you now, boy,—I've forgiven you now, for that marriage has been the means of the greatest happiness I ever experienced. It gave Gipsy to me. Where is Mildred, Richard ? Why don't she come to see her granddad?"

11 She's upstairs, tissin' a man," interposed little Edith, who had just entered the room, her brown eyes protruding like marbles, as if utterly confounded with what they had beheld. " She is," she continued, as Oliver tried to hush her : " I seen her, and he tissed her back just as loud as THAT !" and by way of illustration she smacked her own fat hand.

"Come here, you mischief! " and catching her before she was aware of his intention, the delighted Judge threw her higher than his head, asking her to tell him again "how Mildred tissed the man."

But Edith was not yet inclined to talk with him, and so we will explain how it happened that Mildred was with Lawrence. After leaving her father, her first visit was to her own room, which she found occupied by Lilian, who, having a slight headache, had retired early, and was fast asleep. Not caring to awaken her, Mildred turned back, and seeing the door of Lawrence's chamber ajar, could not forbear stealing on tiptoe toward it, thinking that the sound of his breathing would be better than nothing. While she stood there listening she heard him whisper,

" Mildred," for he was thinking of her, and unconsciously he repeated the dear name. In an instant she forgot everything, and springing to his side, wound her arms around his neck, sobbing in his ear :

" Dear, dear Lawrence, I've comeback to you, and we shall not be parted again. It is all a fraud,—a wicked lie. I am not Mildred Hawley,—I am Mildred Howell,— Richard's child. He's down-stairs, Lawrence. My own father is in the house. Do you hear ? "

He did hear, and comprehended it too, but for some moments he could only weep over her and call her his "darling Milly." Then, when more composed, he listened while she told him what she knew, interspersing her narrative with the kisses which had so astonished Edith and sent her with the wondrous tale to the drawing-room, from which she soon returned, and marching this time boldly up to Mildred, said :

" That big man says you mustn't tiss him any more," and she looked askance at Lawrence, who laughed aloud at the little creature's attitude and manner.

"This is to be your brother," said Mildred, and lifting Edith up, she placed her on the bed with Lawrence, who kissed her chubby cheeks and called her " little sister."

"You've growed awfully up in heaven," said Edith, mistaking him for the boy-baby who had died with her mother, for in no other way could she reconcile the idea of a brother.

"What does she mean ?" asked Lawrence, and with a merry laugh Mildred explained to him how Edith, who had been taught that she had a brother and sister in heaven, had mistaken her for an angel, asking to see her wings, and had now confounded him with the baby buried in her mother's coffin.

"I don't wonder she thinks I've grown," said he; " but she's right, Milly, with regard to you. You are an angel."

Before Mildred could reply, Richard called to her, bidding her come down, and leaving Edith with Lawrence, she hastened to the parlor, where the Judge was waiting to receive her. With heaving chest and quivering lip, he held her to himself, and she could feel the hot tears dropping on her hair, as he whispered :

" My Gipsy, my Spitfire, my diamond, my precious, precious child. If I hadn't been a big old fool, I should have known you were a Howell, and that madame couldn't have imposed that stuff on me. Hanged if I ever believed it! Didn't I swear all the time 'twas a lie ? Say grand pa once, little vixen. Say it once, and let me hear how it sounds !"

" Dear, dear grandpa," she answered, kissing him quite as she had kissed Lawrence Thornton.

" And Clubs went for you," he continued. " Heaven bless old Clubs, but how did he find it out ? Hanged if I understand it yet."

Then as his eye fell on Geraldine, who still sat in the corner, stupefied and bewildered, he shook his fist at her threateningly, bidding her tell in a minute what she knew of Esther Bennett and the confounded plot.

"Yes, Geraldine," said Mr. Thornton, advancing toward her, " you may as well confess the part you had in this affair. It is useless longer to try to conceal it. Oliver heard enough to implicate you deeply, and Mrs. Thompson," turning to Hepsy, whom greatly against her will Oliver had managed to keep there, " Mrs. Thompson will, of course, tell what she knows, and so save herself f rom »

" Utter disgrace," he was going to add, when poor, igno rant Hepsy, thinking he meant "jail" screamed out :

"I'll tell all I know, indeed I will, only don't send me to prison," and with the most astonishing rapidity, she repeated all the particulars of her interview with Geraldine, whose face grew purple with anger and morti fication.

" She brung me that half sheet to-night," said Hepsy, in conclusion, " and told me what to do, and said how all she wanted was for Mr. Lawrence to marry Lilian. There, dear sir, that's all I know, as true as I live and draw the breath of life. Now, please let me go home, I'll give up the fifty dollars and the silk gown," and without waiting for permission, she seized her green calash, and darting from the room went tearing down the walk at a rate high-

.y injurious to her corns, and the " spine in her back," of which she had recently been complaining.

Thus forsaken by Hepsy, Geraldine bowed her head upon the table, but refused to speak, until Richard said to her:

" Madame, silence will avail you nothing, for unless you confess the whole, I shall to-morrow morning start in quest of Esther Bennett, who will be compelled to tell the truth."

There was something in Richard's manner which made Geraldine quail. She was afraid of him, and knowing well that Esther would be frightened into betraying her, she felt that she would rather the story should come from herself. 'So, after a few hysterical sobs and spasmodic attempts to speak, she began to tell how she first over heard Mr. Thornton talking to his son of Esther Bennett, and how the idea was then conceived of using that infor mation for her own purposes if it should be necessary. Once started, it seemed as if she could not stop until her mind was fully unburdened, and almost as rapidly as Hepsy herself she told how she had gone to New York, ostensibly to buy the wedding dress, but really in quest of Esther Bennett, who was easily found, and for a certain sum enlisted in her service.

" I was well acquainted with the particulars of Cousin Helen's marriage," she said, " well acquainted with Mil dred's being left at Beech wood, and this made the matter

easy, for I knew just what to say. I had also in my pos session one of Helen's letters ; her handwriting was much like my own, and by a little practice I produced that let ter which deceived even Uncle Thornton. I told Esther what to say and what to do, when to come to Mayfield and how to act."

" The Old Nick himself never contrived a neater trick," chimed in the Judge; " but what in Cain did you do it for?"

" For Lilian,—for Lilian," answered Geraldine. " She is all I have to love in the wide world, and when I saw how her heart was set on Lawrence Thornton, I deter mined that she should have him if money and fraud could accomplish it! "

" Yes, my fine madame," whispered the Judge again, " but what reason had you to think Lawrence would marry Lilian, even if he were Milly's uncle ?"

"I thought," answered Geraldine, "that when re covered from his disappointment he would turn back to her, for he loved her once, I know."

" Don't catch me swallowing that," muttered the Judge ; " he love that putty head !"

"Hush, father," interposed Richard, and turning to Geraldine, he asked, " Did you suppose Esther and Hepsy would keep your secret always ?"

" I did not much care," returned Geraldine. " If Lilian secured Lawrence, I knew the marriage could not

be undone, and besides, I did not believe the old women would dare to tell, for I made them both think it was a crime punishable with imprisonment."

"And so it should be," returned the Judge. "Every one of you ought to be hung as high as Hainan. What's that you are saying of Lilian ?" he continued, as he caught a faint sound.

Geraldine's strength was leaving her fast, but she man aged to whisper :

" You must not blame Lilian. She is weak in intellect and believed all that I told her; of the fraud she knew nothing,—nothing. I went to a fortune-teller in Boston, and bade her say to the young lady I would bring her that though the man she loved was engaged to another, some thing wonderful, the nature of which she could not exactly foretell, would occur to prevent the marriage, and she would have him yet. I also gave her a few hints as to Lawrence's personal appearance, taking care, of course, that she should not know who we were. Then I sug gested to Lilian that we consult Mrs. Blank, who, receiv ing us both as strangers, imposed upon her credulous nature the story I had prepared. This is why Lilian be came so quiet, for, placing implicit faith in the woman, she believed all would yet end well."

" You are one of the devil's unaccountables," exclaimed the Judge, and grasping her arm, he shook her again, but Geraldine did not heed it.

The confession she had made exhausted her strength, and laying her head again upon the table, she fainted. Mr. Hovvell and her uncle carried her to her room, but it was Mildred's hand which had bathed her head and spoke to her kindly when she came back to consciousness. Mildred, too, broke the news to the awakened Lilian, who would not believe the story until confirmed by Geral-dine; then she wept bitterly, and upbraided her sister for her perfidy until the wretched woman refused to listen longer, and covering her head with the bedclothes, wished that she could die. She felt that she was everlastingly disgraced, for she knew no power on earth could keep the Judge from telling the shameful story to her Boston friends, who would thenceforth despise and shun her just as she deserved. Her humiliation seemed complete, and it was not strange that the lapse of two days found her in a raging fever, far exceeding in violence the one from which Lawrence was rapidly recovering.

" I hope the Lord," growled the Judge, "that the jade will get well pretty quick, or "

He did not say " or what," for Edith, who was in his lap, laid her soft hand on his mouth, and looking mournfully in ' his face said :

" You'll never see my mamma and the baby."

" Why not ? " he asked.

And Edith answered: "You sweared, you did, and such naughty folks can't go to heaven."

It was a childish rebuke, but it had an effect, causing the Judge to measure his words, particularly in her pres ence ; but it did not change his feelings toward Geraldine; and as the days went on and she still grew worse, scolded and fretted, wishing her in Guinea, in Halifax, in Tophet, in short anywhere but at Beechwood.

Owing to Mildred's interference, his manner changed somewhat toward Lilian. She was not to blame, she said, for knowing as little as she did, and when he saw how really anxious she was to atone for all she had made Mil dred suffer he forgave her in a measure, and took her into favor just as Lawrence had done before him. It took but a week or so to restore the brightness to her face and the lightness to her step, for hers was not a mind to dwell long on anything, and when at last Geraldine was able to be moved, and she went with her to Boston, she bade both Lawrence and Mildred good-by as naturally as if nothing had ever happened. Geraldine, on the contrary, shrank from their pleasant words, and without even thank ing Mildred for her many friendly offices in the sick-room left a house which had been too long troubled with her presence, and which the moment she was gone assumed a more cheery aspect. Even little Edith noticed the dif ference, and frisking around her grandfather, with whom she was on the best of terms, she said:

" You won't swear any more, now that woman with the black eyes has gone ? "

** No, Beauty, no," he answered; " I'll never swear
n, if I think in time,"—a resolution to which, as far as
;ible, he adhered, and thus was little Edith the source
ood to him, inasmuch as she helped to cure him of a
iabit which was increasing with his years, and was a mar
to his many admirable traits of character.

CHAPTER XXII.

NATURAL RESULTS.

N a bright September morning, just eighteen years after Mildred was left at Judge Howell's door, there was a quiet wedding at Beechwood, but Oliver was not there. Since his return from Dresden he had never left his room, and on the day of the wedding he lay with his face buried in the pillows, praying for strength to bear this as he had borne all the rest. He would rather not see Mildred until he had become accustomed to thinking of her as another's. So on the occasion of her last visit to him he told her not to come to him on her bridal day, and then laying his hand upon her hair, prayed: " Will the Good Father go with Mildred wherever she goes. Will He grant her every possible good, and make her to her husband what she has been to me, my light, my life, my all."

Then kissing her forehead, he bade her go, and not come to him again until she had been some weeks a happy wife. Often during her bridal tour did Mildred's thoughts turn back to that sick-room, and after her return, her first question was for Oliver.

" Clubs is on his last legs," was the characteristic answer of the Judge, while Richard added : "He has asked for you often, and been so much afraid you would not be here till he was dead."

" Is he so bad ? " said Mildred ; and calling Lawrence, who was tossing Edith in the air, she asked him to go with her to the gable-roof.

At the sight of them a deep flush spread itself over the sick man's cheek, and Mildred cried :

" You are better than they told me. You will live yet many years."

" No, darling," he answered; " I am almost home, and now that I have seen you again, I have no wish it should be otherwise. But, Milly, you must let me have your husband to-night. There is something I wish to tell him, and I can do it better when it is dark around me. Shall it be so, Milly ? "

" Yes, Oily," was Mildred's ready answer.

And so that night,, while she lay sleeping with Edith in her arms, Lawrence sat by Oliver listening to his story.

" My secret should have died with me," said Oliver, " did I not know that there is some merit in confession, and I hope thus to atone for my sin, if sin it can be, to love as I have loved."

"You, Oliver?" asked Lawrence, in some surprise; and Oliver replied:

" Yes, Lawrence, I have loved as few have ever loved, and for that love I am dying long before my time. It began years and years ago, when I was a little boy, and in looking over my past life, I can scarcely recall a single hour which was not associated with some thought of the brown-haired girl who crept each day more and more into my heart, until she became a part of my very being."

Lawrence started, and grasping the hand lying outside the counterpane, said :

" My Mildred, Oliver ! " I never dreamed of this. .

" Yes, your wife," Oliver whispered, faintly. " Forgive me, Lawrence, for I couldn't help it, when I saw her so bright, so beautiful, so like a dancing sunbeam. She was a merry little creature, and even the sound of her voice stirred my very heartstrings when I was a boy. Then, when we both were older, and I awoke to the nature of my feelings toward her, I many a time laid down upon the grass in the woods out yonder, and prayed that I might die, for I knew how worse than hopeless was my love. Oh, how I loathed myself!—how I hated my deformity, sickening at the thought of starry-eyed Mildred wasting her regal beauty on such as me. At last there came a day when I saw a shadow on her brow, and with her heau in my lap, she told me of her love for you, while I com-

pelled myself to hear, though every word burned into my soul. You know the events which followed, but you do not know the fierce struggle it has cost me to keep from her a knowledge of my love. But I succeeded, and she has never suspected how often my heart has been wrung with anguish when in her artless way she talked to me of you, and wished /could love somebody, so as to know, just what it was. Oh, Lawrence ! that was the bitterest drop of all in the cup I had to drain. Love somebody ! —ah me, never human being worshipped another as I have worshipped Mildred Howell; and after I'm dead, you may tell her how the cripple loved her, but not till then, for Lawrence, when I die, it must be with my head on Mil dred's shoulder. Hers must be the last face I look upon, the last voice I listen to. Shall it be so ? May she come ? Tell me yes, for I have given my life for her."

" Yes, yes," answered Lawrence, " she shall surely come," and he pressed the poor hands of him who was indeed dying for Mildred Howell.

Twenty-four hours had passed, and again the October moon looked into the chamber where Oliver lay dying. All in vain the cool night wind moved his light-brown hair, or fanned his feverish brow where the perspiration was standing so thickly. All in vain were Hepsy*s groans and the Judge's whispered words, " Pity, p'ty, and he so

young." All in vain the deep concern of Richard Howell and Lawrence, for nothing had power to save him, not even the beautiful creature who had pillowed his head upon her arm and who often bent down to kiss the lips, which smiled a happy smile and whispered:

" Dear, dear Mildred."

" Let my head sink lower," he said at last; " so 1 can look into your eyes."

Very carefully Lawrence Thornton adjusted the weary head, laying it more upon the lap of his young bride, and whispering to Oliver :

" Can you see her now ? "

" Yes," was the faint reply, and for a moment there was silence, while the eyes of the dying man fixed them selves upon the face above them, as if they fain would take a semblance of those loved features up to heaven.

Then in tones almost inaudible he told her how happy she had made his short life, and blessed her as he had often done before.

" Mildred, Mildred, dear, dear Mildred," he kept repeat ing, " in the better land you will know, perhaps, how much I love you, dear, darling Mildred."

The words were a whisper now, and no one heard them save Mildred and Lawrence, who, passed his arm around his bride and thus encouraged her to sit there while the pulse grew each moment fainter and the blue eyes dim mer with the films of coming death.

" Haven't you a word for me ? " asked Hepsy, hobbling to his side, but his ear was deaf to her and his eyes saw nothing save the starry orbs on which they were so intently fastened.

" Mildred, Mildred, on the banks of the beautiful river I shall find again the little girl who made my boyhood so happy, and it will not be wicked to tell how much I love her,—Milly, Milly, Milly."

They were the last words he ever spoke, and when Lawrence Thornton lifted the bright head which had bent over the thin, wasted face, Richard Howell, said to those around him :

" Oliver is dead."

Yes, he was dead, and all the next day the villagers came in to look at him and to steal a glance at Mildred, who could not be persuaded to leave him until the sun went down, when she was taken away by Lawrence and her father.

Poor Milly, her bridal robes, were exchanged for the mourning garb, for she would have it so, and when the third day came she sat with Hepsy close to the narrow coffin, where slept the one she had loved with all a sister's fondness. She it was who had arranged him for the grave, taking care that none save herself and Lawrence should see the poor twisted feet which during later years he had kept carefully hidden from view. Hers were the last lips which touched his,—hers the last tears which dropped

upon his face before they closed the coffin and shut him out from the sunlight and the air.

It was a lovely, secluded spot which they chose for Oliver's grave, and when the first sunset light was falling upon it Lawrence Thornton told his wife how the dead man had loved her with more than a brother's love, and how the night before he died he had confessed the whole by way of an atonement.

"Poor, poor Oily!" sobbed Mildred. "I never dreamed of that," and her tears fell like rain upon the damp, moist earth above him.

Very tenderly Lawrence led her away, and taking her home endeavored to soothe her grief, as did the entire household, even to little Edith, who, climbing into her lap, told her "not to ty, for Oiler was in heaven with mamma and the baby, and his feet were all straight now."

Gradually tfie caresses and endearments lavished upon her by every one had their effect, and Mildred became again like her former self, though she could never forget the patient, generous boy, who had shared her every joy and sorrow, and often in her sleep Lawrence heard her murmur : " Poor dear Oliver. He died for me."

CHAPTER XXIII

CONCLUSION.

FEW more words and our story is done. For one short year has Mildred been a happy wife, and in that time no shadow has crossed her pathway save when she thinks of Oliver, and then her tears flow at once; still she knows that it is well with him, and she would not, if she could, have him back again in a world where he suffered so much. Well kept and beau tiful is the ground about his grave, for Richard's tasteful hand is often busy there, and on the costly marble which marks the spot are inscribed the words:

IN MEMORY

OP

OUR BELOVED BROTHER.

In the distant city there is a handsome dwelling, looking out upon the Common and the

passers-by speak of it as 14*
the home of Lawrence Thornton, and the gift of Richard Ho well, who made his daughter's husband rich and still retained a princely fortune for himself and little Edith.

Dear little Edith, how she frisks and gambols about her Beechvvood home, filling it with a world of sunshine, and sometimes making the old Judge forget the aching void left in his heart, when Lawrence took Mildred away. That parting was terrible to the old man, and when Mil dred suggested that Edith should live with her, he cried aloud, begging of her not to leave him all alone,—to spare him little Beauty. So " Beauty " stayed, and every pleasant summer evening the Judge sits on the long piazza with Edith on his lap, and tells her of another little girl who came to him one winter night, stealing in so quietly that he did not know she was there until reminded by her of his falling glasses. Of this story Edith is never weary, though she often wonders where she was about those days, and why she was not there to help eat up the prunes, which she guesses "must have made Milly's stomach ache!"

As the Judge cannot enlighten her in the least degree, she usually falls asleep while speculating upon the matter, and her grandfather, holding her lovingly in his arms, in voluntarily breathes a prayer of thanksgiving to the kind Providence which has crowned his later life with so many blessings.

Richard is a great comfort to his father, and a great favorite in the village, where his genial nature and many virtues have procured him scores of friends, and where even Widow Simms speaks well of him.

The Judge has made another will, dividing his property equally between Spitfire and Beauty, as he calls his two grandchildren, and giving to the "Missionaries," once defrauded of their rights, the legacy intended for poor Clubs.

Old Hepsy lives still in the gable-roof, and when her rent comes due, Judge Howell sends her a receipt,—not for any friendship he feels toward her, but because she is Oliver's grandmother, and he knows Mildred would be pleased to have him do so.

Esther Bennett is dead ; and the Judge, when he heard of it, brought his fist down upon his knee, ex claiming :

" There's one nuisance less in the world ! Pity Mad ame Geraldine couldn't follow suit !"

But Geraldine bids fair to live to a good old age, though she is now seldom seen in the streets of Boston, where the story of her perfidy is known, and where her name has become a by-word of reproach. A crushed and miserable woman, she drags out her days in the pri vacy of her own home, sometimes weeping passion ately as she reviews her sinful life, and again railing bitterly at Lilian, not for anything in particular, but because she is unhappy, and wishes to blame some one.

In Lilian there is little change. Weak-minded, easily influenced, and affectionate, she has apparently forgotten her disappointment, and almost every day finds her at Lawrence's handsome house, where Mildred welcomes her with her sweetest smile. In all the city there is no one so enthusiastic in their praises of her cousin as herself, and no one who listens to said praises as complacently as her Uncle Robert.

He is very fond of his daughter-in-law, very glad that she was not a beggar's child, and very grateful for the gold she brought him. In his library there are two portraits now instead of one, and he often points them out to strangers, saying, proudly:

" This was taken for my wife, the famous beauty, Mil dred Howell; while this, is my son's wife, another Mil dred Howell, and the heiress of untold wealth. Hers is a strange history, too," he adds, and with a low bow, the strangers listen, while in far less words than we have used, he tells them the story we have told,—the story of Mildred with the starry eyes and nut-brown hair.

THE END.

Copyright by
DANIEL HOLMES.
1877.

Trow's
Printing and Bookbinding Co.,
205-213 *East 12th St.*,
New York.

Made in the USA
Monee, IL
11 March 2023